WHY AREN'T THEY SCREAMING

Why Aren't They Screaming

JOAN SMITH

faber and faber

LONDON · BOSTON

First published in 1988
by Faber and Faber Limited
3 Queen Square London WC1N 3AU
This paperback edition first published in 1989

Photoset by Parker Typesetting Service Leicester
Printed in England by Clays Ltd, St Ives plc
All rights reserved

British Library Cataloguing in Publication Data

A CIP record for this book is
available from the British Library

ISBN 0–571–15476–X

for Carol Baker and Jennifer Benjamin

'A mistress, that's all I am,' John Tracey announced with gloomy satisfaction. 'It doesn't matter what happens, her husband always comes first. D'you know, Loretta, she didn't even come round last week after I'd been to the dentist. She knew I was in agony, but oh no, she said, he'd get suspicious if she suddenly went out on her own in the evening. I mean, she could have said she was nipping out to get some fags, couldn't she? She only lives round the corner.'

He leaned across the table, grasped the bottle of cheap red wine he'd bought in a nearby off-licence and refilled his glass.

'It's no good telling me to give her up,' he went on, although Loretta hadn't spoken for some time. Picking up a foil container, he scraped the last few pieces of beef in black-bean sauce on to his plate. 'You haven't got any soy sauce, have you, Loretta?' He pushed the food around with a fork, examining it critically. 'This looks a bit dry to me.'

Loretta heaved herself out of her chair and knelt in front of one of the kitchen cupboards. There was a bottle of it somewhere, she thought, rummaging among half-empty jars of jam and honey. If only Tracey would finish his meal and go home, she prayed silently, wishing she hadn't accepted his offer to bring round a Chinese takeaway and cheer her up. His concern for her welfare had been forgotten as soon as he got on to the subject of his current girlfriend, a gym teacher he'd met early one Sunday morning in his local launderette in Brixton. It wasn't even as if Loretta was hearing his tale of woe for the first time. The affair had been going on for a good three months and she had recently begun to suspect that her ex-husband was relishing his unaccustomed role as the wronged sweetheart. He was still an attractive man: apart from his prematurely grey hair, he had weathered his forty-one years with remarkably little evidence of ageing; his job, as a journalist on a Sunday newspaper, was glamorous enough if you liked that sort of thing. So why couldn't he find a girlfriend who would appreciate all his sterling qualities?

'A plaything,' she heard him say as she finally spotted the soy sauce bottle on its side at the back of the cupboard. 'She just picks me up and drops me at her own convenience. Oh, thanks, Loretta.'

Tracey spooned more fried rice on to his plate and followed it with a generous sprinkling of soy sauce; Loretta reflected that the vicissitudes of his love life had had no appreciable effect on his appetite. She watched as he emptied the last of the red wine into his glass and held up the bottle hopefully. When she didn't respond he put it down and peered anxiously at her.

'You all right? You're very quiet.'

A potent mixture of irritation and self-pity welled up in Loretta and, to her dismay, she found she was on the verge of tears. Tracey was saved from the stream of bile that was about to pour out by the opportune ringing of the telephone.

'I'll get it,' he said quickly, sensing he'd been reprieved. He got to his feet, seized the receiver and murmured Loretta's number. Then his face fell.

'Oh, hello,' he said off-handedly. 'Just a minute, I'll get her. It's for you,' he told Loretta unnecessarily. 'Bridget.'

Loretta took the phone, at once feeling more cheerful.

'I gather John Tracey is his usual charming self,' said the voice at the other end of the line. 'He is one for bearing grudges, isn't he?'

'Ye-es,' said Loretta, suppressing a smile. Tracey had picked up a day-old copy of the *Guardian* and appeared to be giving it close attention, but she was in no doubt that he was listening. Bridget had been a member of the women's group Loretta joined when her marriage to Tracey was breaking up, and he persisted in regarding her with the wariness of a flying ant that has just seen one of its number snapped up by a Venus fly-trap.

'Well, never mind that, are you feeling any better?' Bridget demanded. 'Because I think I've found the answer to all your problems.'

Loretta stiffened. Bridget's urge to rescue her women friends from whatever their current predicament happened to be was notorious for leading to awkward situations – she was for ever introducing them to wildly unsuitable men or lending them cars that promptly broke down. In any case, the cause of Loretta's depression, which she had foolishly recounted to Bridget only that morning, was a particularly intractable problem. Her GP had just announced that the prolonged bout of sore throats, low spirits and general debility she'd recently experienced was probably a mild dose of glandular fever. If Loretta wished to make a speedy recovery, the doctor had said, she must immediately take time off work for a complete rest, preferably well away from London. These instructions, delivered as her third-year students were coming up to their final exams – Loretta lectured in English at London University – could not have come at a worse time. Not only was it difficult to take sick leave at this point in the summer term, but she was also flat broke as the result of expensive repairs to the roof of her flat in Islington.

'Loretta? Hello? Are you there?'

Bridget's voice broke into this unhappy reverie. Embarrassed, Loretta apologized for her inattention and asked Bridget to start again from the beginning.

'I was just saying', Bridget said patiently, 'that I've got a friend – you are listening, aren't you?' Loretta assured her that she was. 'Well, you know I've got a friend called Clara Wolstonecroft, the one who's a painter?'

Loretta did. Knowing Loretta's fondness for cats, Bridget had once shown her one of the children's books Clara wrote and illustrated herself and which featured a couple of beautiful grey cats.

'Yes, well, I happened to be speaking to Clara last weekend and she mentioned that her tenant was moving out earlier than expected. She's got a cottage near her house, you see, it used to be the gamekeeper's cottage in the days people went in for that sort of thing. She lets it out to visiting academics, quite a few of them like the idea of living in the real English countryside and all that.' Bridget tried, and failed, to put on an American accent for the last phrase. 'Anyway, she said she was feeling terribly cheerful 'cause this chap, Wayne something or other, was going home early – he's been asked to do a lecture tour on *Hemingway*, if you can believe it – and Clara can't stand him. So after you rang this morning I suddenly remembered the cottage might be free, and it is. Wayne thing is moving out this Saturday and it's all yours. If you want it, that is,' she added hastily. 'You really should think about it, Loretta, it would do you the world of good to get out of London. And you wouldn't be completely on your own. You'll like Clara, and her house is only yards away. And it's not far from Oxford, so I could pop over and see you. Bring you flowers or something,' she added vaguely. Bridget taught at one of the oldest colleges in Oxford, and lived in a pleasant semi in Summertown.

Loretta wasn't enthusiastic. A dedicated city dweller, she found it hard to imagine what she would do with herself stuck out in Oxfordshire. No cinemas – she was used to popping into the Screen on the Green just down the road; no restaurants; no bookshops within walking distance: she would be mad with boredom in days. On the other hand, she didn't want to appear ungrateful.

'What's it like, this cottage?' she asked non-committally.

'Small, but then you wouldn't be staying there for too long,' Bridget said. 'It's a sort of one-up, one-down.'

'Very small,' Loretta observed disparagingly.

'All right, but it's beautiful inside,' Bridget persisted. 'It was derelict for ages and then Clara did it up three or four years ago. She picked all the wallpaper and furniture, and she's got exquisite taste. There's a biggish kitchen-cum-living room downstairs, and it's got a what d'you call it, one of those old stove things you cook on. And upstairs there's a bedroom with a wonderful view across the valley. It's even got a desk, in case you can't tear yourself away from work completely. You could get on with your Edith Wharton book – oh dear, I suppose I shouldn't have mentioned that.'

'Doesn't matter,' mumbled Loretta, pushing away thoughts about her much-delayed work on the American writer. She had enough troubles on her plate without adding that one.

4

'It's very kind of you to go to all this trouble, but how can I take time off with finals coming up?'

'I thought you didn't have any choice,' Bridget countered. 'I thought you said your GP had signed you off. Don't you *want* to get better?'

'Yes, but there's still the money problem,' Loretta persisted weakly, admitting the force of Bridget's argument.

'Oh, but that's the best part of it! Didn't I explain? You can have the cottage *for nothing*.' She paused to let these words have their effect. 'Wayne thing has paid the rent till the end of July and Clara says she's damned if she's giving it back, all the money he's going to make from this lecture tour. Just think, flying round America to talk about that old bore *and* getting paid for it!'

It wasn't clear from Bridget's tone whether her incredulity stemmed from her distaste for modern literature – she tended to the view that nothing of much interest had been written since the demise of George Eliot – or from a feminist disgust for Hemingway's male chauvinism.

'Anyway,' she added, returning to the point at issue, 'you're not going to look a gift horse in the mouth?'

Loretta felt her resistance crumbling. It was true that she didn't have much desire to sample rural life, but a calculation on the back of an envelope that morning had been enough to demonstrate she couldn't afford a *real* holiday, by which she meant a leisurely trip to Venice by train or a month in Tuscany.

'All right, you've talked me into it. You'd better give me Clara's number.' She reached across to the table for a pen. 'And thanks, Bridget,' she added, fearing that her response so far to her friend's offer had been little short of churlish.

When Loretta put the phone down, Tracey looked at her with raised eyebrows, visibly hostile.

'What was all that about then?' he asked in a sulky voice. 'I suppose she's booked you into a rest home for vegetarian lesbians? With basket-weaving classes and radical flower arranging?'

Loretta laughed for the first time that day.

'How did you guess? And I'm afraid that you, my love, will have to be on your way. I have to arrive first thing if I'm going to sign up for the refresher course in man-eating. How much do I owe you for the takeaway?'

She shooed a reluctant Tracey out of her flat, determined not to listen to another word of his complaints about his love life.

'But how will I get hold of you?' he called up the stairs, turning to peer up at her.

Loretta realized she didn't even know whether Clara's cottage was on the phone.

'Don't call me, I'll call you,' she shouted cheerfully.

The slamming of the street door two floors below told Loretta that her sally had not been well received. She shrugged, crossed the landing and went back into her flat, looking at her watch as she did so. It was just after ten and she wondered whether it was too late to ring Clara Wolstonecroft. On balance she decided that it was. The woman was a stranger, and her habits entirely unknown to Loretta; for all she knew, people kept different hours in the country. And though she was feeling more light-hearted than she had for days, the prospect of an early night was decidedly appealing. Thinking that she'd watch a few minutes of *News at Ten* before retiring, Loretta went into the drawing room and was about to switch on the television when the phone rang again.

'Loretta Lawson?' The woman's voice was brisk and upper middle class, not one that Loretta recognized. 'Ah, good,' she said when Loretta had identified herself. 'So glad to have caught you. You weren't in bed, I hope? Clara Wolstonecroft here, I'm a friend of Bridget Bennett's. Has she spoken to you?'

Loretta murmured that she had.

'I thought so. I tried your number earlier and it was engaged. She's told you about the cottage?'

Clara's diction was loud and clear, as if she was used to communicating with foreigners whose grasp of English could not be relied upon. Loretta had a momentary flashback to her schooldays when she had habitually been addressed in this manner by her rather grand Latin teacher. She struggled to repel the vision of herself in bottle-green uniform that Clara had unknowingly conjured up.

'So do you think you might be able to move in for a few

6

weeks? Actually' – Clara's voice dropped to a tone that was probably intended to be confiding – 'you'd be doing me the most tremendous favour. It's a trifle delicate, as a matter of fact. The thing is – goodness, how thoughtless of me, bothering you with all my problems when you're feeling like a squashed hedgehog! My niece had glandular fever once, she looked quite appalling. How about it?'

'It's very kind of you . . .' Loretta began, her doubts about the project suddenly returning. Clara's eagerness to have her as a tenant, combined with the mysterious reference to a 'tremendous favour', had unnerved her. Did Clara have an ulterior motive for wanting her there? And what could it be? Loretta was still trying to frame a tactful inquiry that might elicit answers to these questions when Clara interrupted her.

'That's settled then,' she announced, either misinterpreting Loretta's hesitant response or pretending that she had. 'How soon can you move in? Is Saturday all right? Let's make it Saturday – Wayne's moving out in the morning, thank God, and I'll invite some of the neighbours round to supper to meet you. We don't want you to be lonely! Come around five, that'll give Mrs Abbott time to clear up the mess in the cottage. By the way, you don't have any unusual hobbies, do you?'

Loretta said that she didn't, even more perplexed. What on earth had her predecessor as Clara's tenant been up to? All she'd gathered about Wayne was that he was American and lectured on Ernest Hemingway: did that offer any clue? Casting her mind back to her meagre store of knowledge on Hemingway, the first thing Loretta came up with was bullfighting, which was obviously out; it seemed highly unlikely that Wayne had rustled a local cow and made passes at it with his gown in the garden outside the cottage. The other pastimes she associated with Hemingway, drinking and shooting, seemed much more possible. Wrinkling her nose, Loretta hoped she wouldn't find a cache of empty bottles under the bed, or, even worse, the remains – feathers perhaps? – of any harmless creature Wayne had blasted out of the sky. Deciding that these reflections were further evidence of her feverish state, Loretta turned to the business of taking down Clara's instructions on how to get to her house to collect keys to the cottage. Ten minutes later she went to bed, more than a little concerned about what to expect from her hastily arranged visit to Oxfordshire.

Moving out of London at three days' notice, even for a short period, posed more problems than Loretta had anticipated. There were discussions at college as to how her work should be shared out among colleagues over the next few weeks; clothes to be cleaned and packed (a task made all the more difficult by Loretta's resistance to what she thought of as 'country' clothes and their consequent absence from her wardrobe); books to be returned and borrowed from the London Library; and arrangements to be made with her downstairs neighbour to water plants and forward mail. She was quite relieved when she shut the front door of her flat on Saturday morning and carried her bags down to her white Panda. She had arranged to stop for lunch at an Indian restaurant in Holloway Road with a friend from her department, and it was just after three when she finally set off for Clara's.

The weather was warm and sunny, just as it should be but rarely is in mid-May, and she was in high spirits. These slumped suddenly on the M40 just beyond High Wycombe as a bout of tiredness combined with an unwelcome thought: she had not travelled along this road since the previous autumn, when she'd had a brief and exceedingly painful affair with someone she'd met at Bridget's house in Oxford. She wondered fretfully whether this was an omen for the present trip, then laughed at herself. Usually the least superstitious of people, she had recently discovered a morbid tendency, which she attributed to her illness, to seek out signs and coincidences. Pop music was the answer to this nonsense, she decided; picking up a tape from the parcel shelf, she pushed it into the cassette player and filled the car with Tina Turner. She sang along happily, and in no time at all she was at the end of the motorway and had spotted the right turn off the A40 to Forest Hill.

Turning off the main road, Loretta drove along a twisting lane through the village and found herself in what seemed like another world. The hedgerows to either side groaned under a weight of white blossom, and the fields were a patchwork of bright and mossy greens. She passed thatched cottages so overgrown with lilac and white flowers that they themselves might have been rooted to the spot. A herd of long-horned cattle gazed incuriously at her from a field; one of them, larger than the rest, rubbed his head patiently against the top strand of the wire fence. A couple of miles further into this paradise Loretta saw a road to her right and a sign pointing along it to the village of Flitwell. Although this was Clara's postal address, Loretta followed her instructions and drove on, keeping an eye out for the narrow lane which apparently preceded the house. In the event, she saw the house first, a long and slightly forbidding building standing alone on the right-hand side of the road, flanked on either side by trees. The lane, down which Loretta had been told to drive, was so overhung that it looked like the entrance to a tunnel; the diminution of light when the car began to make its way down the narrow hill was startling. At the bottom she saw a dusty lay-by to her left, empty even though it was large enough for several cars, and parked. Deciding to leave her luggage in the car for the time being she made her way back up the hill. It was steep, and she found herself panting before she reached the top. Turning right at the main road, she stopped for a moment to get her breath back and take in the details of Clara's house. She was in the right place; a modest wooden sign above the front door bore the name 'Baldwin's'. Loretta wondered whether it had been built, or at least owned, by someone of that name. A member of Clara's family, perhaps? The house was low and, had it not been constructed of a honey-coloured stone which Loretta took to be local, might well have appeared – unfriendly? It seemed the wrong sort of word to apply to a house, but the building certainly hadn't been designed to impress the visitor with its open charm. It was asymmetrical in shape, the front door and window to each side being bunched at one end, next to the lane. To the left, a blank wall stretched for several yards. It looked, in fact, as though a barn and a house had lurched drunkenly together after some bucolic revel and failed to part. The upper storey showed even less evidence that it was part of a dwelling; only one window, situated directly above

9

the front door, provided a break in the façade. Loretta wondered if the builder had been particularly unsociable, or whether he had simply intended to shield his affairs from the gaze of passers-by. Not that there could be many of those; peering in both directions, she noticed that Baldwin's was the only house in sight.

Realizing she had been standing in the road for several minutes, Loretta stepped forward and lifted the knocker, an evil-looking brass sprite with one leg folded across the other. As she brought it down, the sound was completely drowned by the sudden roar of a plane passing low overhead. She stepped back and stared up into the sky, but it was gone. Loretta moved closer to the door and tried again. This time the sound echoed through the house, but she heard no evidence of occupation. Loretta looked at her watch, satisfied herself that she wasn't early, and knocked a third time. Just as she was beginning to think no one was in, the door finally opened.

'Sorry,' said the young woman half-hidden behind it. 'I was in the bath.' As she opened the door wider, Loretta saw that the girl was wearing nothing but a large white bath towel which she had clutched to her chest; it made a rather fetching contrast to her thick chin-length black hair. 'I hoped I'd have finished by the time you got here,' she went on, stepping back so that Loretta could enter the hall.

It was light and spacious, with a colourful tiled floor, and Loretta's first impression of the house as unwelcoming was immediately dispelled. She was facing a back door which led into a conservatory; to her right, a door stood open into the kitchen, and wide stairs rose to the upper floor. To her left, a long corridor stretched along the blank front wall of the house. The wallpaper, wild flowers on an off-white background, was dotted with a startling collection of watercolours, oriental prints and china plates.

'I was absolutely filthy, everything's in chaos today,' the girl went on. 'Clara's still up at the peace camp, they're trying to get enough tents up before it gets dark. She was going to ring you to let you know about Wayne but I expect she forgot. She's been at the camp most of the day. Anyway, I'm sure we can sort something out. Why don't you put the kettle on and

I'll be down in a minute. Through there,' she said, indicating the kitchen door and heading for the stairs.

Loretta made to follow her, and realized she didn't know the girl's name, or who she was.

'Wait a minute – you said something about Wayne – is there a problem?' Her heart was sinking at the prospect of having to turn round and drive back to London.

'Only that the little shit has decided not to move out till tomorrow,' the girl called cheerfully from the top of the stairs. She stopped and leaned over the banister. 'But Clara said not to worry, we'll fix you up here and you can still meet the neighbours. Though God knows what they're going to eat, I don't think Clara's thought about food. But I dare say she'll manage, she always does. I'm Imogen, by the way, Clara's my mother. You can call me Imo. I take it you're Loretta? Bit silly if you weren't.'

With this she disappeared, leaving Loretta to make her way to the kitchen. It was an L-shaped room, with one window giving on to the main road and another, which hadn't been visible from the front, looking out on to the trees which overhung the side lane. It was a dark room, but not unpleasant; a deep red Edwardian wallpaper covered the walls and gave an impression of cosiness which was enhanced by the presence of an Aga. Suddenly aware of how weary she was – this damned illness, she thought – Loretta pulled out a chair and sat down at the table. She was very glad that she wouldn't have to return to London that night, even though Imo's promise of alternative accommodation had been a bit vague. She wondered if Imo, with her dark hair and white skin, resembled her mother. Bridget hadn't mentioned Clara's daughter, perhaps because the girl looked the sort of age at which she might be away at university or college. Maybe Imo was home for the weekend? And was the girl's father about to appear? Loretta assumed all would become clear in the course of the weekend.

Remembering Imo's suggestion that she put the kettle on, Loretta got up and looked for an electric kettle. It took her a couple of minutes to realize there wasn't one. Instead, a heavy, old-fashioned whistling kettle of a type she hadn't seen since childhood was standing half-full on the shelf above the Aga. Loretta lifted it down, added more water, and raised one of the two chrome lids which covered the hob. She had an idea that one end would turn out to be hotter than the other and was about to try the second when she was startled by a crash from the hall. Her first thought was that she was about to come face to face with a burglar, and she looked round wildly for anything that might serve as a weapon. At the same time she heard a sliding noise, as if a heavy object was being pushed or pulled laboriously across the floor. Next came a series of panted curses.

'*Bloody* thing!' she heard, then a noise like a kick and a muttered 'ow'. This was followed by the same voice uttering, or rather bellowing, a single word: '*Clara!*'

Loretta unfroze and moved towards the door. Since the newcomer knew her hostess, it seemed unlikely that he was a burglar. But how had he got into the house? Loretta was sure she had closed the front door behind her.

'*Clara!*' The voice was even more impatient. 'Oh God, where *is* the woman?'

Loretta opened the kitchen door and collided with the owner of the voice. As she fell back into the room she realized she was still clutching the pewter jug of dried flowers she had grasped a moment before in lieu of a weapon. She thrust it behind her, feeling for the edge of the table, meanwhile surveying the newcomer with as much equanimity as she could muster. He was looking at her oddly, and Loretta felt she couldn't blame him in the circumstances.

'Can I help?' she asked brightly, crossing her arms in front of her as though she'd never been near the flowers, which were now back in place on the table.

'I'm looking for Clara,' the man said, still observing her warily. He was in his late thirties or early forties, thin and dark, with rather intense eyes.

'She isn't here, she's at the peace camp.' Loretta repeated the information Imo had given her, realizing as she did so that she knew nothing about the camp – its location, or Clara's connection with it. She hadn't even been aware that there *was* a peace camp anywhere in the vicinity of Flitwell.

'Oh *hell*,' the man said in a slow voice which expressed perplexity more than annoyance. He stepped back into the hall and Loretta followed. She found him staring at a large square box which was sitting in the middle of the hall floor. There were fingermarks all over its dusty mahogany surface and scuff marks on the tiled floor as though he had pushed it from the back door.

'So what do I do with this?' he asked, running a hand through his hair – the picture of puzzlement, Loretta thought. 'Wait a minute, do you have a car?' he asked, suddenly hopeful.

'Yes, but – '

'That's it then. You'll be going back there shortly, I suppose? I'll load it up and you can take it with you.'

'To the peace camp? But I don't know where it is. Or what *that* is,' she added, taking a second look at the object he'd delivered.

The stranger ignored the second part of her remark.

'You're not from the peace camp?'

Loretta admitted she wasn't.

'I thought – ' Her interlocutor began to laugh. 'Sorry, it's just that you had me puzzled,' he explained. 'When I saw you here I assumed you must be one of the peace women, but you didn't look quite – right. You know what I mean.' His gaze travelled down her fine grey wool jumper, her matching straight skirt, and hovered for a second at her grey suede high heels. Loretta took his meaning and bridled.

'I've been to Greenham loads of times, as a matter of fact,' she said stiffly.

'Look, I didn't mean – '

'I was arrested at Christmas,' she continued, ignoring his attempt at an apology. She decided against revealing that she had later been released without charge. Bridget, to whom this had happened twice before, had been most put out when they hadn't been required to appear in court; Loretta had secretly been relieved. She realized that the stranger was waiting with amusement for her next remark and decided to change the subject.

'I'm Clara's new tenant, by the way. I was supposed to move into the cottage today, but the chap who's there at the moment isn't going till tomorrow, apparently. So here I am.'

'Oh, re-ally.' He had a way of drawing out short words

13

which invested them with a significance Loretta couldn't fathom. 'Another sin to add to the catalogue. Clara must be furious.' He smiled absently, gazing into the middle distance. 'It's Great-aunt Idena's commode. That thing.' He gestured towards the wooden box. 'Hasn't been used for years. But it's all there.'

Obviously proud of this fact, he lifted the hinged lid to reveal the white porcelain chamberpot inside. Loretta giggled, suddenly assailed by a vision of full-skirted Victorian ladies emerging from benders to form a sedate queue in the bushes.

'They want *that* at the peace camp?'

'So Clara says – ' He looked at her for a moment, puzzled, then joined in her laughter.

'Robert?' It was Imo's voice, and a moment later she ran lightly down the stairs, dressed now in a denim mini-skirt. 'What's the joke?' A smile hovered about her lips as she looked from Robert to Loretta, waiting for enlightenment.

'It's all your mother's fault, as usual,' Robert explained. 'She rang this morning to ask if I still had Idena's commode. I've spent half the afternoon crawling about in the loft looking for it. And now it's here your mother isn't. I don't know what to do. *I* can't take it up there, can I?'

'Hardly,' Imo agreed. 'It's women only,' she added, turning to Loretta. 'And even if it hadn't been up to now, after last night . . .' She trailed off.

'Last night?'

'Haven't you heard? There was even something on the radio about this morning,' Imo said. 'It happened about three o'clock this morning. A bunch of men appeared out of nowhere and started smashing up the camp, they even tried to set fire to the caravan.'

'Was anyone hurt?' Loretta was horrified.

'A couple of women had to go to hospital. Fortunately they ran off as soon as everyone started coming out of their tents. It's amazing no one was badly hurt, really.'

'But why do they want a commode?' queried Loretta. 'Haven't they dug, er, trenches?'

'Yes, but Clara thought it would be safer if they didn't have to walk all the way to the trenches at night. She's been

14

ringing round all day trying to find people who've got those old things. With Robert's we've got three. She's a terrific organizer, my mother. Tell you what, Robert, why don't you lend me your car and I'll take it up there? I've passed my test, you know.' Robert seemed to be hesitating. 'Oh, go on, Robert. It's not very far. And how else are you going to get it up there?'

Robert sighed. 'All right. I suppose you want me to put it back in the car for you?'

'Please. By the way, this is Loretta, she's staying with us tonight. Robert's one of our neighbours, he lives in Flitwell. He's coming to dinner this evening, you're not supposed to have met him yet.'

Robert was leaning over the commode, preparing to lift it. Loretta moved to help but he waved her away.

'I can manage. See you later.'

Imo opened the back door, which was unlocked, and Robert trundled the commode out of it. Loretta returned to the kitchen where she was joined by Imo, who asked if she'd made some tea. Loretta explained she'd been interrupted by Robert's arrival, and Imo placed the kettle on the hob.

'I'll just have a cup before I go back to the camp,' she said. 'Robert's left me his keys.'

'I had no idea there was a peace camp near here,' Loretta said. 'Where is it exactly?'

'About a mile along the road. You must have heard of Dunstow, RAF Dunstow? Though it's not really an RAF base at all, it's American. Just like Greenham. Except they don't have Cruise missiles here, they have F1-11s. Remember all the fuss last month when they bombed Libya? Well, some of the planes came from here. That's when the peace camp was set up, the first women arrived the day after.'

'I *see*, that's why I hadn't heard of it.'

'Oh yes, the camp's only been going about four weeks. But the fuss it's caused – you wouldn't believe it. When they first arrived, they put up tents outside the main gate. But the council evicted them – it turned out they'd passed some by-law ages ago in case a peace camp was set up here, and no one had noticed. Milk? Sugar?'

Loretta shook her head.

'That's when Clara got involved. She was so cross when the Americans attacked Libya – I rang her up that night and she was . . . well, I've never heard her so angry. When the peace camp got evicted, she offered them a site on her land. She owns part of the wood along the side of the base, you see. And everyone's furious with her. She's been banned from the Green Man in Flitwell, and half the village isn't speaking to her. Mind you, a lot of people are on her side – the vicar got up a petition and took it to the base, but the man in charge refused to meet him. So he's written an absolute diatribe in the parish magazine. You can imagine the ructions that's caused.'

'But the attack last night – is this the first time it's happened?'

'More or less. I mean, it's not the first time people have turned up at the camp and yelled abuse, that sort of thing. Some of the Americans from the base, they come down at night and throw the odd stone, apparently. You'll have to ask Clara, this is the first time I've been home when anything's happened. But last night was really vicious. They wore masks, the sort you get in joke shops. The women woke up and found these men with horrible faces trying to set fire to the caravan.'

'What about the police?' Loretta asked the question without much hope.

Imo shrugged. 'They say there's nothing they can do.' She leaned back against the Aga and sipped her tea. 'I suppose they're right. The women can't identify anyone 'cause of the masks. And they say they haven't enough men to put a guard on the camp at night. Gosh, is that the time?' A clock was chiming six somewhere in the house. 'I hope Clara comes back soon.'

'What time is everyone coming?'

'Eight,' said Imo. 'I should have asked her what needed doing. But I expect she'll manage. There's bound to be something in the freezer.' She pulled a face.

'Shouldn't I be doing something?' Loretta was becoming anxious on Clara's behalf. Her own dinner parties were always carefully planned to give her plenty of time to shop and cook. The idea that there were only two hours to go before the arrival of Clara's guests appalled her. At that moment a door slammed and a woman's voice sounded in the hall.

'Imo? Are you there, darling?'

'In here, Clara.'

The kitchen door opened and a striking figure strode in.

'Is Robert here? I saw his car in the lane. Ah, you must be Loretta.'

Loretta stood up and took Clara's extended hand, feeling much like a schoolgirl meeting her new headmistress.

'Sorry I wasn't here when you arrived. I see Imo's made some tea, good. I gather you're supposed to be having *complete* rest. Where *is* Robert? Has he brought the commode?'

She moved across the kitchen to the sink and dried a mug on a rather scruffy tea-cloth. Imo explained that she was about to take the commode up to the peace camp in Robert's car, and Loretta had time to study her hostess.

Clara Wolstonecroft was slightly above average height, and well built. Her most commanding feature was a matronly bosom whose prominence was not disguised by the loose flowered dress she was wearing. Her hair was an attractive iron-grey, cut, like Imo's, to chin length so that it framed her strong face.

'I'm sorry about the cottage,' she said, joining Loretta at the kitchen table. 'The little rat swears he told me Sunday and I know he's lying. He's just changed his mind and didn't have the manners to tell me. But he'll be out tomorrow, no doubt about that. I told him – if you don't shift your belongings by lunch time, my lad, I'll move them myself.' She bestowed a satisfied smile on Loretta. 'You don't mind sleeping in my study tonight? It's quite comfortable. I have a couch in there for when I'm working on a book – I tend to sleep odd hours.'

Loretta assured her that this arrangement suited her very well. Anything, she thought privately, rather than face the journey back to Islington. 'Can I help with dinner?' she asked, aware of the moments ticking past.

'Certainly not.' Clara was affronted. 'You must be exhausted, driving all the way from London. I think the best thing is if I take you upstairs so you can have a nap before dinner.' It was said in the tone of a matron packing off her charge to the sick bay. Suddenly suspecting that Bridget had greatly exaggerated the extent of her debility, Loretta summoned up the courage to defy her hostess.

'I feel fine, honestly,' she said firmly. 'I'd be much happier if I had something to do. I could scrub some potatoes,' she suggested, catching sight of the vegetable rack.

Clara's gaze slid across to the clock on the wall and back to Loretta.

'Well, I suppose you don't look too bad,' she admitted. 'If you insist . . .'

Loretta got up and busied herself finding a bowl in which to heap the potatoes. In the background, Clara was talking to herself.

'Now where's my list?' She began to search through the heap of letters, bills and envelopes which lay at the window end of the table, finally drawing out a crumpled piece of paper.

'Bridget can't come, so that's one less,' she murmured. 'That leaves me, Loretta, Imo – are you here for dinner, Imo?'

'Certainly am!'

'Plus Robert. Not the Etterbekes, silly old fools. Did I tell you, darling, Charles Etterbeke won't come to dinner because of the peace camp? Ellie and Herc, that makes, um, six. And Gilbert. Oh, and one of the girls from the camp will be here,' she added, looking first at Imo and then at Loretta. 'She only arrived yesterday, poor thing, and she got rather a bang on the head when they pulled her tent down. The hospital says she's all right but I want to keep her here for a couple of days just to make sure. Perhaps you can bring her back in Robert's car, darling? I said I'd collect her but as you're going up there anyway . . . Her name's Peggy and she's got blonde hair. So that's how many?'

'Eight,' supplied Loretta.

'And can I leave pudding to you, my sweet? I thought we'd have hate cake. The biscuits are in the top cupboard.'

'Oh, goody,' said Imo in a surprisingly childish voice.

'Hate cake?' queried Loretta.

Clara smiled. 'An old family recipe,' she said. 'We call it

that because we love it so much. Biscuit crumbs and chocolate and honey. Delicious.'

Loretta wasn't so sure; it sounded just the sort of disgusting mess that children would have been expected to eat in the nursery eighty or a hundred years ago. But she maintained a tactful silence.

'I think we'll have to have that *boeuf bourgignon* I put in the freezer last week,' Clara went on. 'It's no good looking like that, darling, there isn't anything else. Are you sure you can cope with all those potatoes, Loretta?'

Loretta nodded vigorously, fearing that the potatoes might well turn out to be the most edible part of the meal. As the others got on with various tasks connected with the meal – Loretta watched in secret horror as Imo mixed together the ingredients of the hate cake – she began to wonder how Clara intended to fit eight people into such an awkwardly shaped room. The kitchen table was hardly big enough even for six and any attempt to move it into the centre would bring it into contact with the handsome oak dresser on the opposite wall. Her question was answered, however, when she finished the potatoes and Imo suggested taking her upstairs to the study.

'I'll come too,' said Clara, wiping her hands. 'We'll have to bring my work table down before anyone arrives – I thought we'd eat in the hall.'

Loretta followed the two women up the stairs and found herself on a spacious landing. A sash window looked out on to the road; at the back of the house its double gave on to the back garden. As she faced the front of the house the wall to her left was completely taken up with bookshelves; that to her right was dominated by a large abstract painting.

'Come and admire my view,' Clara instructed, leading the way to the window overlooking the garden.

Loretta obeyed, unprepared for the sight that met her eyes. It was, she thought, as though she had been transported back several decades. A grassy terrace ended in a low stone wall, beyond which fell away a lawn starred with wild flowers. Towards the bottom of the lawn, slightly to the right, was a disused circular pond, its cracked stone base suggesting it had weathered innumerable dry summers. To one side a magnolia dripped its heavy blossom over the pond's edge.

All that was needed to complete the scene was a group of women in trailing white dresses. The lawn ended in another stone wall, this one of much more rough-hewn appearance, beyond which a row of outbuildings struggled to survive an onslaught of weeds and brambles. On the far side of the outbuildings, a thick green wood stretched up the other side of the valley.

'Isn't it wonder– ' Clara's voice, loud as it was, was lost in the noise of another plane passing overhead. 'Bloody machines,' she snapped as the noise died away. 'They're not supposed to fly at weekends. This way.'

She turned abruptly and led Loretta down the long corridor stretching to the right at the front of the house.

'Spare room,' she said, indicating a door half-way down. 'I'm going to put Peggy in there.' She opened a door at the very end of the corridor and went in. 'This is where I work,' she said, a note of pride in her voice.

It was a delightful room. There were no fewer than three sets of windows, one at each side of the black marble fireplace and a bay window with white wooden shutters on the wall facing the door. The walls were painted off-white and were covered with sketches of cats, many of them the originals of Clara's books. It took Loretta a moment to realize there was also a live cat in the room, a sinuous grey creature stretched out on a *chaise-longue* upholstered in faded yellow velvet. This animal suddenly sat up, let out a conversational wail, and padded over to Clara, who picked him up. He immediately clambered up on to her shoulders, draped himself elegantly across the back of her neck, and began to purr.

'This is Bertie,' said Clara, reaching up to stroke the cat's head. 'I suppose you haven't seen the cottage yet?'

She moved across the room to the bay window, lifting the heavy metal bar to open the shutters. They folded neatly back on themselves and Loretta caught her first glimpse of Keeper's Cottage.

It was much closer to Baldwin's than she had imagined – Loretta realized she had pictured the cottage in some far corner of Clara's garden. It was separated from Baldwin's by a privet hedge which stood about five feet tall, a small path leading from a gap in the hedge to its front door. The high stone wall which hid Clara's garden from the road actually joined the cottage at its far end, and there were double wooden doors in it to allow direct access to the cottage. As Bridget had warned, Keeper's Cottage was very small; it was also beautiful, with the mauve blossom of a long-established wistaria obscuring most of its front elevation. There were two doors, one in the main building, a second in the two-storey extension to the right. Upstairs a modern window, set into the roof, provided the cottage with both light and privacy. The only discordant note in this charming rustic scene was a large and unmistakably American car parked between the privet hedge and the front door, next to the wooden gates that led to the main road.

'Wayne's?' Loretta turned to Clara.

'Of course. Imo, if I take this end of the table, can you do the backwards bit?'

Imo, who had been piling various pieces of paper on a desk in the corner, grasped the far end of the table as her mother took the other, the cat still balanced precariously on her shoulders. Loretta's offer of help was firmly refused, and she trailed down the corridor in their wake feeling rather useless.

'Bathroom's through there,' called Clara, indicating a door towards the back of the house. 'You go off and get ready. Come down for drinks at eight.'

Loretta accepted her dismissal, observing that Clara seemed accustomed to having her orders obeyed. Returning to the study she sat down gingerly on the *chaise-longue* which the cat had recently vacated. This, she presumed, was where she was to sleep tonight; it felt unexpectedly sturdy for so delicate a piece of furniture. Looking round the room she noticed a chest of dark wood against a wall. She went over and lifted the lid, discovering sheets, blankets and a worn patchwork quilt. She glanced at her watch and decided there was time for a bath before supper, then remembered that her luggage, including her soap bag, was still in the car.

She returned to the landing and descended the stairs. The long table was now in the hall, laid with a white tablecloth and place mats for eight. Towards each end stood huge branching candelabra, precariously filled with candles of assorted length and design – straight-sided, twisted, even a couple of red ones with paper holly leaves left over from Christmas. Each place was set with a quantity of large, old-fashioned silver, much in need of polishing. The overall effect was rather pleasing, like a stage set artfully designed to suggest careless grandeur.

Loretta turned sideways to slide past the table and put her head round the kitchen door. The grey cat was now on the floor, she noticed, leaning with closed eyes against the lower oven door of the Aga.

'I'm just going to get my things from the car,' she said. 'Is there a short cut across the garden?'

Clara tossed a heap of chopped vegetables into the saucepan and came to the door.

'You go out of the conservatory, across the terrace and on to the lawn,' she said. 'There's a gate in the trees that brings you out into the lane just above the lay-by. Leave your car there for tonight and you can put it outside the cottage when Wayne leaves. I'll be delighted to see the back of that wretched Pan-Am.'

'*Trans*-Am,' Imo called from the kitchen, her tone suggesting this was not the first time Clara had made the mistake.

'Oh, Loretta, don't feel you *have* to dress for dinner.' Clara's voice followed Loretta as she stepped into the conservatory. She paused for a moment, wondering how to interpret this remark. It hadn't occurred to her to change, but the way Clara had spoken suggested that it might be the usual practice at Baldwin's. It was just as well, Loretta thought, that she'd brought a couple of dresses with her.

Just under an hour later, as Loretta was outlining her eyes with a kohl pencil, the sky suddenly darkened. Through the windows Clara's garden abruptly drained of colour, the multitude of greens turning to tones of grey as the sky filled with rain. When it came, the first fork of lightning briefly restored a washed-out colour, as though someone had let off a giant flashgun. Loretta drew back into the room, disturbed not so much by the lightning as by a sense of unaccustomed closeness to the elements; she had a heightened awareness of her surroundings which was lacking in London, as though some sort of protective film had temporarily dissolved. Feeling a momentary yearning for the familiarity of her flat, she tried to dispel her unease by switching on the red-shaded table lamp which stood on Clara's desk. It cast a deep, warm glow across the room and she relaxed in spite of the lightning which again disfigured the sky.

She had already unpacked some of her clothes; she took down a drop-waisted dress of black and white silk from its hanger on the back of the door and slipped it over her head. Crossing to the mantelpiece, she took a pair of jet earrings from her jewellery box and fixed them in her ears. She wasn't looking too bad, she thought, examining her reflection critically in the mirror; her bobbed blonde hair would soon need cutting, but there was a bit of colour in her cheeks and her eyes were less sunken than they had been for weeks. She applied a touch of lipstick, stood back, and decided that she'd do. It wasn't that she minded being thirty-two, she thought, crossing the room to close the shutters; what bothered her was feeling a good ten years older, as she had since the start of her illness. Well, perhaps things were looking up at last. She closed the curtains to either side of the fireplace, had a last look round the room, and went downstairs.

'Good timing,' said Imo, who was crossing the hall from the kitchen. 'This way for drinks.'

She led the way into a room to the left of the back door which turned out to be the drawing room. A large square bay looked out on to the back garden, and an assortment of comfortably shabby chairs and a sofa were grouped before an unlit grate. There were pictures everywhere, most of them Victorian portraits and landscapes; a couple looked like copies – surely not originals, Loretta thought – of lesser-known Pre-Raphaelites.

'Who are you?'

There were three people already in the room, and the voice came from one of them, a woman sitting to one side of the fireplace in an attitude of complete relaxation: her legs, encased in elderly corduroy trousers with splashes of mud round the ankles, were stretched out before her as she lounged in her chair. An old bottle-green jumper completed her *ensemble*, and her gaze was directed unwaveringly at Loretta in spite of the fact that she was engaged in relighting an obviously troublesome pipe. Loretta swallowed, suddenly self-conscious, and was relieved to be rescued by Imo.

'Loretta's our new tenant,' the girl said. 'She's moving into the cottage.'

'Makes a change,' the woman said, smiling widely. 'You're an improvement on the dreadful Wayne. Isn't she, darling?' This remark was directed at a man seated on a high-backed chair on the other side of the fireplace. He was of small, stocky build, and had a mass of dark, curly hair. Before he could speak she went on, 'I'm Ellie Barker, and this is my husband, Herc Parker.'

She beamed at Loretta, who was beginning to realize that the woman's manner was simply direct, rather than hostile as she had at first thought.

'Don't worry about getting them mixed up,' said Imo, who had taken a seat in the bay where she was half-obscured by a full-length velvet curtain. 'Everyone does. Clara says they should toss a coin and choose one or the other, but they won't. It's very confusing.'

'No, it isn't,' objected Ellie. 'You've known me all your life, Imogen, and I've always been Ellie Barker. I don't believe in this nonsense of women having to change their names when they get married.'

'Neither do I,' said Herc firmly, revealing a strong New England accent. 'But I did say to Ellie, the day she proposed to me, this name business is not going to be easy. Why don't we combine them, I said, and call ourselves the Barker-Parkers? See, I even offered to put hers first. But would she? Oh no.'

'Course not, darling,' Ellie said indignantly. 'It makes us sound like chinless wonders out of a P.G. Wodehouse novel.'

'Lovely, when you've spent forty-eight years of your life as Hercules Parker, it don't seem important what people think.'

'I, on the other hand, am plain Gilbert Brown,' said the third person in the room, rising to his feet and extending a hand courteously to Loretta.

He was tall, Loretta noticed, though his height was slightly disguised by what appeared to be an habitual stoop. His age, she thought, could be anything between sixty and seventy.

'Like you,' he went on, 'I am one of Clara's tenants.' He relinquished her hand and sat down. 'Though pensioner might be more accurate in my case. I've lived in one of Clara's cottages in the village for fourteen years, on and off. A very good landlady she is, too.'

He had a slow, pedantic way of speaking, Loretta noticed, nonplussed by this strange gathering. The thought uppermost in her mind, in fact, was that she had misread Clara's remark about dressing for dinner; Herc and Ellie had obviously come as they were – Loretta wondered if they were farmers, and had been engaged in one of the innumerable messy tasks of which, she assumed, farmers were fond – and Gilbert was wearing an old pullover under his shabby sports jacket. Nor did it seem likely that the woman from the peace camp had arrived at the house with a trunkful of evening clothes among her luggage. Her only hope was Robert, and he hadn't struck her as a man with a great interest in his appearance.

To cover her sense of being out of place, Loretta took a seat near Herc and inquired how long he'd lived in England. Ten years, he told her, dispelling her vision of him as a farmer with the information that he was a freelance journalist specializing in financial affairs. His contact with the soil, she discovered, was limited to an allotment in the village where he was experimenting with various kinds of marrow that he hadn't been able to get since moving from the States. 'Butternut squash,' he sighed, reminiscing about the soup his mother used to make.

'He's not boring you with his marrows?' Ellie demanded, smiling broadly. 'Darling, you'll never get squash to grow over here, the climate's wrong. You ought to write to the manager of Sainsbury's, I've told you.'

At that moment, the door opened and Clara swept into the room. Loretta was at once glad she'd taken trouble with her appearance; her hostess was resplendent in a full-length caftan in a brilliant green and yellow material. It was much admired, until Clara whirled round and propelled into their midst the slight figure who had been standing behind her.

'Everybody, this is Peggy,' she announced, a hand on the

girl's shoulder. 'She got a nasty bang on the head last night, so I'm keeping an eye on her. How *is* your head?'

'All right.'

The girl – she didn't look more than twenty, Loretta thought – seemed uncomfortable in her role as Clara's protégée. Loretta sympathized. Peggy was dressed in painfully tight jeans, a pastel pink sweatshirt which had been through more washes than was good for it, and a battered pair of training shoes. Her short, dyed blonde hair was already showing dark at the roots and she was wearing gold sleepers in her ears. Loretta guessed her discomfort was as much to do with being in unfamiliar surroundings as it was to the blow she'd sustained to her head. An impulse to help her led her to catch the girl's eye and pat the sofa beside her.

'Come and sit down,' she said in a friendly voice.

Peggy looked a little mutinous but, realizing her retreat was amply blocked by Clara, decided to comply. She crossed the room and sat down next to Loretta, her body unrelaxed and her knees drawn stiffly together.

'Have you come far? To get to the peace camp, I mean?' Loretta spoke in a low voice, hoping to draw the girl out and put her at her ease.

Peggy's response was not encouraging.

'Yeah,' she said, absently fingering one of her earrings. 'London, sort of.'

Loretta noticed a band of white skin on the third finger of the girl's left hand, as though she had worn a ring until very recently.

'Are you staying at the peace camp for long? Or did you come for the weekend?'

'Depends.' She was apparently bent on keeping her replies to the minimum consistent with good manners.

Before Loretta could try another gambit, Clara finished a conversation with Herc and swept down on them.

'Now, Peggy, what can I get you to drink? Some wine perhaps, or a gin and tonic? I know, why not have a kir, that's just the thing for a spring evening. Oh dear, you don't seem to have anything either, Loretta – Imo, what *were* you thinking of, darling? Loretta hasn't got a drink. Right, that's two kirs.'

Loretta opened her mouth. She had been quite unable to face the latter drink since it had featured in a highly emotional scene in Paris the previous year when she had parted from a lover in distressing circumstances. Beside her, Peggy was looking blank, and Loretta realized the girl had no idea what a kir was. Clara, it was becoming clear, was not the most sensitive of women. She was about to make a polite protest on both their behalfs when Clara clapped a hand to her forehead.

'Heaven, what am I thinking of? Here's poor Peggy with a bang on the head and I'm offering her alcohol! Tell you what, Peggy, I'll get you a nice glass of freshly squeezed orange juice. And a kir for Loretta. Anyone else? No? Right.'

She swept from the room; Peggy, sensing Loretta's dismay, thawed a little.

'Bossy, i'n't she?' she said in a low voice, raising her eyebrows theatrically. 'Bet she's used to getting her own way.'

They exchanged complicit smiles and then Loretta, feeling slightly guilty about this disloyalty to her hostess, turned back to Herc and asked which papers he worked for. He was explaining that his main source of income was specialist magazines when Clara came back with the drinks. Handing them over – Loretta took hers with a shiver – Clara pulled up a chair and joined them, settling her dress in vivid folds about her feet.

'Now, Clara, do tell us what happened at this settlement of yours last night,' said Gilbert.

He meant the peace camp, Loretta guessed, although she had never heard it described in this way before. It occurred to her, correctly as it turned out, that Gilbert Brown was not an admirer of the peace women.

'Well, Gilbert, I'm afraid some of our neighbours decided to take the law into their own hands,' Clara said combatively. 'And it's a miracle no one was killed. Burning branches, that's what they used – they very nearly set fire to the caravan with two people inside it. They wore masks, of course, that shows how brave they are. Even so, we all know who's behind it, don't we? It's RALF again.'

'Oh, come on, Clara, you've got no proof –'

Loretta interrupted Gilbert. 'Who's Ralph? If you know who he is, why – '

'No, no, RALF's not a person,' Clara explained impatiently. 'It's a what d'you call those things made of initials, an acronym. Residents Against Loony Feminists, that's what it stands for.'

'Females, not feminists,' put in Imo. 'Those people wouldn't know how to spell feminists.'

'It's not called that any more, as you're perfectly well aware,' Gilbert protested. 'It was changed at the second meeting. It's the Flitwell Residents' Association.'

'Whatever it's called, they ought to be ashamed of themselves,' Clara said hotly. 'They're nothing more than a bunch of vigilantes. It was them who got the camp evicted from the main gate,' she told Loretta ungrammatically, 'and now they're furious because it's on my land. And *staying* there,' she added.

'Clara, I'm sure you haven't got a shred of evidence,' Gilbert objected. 'The association's just a group of local people who support the base and don't like it being disrupted by a bunch of agitators from outside the area. It's got some very respectable members' – he seemed to be addressing Loretta now – 'like James Silbey, he's an economist, very highly respected, he lives in the Old Rectory. And there's Colin Kendall-Cole, he's our MP. You've known Colin for years, Clara, you know he wouldn't touch the association if there was the merest hint of violence . . . For all you know, it was just a group of local lads who'd had a bit too much to drink in the Green Man. And to be frank, if those women insist on staying here and making a fuss, they're going to have to expect a backlash. After all, we've lived with the base for years, since the last war in fact, and we know the Americans are here for our protection as much as theirs.'

'Now wait a minute – ' Herc began to speak but was interrupted.

'The trouble with you, Clara,' Gilbert pressed on, 'is you've suddenly changed your tune and you want everyone else to do the same. The worst bigots are always the ones who've just seen the light. You were quite happy to live next door to the base until last month.'

'*Exactly.*' Clara pounced. 'And what happened last month? These so-called *allies* of ours, these people who are here to defend democracy, they suddenly took off and bombed a country we're not even at war with! Didn't you see the pictures on the news, all those women and children in hospital in Tripoli? It was planes from here, from Dunstow, that did that!'

'Maybe it was a mistake,' Gilbert conceded in the most reasonable of tones. 'But we're talking with hindsight. And it doesn't change the essential point – that the Americans are here to defend us from the Russians.'

'The *Russians*.' Peggy joined in unexpectedly. 'I'm sick of hearing about the *Russians*. You people' – she looked accusingly at Gilbert – 'you people always dress it up in long words, but what it's about is our kids. Is there gonna be a world for them to grow up in, or are we supposed to sit here and watch it get blown apart? Those blokes over there' – she gestured, presumably in the direction of the base – 'if they can bomb one place we're not at war with, they can bomb another. I don't want my kid to die 'cause the Americans decide to attack Russia. They're welcome to their atom bombs and their missiles – if they like them so much why don't they keep them in America? Sorry,' she said suddenly, casting an embarrassed look at Herc as though she had just remembered his accent. 'I didn't mean anything personal.'

'Don't worry,' said Herc. 'I used to be in the US navy, but as it happens I agree with you. In fact–'

At this moment the door opened and the last guest appeared. Loretta's first thought, apart from her regret that the discussion had been interrupted at so interesting a point, was that Robert had, like her, changed for dinner; he was wearing a baggy grey suit and a very cheerful tie. It was a much more fashionable outfit than she'd expected of him.

'Dear Robert, last as usual!' Clara was on her feet; Robert crossed the room to kiss her cheek.

'All in the cause of world peace,' he said innocently, stepping back and looking for a vacant seat.

'Peace?' Clara sat down, a perplexed look on her face.

'Why yes. I loaned my car to Imo in the service of the

peace camp. So I had to wait for the storm to pass before I could walk over.'

His gentle irony seemed to pass over Clara's head. 'Darling, don't forget to give Robert back his keys,' she said instantly. 'Let me introduce Loretta –'

'We've met,' said Robert, inclining his head in Loretta's direction.

'And Peggy. Thanks for the commode, by the way. It's very much appreciated. Now, everybody, let's eat. Into the hall, please.'

They filed obediently out of the room after Clara, bunching uncomfortably near the front door while they waited for instructions on where to sit. Loretta rather hoped she'd find herself next to Ellie or Herc, both of whom had aroused her curiosity. Instead, she was dispatched to the far end of the table by Clara, who suddenly declared that Loretta was that night's guest of honour. Robert and Gilbert were sent to sit on either side of her. Imo made to follow Robert but was collared by her mother.

'No, darling, not up there. I need you to help me with the dishes. Peggy, you can sit by me as well.'

The Barker-Parkers, as Loretta had begun to think of them, fitted themselves into the remaining gaps as best they could, Herc taking the seat between Peggy and Robert, his wife settling herself with Gilbert and Imogen. Loretta had glimpsed a look of disappointment on Imo's face and wondered fleetingly whether Clara's daughter had a crush on Robert. Her thoughts were distracted as a matchbox landed on the table slightly to her left.

'Gilbert, make yourself useful,' declared Clara, who had thrown it. She gestured towards the drunken candles, which Gilbert obediently lit. At the other end of the table, Imo did the same. Clara turned off the overhead light, plunging them into a gloom which made Loretta realize how dark it had become outside. The atmosphere was rather eerie: the long table, the flickering light of the candles, the ill-assorted band of strangers, and the occasional distant roll of thunder combined to produce an air of unreality, even suspense, as though something untoward might happen at any moment. She shivered, and Robert leaned towards her.

'Cold?' he asked. 'Have you got a jacket or something? That dress doesn't look very warm. Though it's very ... elegant.'

Loretta assured him she'd be all right. 'I thought I felt a draught from the back door,' she invented, 'but it's stopped now.'

'I gather you're a don,' Gilbert said from her left. 'Which college?'

Loretta looked at him in surprise, then told him the name of her college in London. Gilbert's face was momentarily blank.

'Oh, I see,' he said, 'so you're not at Oxford. Somehow I'd got the idea you were at the University.'

Loretta's hostility towards Gilbert, its seed sown during the discussion about the peace camp, began to sprout. London was just as much a university as Oxford, she thought crossly. But, for Clara's sake, she held her peace.

'What do you do?' she asked, a little maliciously. She had guessed that Gilbert was retired and, from his remark about being Clara's pensioner, not particularly well off.

'Oh, I potter about, grow a few vegetables,' he said lightly, turning her question away.

'Don't listen to him,' Robert said. 'Gilbert is a distinguished man of letters and he's writing his autobiography. He's just rather shy when it comes to talking about it.'

'One doesn't want to bore people with interminable reminiscence. I have a dread of people moving away when I walk into the pub, like they did with that chap who used to be in the RAF.'

'I think that was slightly different.' Robert grinned.

'Are you a writer? I'm sorry, I don't know your books . . .'

'Not a writer. A publisher. Writing about me is really a way of writing about my authors.'

'Who were your authors? No, I really want to know.' It took Loretta several more attempts to draw Gilbert out, interrupted by the arrival of a very good vegetable soup, but by the time the *boeuf bourguignon* appeared she was listening with genuine interest.

'Congratulations,' Robert said in a low voice as Gilbert passed his plate down for a second helping. 'That's the longest conversation I've ever known Gilbert have with a stranger. You're a good listener.'

Loretta checked nervously to make sure that Gilbert's attention was elsewhere and saw that he was talking to Ellie. 'Mock Georgian coach lamps,' Ellie was saying; they seemed to be discussing the latest piece of architectural vandalism in Flitwell.

'I'm feeling rather guilty,' Loretta admitted in a low voice. 'I took against him before you arrived – he was being sniffy about the peace camp. But he's very engaging when you get to know him.'

Robert looked at her quizzically. 'Do you always judge people on the basis of their politics?'

Loretta was taken aback. 'Well, yes, I suppose I do. But then, the people I meet in London, we're all pretty much the same – anti-nuclear, feminist, green, that sort of thing.'

'Then it's a very good thing you're not in London,' Robert said. 'It's bad for you, always mixing with people who agree with you. Lets the mind get flabby. More wine?'

Loretta nodded, not knowing what to say. It had sounded like a snub, yet Robert was smiling affably at her.

'I'm not sure it's as simple as that,' she said. 'Surely politics can be a guide to character? But maybe you're right. I'll let you know when I've spent a week or so here.' She had a feeling she'd deliberately ducked a confrontation, but this was, after all, a social occasion. 'What do you do?' she asked, repeating the question that had succeeded so well with Gilbert.

'I write music,' Robert said unexpectedly. He laughed. 'That is, I sit at my piano and think about writing music, and occasionally I actually do it. It's a very pleasant existence.'

'Actually, Loretta' – Imo's voice floated down from the other end of the table – 'Robert's very famous. You *must* have heard of him.'

'Very probably,' Loretta said, hoping her ignorance of contemporary music was not about to be exposed. She turned back to Robert. 'But I don't know your surname.'

'Herrin,' called Imo. 'Didn't I tell you?'

Loretta was relieved; she recognized the name from concert posters she'd seen on the London Underground, even though she had no idea what kind of music Robert composed.

'Of course,' she said. 'Flitwell obviously isn't as rural as I'd supposed. I expected it to be full of farmworkers and smallholders, not publishers and composers.'

There was a slight edge to her remark which Robert was quick to pick up.

'And what about where you live?' he asked. 'What kind of people live there? Islington, I should say, or just maybe Fulham?'

'Islington,' Loretta agreed, wondering where this conversation was about to lead.

'Islington? I used to have a very tiny flat down by the Angel. Where are you?' Gilbert had overheard the last part of the conversation.

Loretta told him she lived in Liverpool Road and they began to compare notes about the area. Robert's attention was distracted by Herc, and Loretta settled back and began to enjoy the evening again.

Conversation flowed unforcedly round the table – even Peggy, coaxed by Herc and Robert, seemed to be joining in. It was not until the hate cake made its appearance, to general acclaim, that Loretta realized how tired she was. Perhaps it was the soft darkness of the room, or the gentle rhythm of the rain overhead, but she longed to curl up on the yellow velvet *chaise-longue* in Clara's study. So seductive was this image that, as Gilbert handed a plate of cake to her, she realized she was in danger of nodding off. Blinking hard, she picked up her spoon, only to drop it with a clatter as a tremendous crash resounded through the room, followed by the noise of a car accelerating.

Confusion reigned; she was aware that Robert and someone else – was it Ellie? – were on their feet and a voice was calling for lights. As the room flooded with light Clara wrenched open the front door. For a moment all Loretta could see was blood – blood running down the brown front door, over the threshold into the hall, and leaving brilliant red stains on the hem of Clara's green and yellow dress. Then she heard Ellie's voice – 'Paint! It's only paint!' – and a collective sigh of relief ran through the room. Everyone began talking at once and Loretta edged round the table behind Robert until she was close enough to see for herself. The smell alone, she realized, was enough to prove it wasn't blood. Of all of them, Peggy was the first to recover her wits.

'You got a floorcloth? And a bucket?'

Imo led the way into the kitchen, leaving the others standing uselessly in the hall. Robert stepped gingerly into the road, avoiding the pool of paint, and returned with something in his hand.

'This is what it came in,' he said, holding up a two-and-a-half litre paint tin with the label clumsily torn off.

'Don't touch it – there may be fingerprints!' Clara's warning was too late.

'Sorry. I expect they wore gloves, anyway.' Robert stood the can on the floor, well away from the front door which Imo and Peggy were now attempting to clean.

'Hadn't we better phone the police?' Gilbert was the first person to think of it.

Robert offered to make the call, and disappeared into the sitting room.

'How did they get away so fast?' Ellie asked.

'There was a car,' Loretta said. 'I heard it accelerate.'

'I did, too,' said Herc. 'I guess they threw that stuff out the door.'

'Now what do you say?' Clara suddenly whirled round to face Gilbert, her face flushed. 'Is this what I have to put up with, just because I don't want the base here?'

'Clara, there's no proof this has anything to do with the peace camp,' Gilbert said weakly. 'Let's leave it to the police to find out. That's their job.'

'You're telling me this is a coincidence? After last night?' Clara was really angry now. 'Since I allowed that peace camp on to my land there's been one thing after–'

'Mum, hadn't you better change your dress? It's got paint all over it.' Loretta wasn't certain but she thought there had been some sort of warning in Imo's tone. What had Clara intended to say?

At that moment Robert returned from the sitting room. As soon as he appeared, Peggy, who was on her knees wiping up paint with old newspapers, jumped to her feet.

'They coming?'

Robert shook his head.

'Not yet. They're sending a car, but it'll be at least three-quarters of an hour. They're short-staffed, apparently. There's been a big crash on the M40 and they're out at that as well as some incident in Oxford. Saturday night, I suppose. So – we wait.' He paused. 'Listen, Clara, why don't you go to bed? You as well, Loretta, and Peggy. There's no point in all of us hanging about down here. I can tell them what happened, I saw as much as you did.'

For a moment Loretta thought Clara was going to argue; then, with a heavy sigh, she gave in.

'I suppose you're right.'

'Sure you can deal with this? You don't want me to stay?'

Robert refused the offer and Herc gathered together the party that was to return to Flitwell. Ellie hugged Clara briefly, then she, Herc and Gilbert stepped out into the night. As the door closed behind them, the women gathered at the foot of the stairs.

'Off you go,' Robert said encouragingly. 'You're quite safe. I'll wait here till they arrive.'

Climbing the stairs, Loretta realized she was trembling very slightly. The attack on the house, so sudden and intimidating, had left her feeling weak and empty. The image of Clara on the doorstep, what looked like blood soaking into the hem of her dress, was more real to her than the brightly lit staircase and landing. At the top of the stairs she turned and said a subdued goodnight to Clara, Imo and Peggy, then started down the long corridor to the study.

'Loretta – I'm so sorry.' Clara's voice followed her down the corridor, her attempt at a normal tone underlining how shaken she had been by the incident.

Loretta turned again, forcing a smile. Inside the study, the door firmly shut, she undressed slowly, folding her clothes in a neat pile and absently brushing dust off her grey shoes. But there was no disguising the taste of bile in her throat as she curled up on the *chaise-longue* with the pretty Victorian quilt drawn up to her ears.

2

She didn't wake with a start, as sometimes happens in a strange place. She was in no doubt about where she was, and at no point did she experience the gut-wrenching stab of fear that hurls the sleeper across the boundary from dream to consciousness after a particularly vivid nightmare. It was more that she gradually became aware of voices, and the fact that she could still hear them now that she was fully awake. It was difficult to make out what they were saying, and she had to strain even to catch one or two phrases. When she did, she had to dismiss her initial assumption, which was that the police had finally arrived and were talking to Robert Herrin in the hall below. For one thing there are too many voices; for another the vocabulary was all wrong.

'– brother was always penny-pinching but it did not occur to me that even he –'

'God be thanked that his poor dear sister is not alive to hear such words.'

'His own flesh and blood –'

'Poor, poor Cousin Maude.'

Loretta sat up and peered into the darkness. Where were the voices coming from? They seemed to be in the room with her, but she had no sense of their direction, perhaps because the drawn curtains and closed shutters had combined to produce an impenetrable darkness. Now completely awake, she sat up on one elbow and listened carefully. What were these people talking about? She caught more phrases.

'To think that the scion of so noble a family could sink to such depths of depravity.'

'Not just depraved, Lord Brownshaw; *unnatural.*'

'"Tis a final and most bitter bequest.'

They were speaking in shocked, subdued tones, and a scene flashed into Loretta's head: a group of people, middle-aged to elderly, dressed in sombre and old-fashioned clothes, sitting in a dark parlour discussing the newly revealed contents of a will. But there was something stagy about the set-up, something not quite right; it was as though she was listening to a bad play on Radio Four.

Of course – someone in a nearby room was listening to the radio. Sound travels in old houses, she told herself, speculating that the wall between the study and the room next door might be unusually thin. But what a time to choose. Then she realized that she had no idea what hour it was. She threw back the quilt, swung her feet to the floor, and took careful steps across the room to the mantelpiece where she had left her watch. Pushing a curtain to one side, she read the time by moonlight: twenty past one. Who on earth could be listening to the radio at that hour? She remembered that Peggy was sleeping in the spare room next door, and felt even more perplexed; the play, if that was what it was, hardly seemed the sort of thing that would interest Peggy. In any case, surely Radio Four would be off the air by now? Even so, there was presumably some sort of local radio station in the area – maybe it was running a drama series for insomniacs? The obvious thing was to go next door and ask. Loretta let go of the curtain, drawing in her breath as the room was plunged again into darkness, and began to feel her way towards the door. As she did so she heard a sudden click, and the voices ceased. So it had been a radio, she thought, relieved that she'd been spared the task of asking Peggy to turn it down. And who could blame the girl for her wakefulness – she had seen the peace camp and Clara's house attacked on consecutive nights. Loretta put out a hand to her left, felt for the edge of the *chaise-longue*, and slipped back under the quilt. Before long she had drifted back to sleep as though the radio incident had never happened.

The second time she woke up with a start. She must have been sleeping much more lightly, for she actually heard the click before the voices began again. As before, Loretta lay very still, straining to make out what they were saying; it took a couple of minutes to realize that something very odd was happening.

'God be thanked that his poor dear sister is not alive to hear such words.'

'His own flesh and blood –'

'Poor, poor Cousin Maude.'

Not only the voices, but what they were saying, were an exact repeat of last time. Loretta's first thought was to wonder what on earth Peggy was up to. The voices obviously weren't coming from a radio; even a local station wouldn't broadcast the same play twice in one night. A tape recorder? To sit up half the night listening to a second-rate play twice over was eccentricity of a high order. Why would Peggy do such a thing?

'Not just depraved, Lord Brownshaw; *unnatural*.'

''Tis a final and most bitter bequest.'

Loretta felt herself getting angry. As if she hadn't had enough to put up with for one night! The last thing she wanted was a row with Clara's other guest. And yet, if she was going to get any sleep at all, it seemed she had little choice. With an impatient sigh she slid her legs out from under the quilt for the second time, stood up, and started to move in the direction of the door. As she reached it she heard an abrupt click. The voices ceased at exactly the same point as they had earlier. Loretta waited for a moment in darkness to make sure the silence wasn't temporary. Then, as it stretched into minutes, she felt her way back to the *chaise-longue* and lay down to sleep for the third time.

A persistent knocking woke Loretta next morning and she realized someone was at the door of her room.

'Come in,' she called, rubbing her eyes and wondering what time it was.

The door opened to reveal Clara, who was wearing a blue dressing-gown and carrying a cup and saucer.

'Brought you some tea. Were you asleep? Sorry, it's just that I'm nearly ready for church. How did you sleep? After that terrible paint business, I mean.' She perched on the end of the *chaise-longue* as Loretta tasted her tea.

'Oh, that,' said Loretta, surprised to find that the events of the previous evening had rather faded from her mind. 'I was so tired when I came to bed, I went out like a light. What did bother me, to tell you the truth, was the radio next door. At least, it sounded like a radio – what's the matter?'

Clara was leaning forward with an air of suppressed excitement.

'A radio? Tell me what you heard.'

Loretta was slightly unnerved by the intensity of Clara's stare.

'Well, there isn't much to tell . . . I mean – I was woken up by voices, I assume from next door, and it sounded as if someone was listening to a play on the radio. Then it went off, and a bit later I heard it again. It was just – voices.'

'What were they saying? What sort of voices?'

'Quiet, sort of subdued. They seemed to be talking about a will –'

'And Cousin Maude? Did they mention Cousin Maude?'

'Well, yes, they did. What is all this?'

Clara sat back, her lips drawn together in a thin line.

'So I'm not going mad. Thank God. I was beginning to wonder.'

'Clara, what's this about?'

Loretta put her empty cup on the floor and moved closer to her hostess.

'It starts with a click, as though a radio's been turned on,' Clara said slowly. 'First you think it's a play, Radio Four or something. Then it stops. And after a while you hear it again, the same piece of dialogue. So you think it's a tape recorder. In here or next door. So you turn the place upside down looking for it. And that's the point. There's nothing in here and nothing next door. Not a thing. So where's it coming from?'

Loretta shivered.

'You mean you've heard it often? But surely –'

'Oh yes, I quite agree. There must be some rational explanation. But if you can tell me what it is I'll be very grateful.'

'How long has this been going on?' Loretta was at a loss and, unwilling to countenance explanations of a supernatural nature, took refuge in seeking facts.

'Two weeks,' Clara said without hesitation. 'I wrote it in my diary. Not straight away. The first time it happened I was inclined to doubt my sanity. After all, I'm fifty-one, and I haven't shown any previous signs of behaving like Joan of Arc. You know what people say about the menopause. But then, when the first letter arrived a couple of days later – well, I thought the two things might be connected. I don't know how. It's one thing to write disgusting letters, anyone can do that. But this –' She stopped and gestured in the air.

'What sort of letters?'

'Anonymous. I'm sure you can guess. "Why don't you get those whores off your land, you dirty lesbian bitch?" That sort of thing. That's not all, I've had phone calls as well. Though I suspect I have someone else to thank for those, they display an altogether more inventive turn of mind. No obscenities. Mostly it's just silence. But someone read part of the burial service to me once. I suppose I'd have got the whole thing if I hadn't put the phone down. And there was another one where I could hear a woman being tortured.' Clara saw Loretta's face and patted her hand. 'Don't worry, Loretta, I'm sure it wasn't real. Anyone could rent a horror film and tape the nastiest bit of the soundtrack. I don't think for a moment she was really being murdered. But the voices – how are they being done?'

Loretta suddenly remembered Clara's eagerness for her to move into the cottage; had it been connected with this? She had gathered the previous evening that Imo was in her second year at Sussex – it would hardly be surprising if Clara had felt the need of a neighbour she could trust in her present predicament. Even so, it would have been nice to be consulted: Loretta wasn't very happy about the way in which she had been allowed to walk all unknowing into this deeply disturbing situation.

'What do the police say?' she asked, a trifle coldly.

'I haven't told them.'

'You haven't –'

'Wait a minute, there is a reason. Think about it. The police don't like the peace camp – oh, it's not political, I'm sure. They have enough to cope with, and the camp is one more problem they could do without. I've had Collins, he's the local superintendent, round here for a quiet word – we sympathize, it's a free country, but can't you turn them off? If I told them about the voices and the phone calls, there's no proof that I'm telling the truth. Even the letters, I could have written those myself. And you know how gossip gets round. The police are human like the rest of us. I've got enough enemies around here as it is without people saying I'm batty as well as a communist.' Clara smiled slightly. 'I'm biding my time, building up a – well, a dossier is too strong a word. I've been keeping notes in my diary – all the phone calls, the dates of the letters, when I've heard the voices. Now there's been these attacks, and you've heard the voices . . . All I need is for someone else to hear some of the phone calls – you or Peggy, say. Then I'll go public on it.'

'Who else knows?' Loretta asked. 'What about Imo?'

'She knows about the letters. Not the voices. You're the only one who knows about those. And you must keep quiet, Loretta. For the time being. Please.'

A new thought struck Loretta. 'Is that why you put me in here last night? To see if I'd hear the voices?'

Clara looked slightly shame-faced. 'Well, it did cross my mind . . . But really, when you think about it, I had no choice. I could hardly put Peggy in here, could I? Not when she'd had that bang on the head. It wouldn't have been fair.'

'Are they always at night?'

'So far. I've been sleeping in here a lot lately.' Clara's cheeks reddened, and Loretta wondered why. 'It's always been at midnight or later. Heavens, look at the time! I must fly or I'll be late for church. Help yourself to breakfast – there's bread in the crock, eggs, bacon, the usual things. Lunch at one. See you later.'

The door closed and Loretta was alone. She lowered herself back on to the pillow and lay with her hands clasped behind her head. Common sense told her this was no place for someone recuperating from even a mild illness; she should pack her things and be ready to leave when Clara returned from church. Loretta swung her legs to the floor, went to stand up, then hesitated. How would she feel if she washed her hands of the whole business and left Clara to get on with it? Was Clara really asking so much? Loretta had often been to Greenham; she had been moved by the dedication of the women who braved appalling weather conditions and constant evictions in pursuit of a cause she, too, believed in. All Clara was asking for was a bit of sisterly support, and for Loretta to act as a witness. How deep was Loretta's commitment if she wasn't even prepared to do that? She sighed, the impossibility of running out on Clara impressing her forcibly. She had made her bed, she thought, running her hand over the worn surface of the patchwork quilt, and she would have to lie on it.

Half an hour later, dressed and ready for breakfast, Loretta made her way downstairs. Clara's work table was still in the hall, empty and waiting to be transported upstairs. She skirted round it and paused by the front door, looking for traces of the previous night's attack. Apart from a darkening of the cement in the cracks between the floor tiles, there was remarkably little damage. She opened the kitchen door, wondering if Peggy or Imo were up, but the room was empty apart from the grey cat who strolled over to meet her. Loretta bent to scratch his head, was rewarded with a loud purr, and set about making tea and toast. Having consumed both she looked at the clock; it was quarter past eleven, and she wondered how to pass the time until Clara returned. Judging by the potatoes sitting in a pan of water on the kitchen table, preparations for lunch were well under way – she could indulge herself with a clear conscience. Picking up that morning's *Observer*, which was lying unopened on a chair, she crossed the hall, went through the untidy conservatory, and found herself on a small paved area adjoining the house. It was a sunny spot, and several chairs and a low wooden table had been placed there to take advantage of this fact. Loretta sat down and began to leaf through the paper; finding nothing much of interest, she took it back to the kitchen and ran lightly up the stairs to Clara's study. A couple of minutes later she returned to her seat outside, this time armed with an early novel by Margaret Atwood that she hadn't had time to look at before. It was easy reading, and it didn't take long for Loretta to become temporarily oblivious of her surroundings. She was not aware that she was no longer alone until her light was suddenly blocked and she looked up to find a man standing in front of her.

'Hello.' His tone was suspicious and far from friendly. 'Is Clara in?'

Another neighbour? Loretta wondered. 'Not at the moment,' she said briskly, ignoring his hostility. 'She went to church, oh' – she looked at her watch – 'about an hour and a half ago. She should be back soon. Or would you like me to give her a message?'

The man looked blank.

'No thanks, I live here. And who are you?'

For a moment, Loretta was lost for words. She stared at the new arrival, trying to work out who he might be. Some sort of relative, she guessed, taking in his dark hair – like Imo's – and pale skin. Clara's son? Much too old; he looked to be in his early forties, although his receding hair could be deceptive. A younger brother? That seemed more likely. But in that case, why was he living at Baldwin's? Loretta realized the man was still waiting for her reply, and hastily introduced herself. He shook her outstretched hand perfunctorily.

'Jeremy Frere,' he announced. 'I'm Clara's husband. You say you're a friend of hers? I don't think I've heard her mention you.'

'More a friend of a friend,' Loretta admitted, still engaged in the process of revising her picture of Clara's domestic arrangements. Why hadn't Clara mentioned the fact that she had a husband? It was hardly the sort of thing that could have slipped her mind. Loretta realized she had simply assumed that Clara was divorced or widowed. But surely this chap Jeremy – what had he said his surname was? Loretta had been so taken aback by his revelation of his relationship to Clara that she hadn't taken it in – wasn't Imo's father? She examined him covertly, taking in his bright blue eyes and unlined skin. If it wasn't for the hair, he might easily pass for thirty-five. Of one thing she was certain: Jeremy was definitely his wife's junior, and by some years. She realized he was speaking to her, and his tone was less unfriendly now they'd been introduced.

'I'd completely forgotten about this church business. Only started a couple of weeks ago.' He laughed, looking back across the valley with absent-minded admiration for the view. 'Clara never went near a church till she found the vicar was on her side about this Libyan business.' He moved towards the conservatory. 'Drink? I'm going to have a lager. I've just driven down from London and my throat's like sandpaper.'

Loretta said she'd like an orange juice. Jeremy returned a couple of minutes later and handed her a half-full glass. 'We seem to be running out. I expect Clara forgot to do the shopping again. You here for the weekend?' He settled into a chair next to hers.

'Actually, I'm moving into the cottage for a few days,' Loretta said, gesturing towards it with her left hand. 'I've been ill and Clara very kindly –'

'*You're* moving into the cottage? But you can't be! I *told* Clara before I went to New York – I'm sorry, there's been some mistake.' He stopped, glowering at her.

'I – I don't *think* so,' Loretta began hesitantly. 'That is, Clara did ring and ask if I wanted the cottage. She didn't say anything about –'

'Shit!' Jeremy sat with pursed lips, his thin fingers drumming impatiently on the arm of his chair. Then, as if he'd suddenly remembered her presence, he leaned across and touched Loretta lightly on the arm. 'Sorry, love, it's not your fault. I'll sort it out with Clara when she gets back from her devotions, or whatever it is she does in church. So tell me, when did Wayne leave? I'm sorry he went without saying goodbye, he was rather a friend of mine. That's how he came to be living in the cottage, as a matter of fact. When did he go?'

Loretta folded her arms, a gesture that succeeded in removing her from contact with Jeremy's hand without actual rudeness. She didn't like being addressed as 'love' at the best of times, and certainly not by this petulant little creep. She was saved from replying to his question by the sudden appearance of Clara at the bottom of the lawn. She waved vigorously in their direction as she toiled up the hill.

'Jeremy, dear, you've met my new tenant,' she said, dropping a light kiss on his forehead. She straightened up, beaming at Loretta and giving the distinct impression of someone who was rather pleased with herself. 'Good trip?'

'Eh? Oh, fine, fine.' Jeremy got to his feet. 'Clara, what's all this about – um' – he looked at Loretta, obviously unable to recall her name – 'about you letting the cottage? I'm sure I told you I wanted it for a friend of mine. Don't you remember? We were talking about it last weekend, before I went to New York.'

'Really?' Clara's forehead wrinkled, as though with the effort of dredging something from the deepest recesses of memory. 'I don't *think* so, darling. Are you sure you mentioned it? Because it's a bit late now. Loretta's here, and I've promised the cottage to her for as long as she likes. So I don't see there's much to be done. Sorry.'

'Clara! I remember the conversation perfectly! You happened to say Wayne was moving out early and I –'

'Darling, I really don't want to discuss it, especially not in front of Loretta. She must be feeling frightfully embarrassed.' This much at least was true, especially as Loretta was pretty sure Clara was faking her memory lapse. Who could blame her, if Jeremy was responsible for installing the unlovable Wayne as her previous tenant? 'Let's leave it,' Clara finished briskly. 'I must see to lunch or we'll have nothing to eat.'

'I'd like another beer,' Jeremy called after his wife's receding back, subsiding into the chair he'd just vacated. Clara showed no sign of having heard him.

Loretta reached for her book and sat with it open on her lap, pretending to read. It had hardly been an affectionate reunion between husband and wife, and her own position was anything but comfortable. She didn't relish the thought of living next door to someone who had made it clear that he resented her presence, and Clara had made no attempt at all to ease the atmosphere. Did she really want to move into the cottage in these circumstances? Her chief reason for staying – her anxiety that Clara shouldn't be left alone to face the consequences of her role as protector of the peace camp – was no longer valid. Unprepossessing as Jeremy might be, he was still Clara's husband, and on hand if anything untoward did happen. At this point in Loretta's deliberations Clara reappeared and plonked a can of lager on the table in front of Jeremy.

'Clara,' Loretta said, seizing her chance, 'I'm feeling very bad about the cottage. If Jeremy wants it for a friend, wouldn't it be better if I went back to London? I'm sure I can find something else if I hunt around for a bit. I don't want to –'

'Heavens, Loretta, don't even *think* of it! Jeremy doesn't mind *really*, do you, darling?'

Loretta waited for Jeremy to say that he did, and was disappointed.

'No, no, now that you're here . . .' he said in resigned tones, picking up the can and pulling the ring to open it.

'But –'

Loretta wasn't allowed to get any further.

'I completely forgot. I've got a message for you, Loretta. Ellie and Herc are going riding this afternoon and they wondered if you'd like a hack. Half past five, they're going. They said to ring and let them know and they'll fix up a horse from the riding school.'

'But I don't ride,' protested Loretta, to whom the word 'hack' was a derogatory term often applied by John Tracey to his colleagues on the *Sunday Herald*. 'I've never been on a horse in my life. Though I did once ride a camel,' she added unwisely, recalling an uncomfortable holiday with Tracey in Morocco.

'There you are then,' Clara said triumphantly. 'If you can stay on a camel, you can stay on anything. It's wonderful exercise, and the fresh air will do you good. You're looking a bit wan. Get them to fix you up with Albert, you won't come to any harm on him.'

Loretta was about to explain that her pallor was probably due to the fact that, on the previous evening, she'd ignored her doctor's instructions and helped herself to a considerable quantity of wine. But Jeremy forestalled her.

'Don't put her on Albert, she'll die of boredom,' he said scornfully. 'I've never come across a dozier animal. He must be twenty-five if he's a day.'

'Age has got nothing to do with it,' Clara objected. 'Albert goes out every day, he's perfect for a beginner.'

'What about George? She'll have fun on George.'

'Good God, Jeremy, are you trying to kill her? George'd

46

have her off in minutes. Nothing like falling off a horse to put you off for life,' Clara said, turning back to Loretta. 'You ask for Albert, he'll do you nicely. Now, where are those girls? They'll miss lunch if they don't come down soon.' Clara disappeared into the house, leaving a bewildered Loretta to wonder what had happened to her resolution to return to London without further ado.

Imo and Peggy having appeared from their respective rooms, they were five for lunch; to Loretta's relief, the atmosphere at the kitchen table was less strained than she'd anticipated of so ill-assorted a gathering. Jeremy had cheered up considerably with the discovery that he was just in time to say goodbye to Wayne, from whom he had parted with mutual promises – overheard by Loretta from her vantage point in the garden – to look each other up in the future. In the course of the meal Loretta discovered that Jeremy was an art dealer, and had just returned from a trip to America. He was, it transpired, arranging the first London show of an artist called Peter Eddy, of whom Loretta had never heard; Jeremy assured her that Eddy's paintings, most of them scenes of the Mid-West during the Great Depression, were going to be a sensation.

'The next big thing,' he enthused. 'They can't fail.'

'Aren't they a bit depressing?' Loretta asked, not meaning any pun.

'That's why they're going to be a success,' Jeremy insisted. 'It's the spirit of the times. Thirties' nostalgia, the fighting spirit, courage in the face of adversity. Besides which,' he added, 'they happen to be very good paintings.'

'But how can someone today know what it was like in the thirties?' Loretta continued. 'Isn't there a danger of romanticizing it?'

'Ah, but Eddy lived through it,' Jeremy said. 'That's the extraordinary thing – he's a genuine undiscovered talent. When he started painting, the people who liked his work couldn't afford to buy it – they were the farmers who'd had their farms taken away, the people who'd lost their homes. And he refused to sell to anyone who was doing well out of the Depression – bankers, speculators, black marketeers. So

47

his pictures just piled up in a barn in Iowa. It's taken me months to track them down, I've been looking ever since I found one in this country, in a house sale near Worcester, of all places.'

'How does he feel about this exhibition?' Loretta asked curiously. If Peter Eddy had been too principled to sell his pictures to people who were making money in the thirties, she couldn't see why he was willing to part with them in the recession of the eighties.

'Oh well, he's dead, as a matter of fact,' Jeremy said off-handedly. 'It's his widow who's letting them go. I mean, why should she be scratching a living on a farm in Iowa when she can sell a few pictures and live comfortably for the rest of her life?'

'When are we going to see one of these wonderful paintings?' Clara asked, stacking their used plates in a dishwasher Loretta hadn't noticed before.

'I thought you might say that.' Jeremy grinned boyishly. 'Wait there.'

Loretta heard him run upstairs; five minutes later he returned with a small picture in a plain wooden frame which he handed reverently to Clara. She took it across to the side window, held it at arm's length, and examined it closely until Jeremy could stand it no longer.

'What d'you think?'

Clara sighed. 'Exquisite. The use of colour – and the light. I can see why he didn't want to part with them.'

She came back to the table and handed the picture to Loretta. It showed a small group of people, their possessions piled high on a horse-drawn cart, standing in attitudes of resignation outside a small clapboarded house. It was signed in one corner by the artist, and a small brass insert in the frame revealed its title to be *The Leave-taking*. As Loretta passed it to Imo, Clara and Jeremy began an animated discussion of Eddy's technique; for the first time, Loretta could see what might have brought so incongruous a couple together. Imo stared at the picture for a moment, then handed it on to Peggy.

'Looks like a Hopper to me,' she said dismissively. 'I can't see what all the fuss is about.'

'A Hopper? God, Imogen, you don't know what you're talking about! There's an energy about these paintings – they make Hopper look washed-out, etiolated. Surely you can see that?' Jeremy stared at her, his anger visible in two red patches on his pale cheeks.

'Yes, darling, he's right. That wasn't really a very intelligent thing to say, was it?' Clara's tone was lighter, lacking in her husband's vehemence, but there was no doubt he and she were on the same side.

'OK, OK, I know I haven't inherited your delicate artistic sensibilities.' Imo scraped back her chair and headed for the door. 'Can I borrow the car, Clara? I promised to go and see Emma, she's home this weekend, too.' She waited, one hand on the door-knob, avoiding her mother's eye.

'As long as you're back in time for your train,' Clara said. 'Imo's got to be back in Brighton tonight,' she added as her daughter left the room. 'She's got her second-year exams tomorrow.'

'It's a nice picture,' Peggy said suddenly, holding out the Eddy painting to Jeremy. He took it, with an air of being surprised by the fact that she was able to speak.

'Half past two already,' Clara said, switching on the dishwasher. 'Loretta, would you like to see the cottage now? Mrs Abbott will still be there, but I expect you'd like a look round. What about you, Peggy, d'you want to come?'

Peggy, who had been largely silent during the meal, stood up immediately. Loretta guessed the girl was grateful for an excuse to escape from Jeremy. Clara led the way to the back door and out into the conservatory.

'I phoned Mrs Abbott and asked her to clean upstairs first so you could dump your things up there,' she said conversationally, following the path that led through the privet hedge to the cottage. 'Oh yes, she's still here – the door's open.'

Clara rapped on the front door with her knuckles and stepped inside. Loretta and Peggy followed, making rather a crowd in the small room. As soon as she crossed the threshold Loretta was assailed by an unpleasant smell, one she associated with antiseptic and hospitals. The grey-haired woman who was standing at the sink turned to face them, and immediately launched into an apology.

'Sorry, Mrs Wolstonecroft, I just can't seem to get rid of that smell. This is the second time I've scrubbed this sink, it just won't go.'

'It's not your fault,' Clara reassured her, turning to Loretta. 'It's those wretched butterflies – Wayne collected them. The place has been stinking of this stuff for weeks, formalin I think it is. Or do I mean formaldehyde?' She moved to her right and opened a door into a room which, from what Loretta could see over her shoulder, appeared to be the bathroom. 'As if the Americans don't do enough killing already,' Clara continued in her carrying voice. 'If it's not Libya or Nicaragua, it's some poor innocent insect.'

Behind Loretta, Mrs Abbott's bucket clinked noisily in the sink.

'She doesn't like me saying that, her son works at the base,' Clara hissed, *sotto voce*. Then, resuming her normal tone, 'How d'you like the stairs? I had them made specially.' She was looking at a wrought-iron spiral staircase which ascended to the first floor from a corner of the bathroom. 'Some people think it's a bit odd, having them in here, but I think it's logical. People often want to go to the loo in the night, I know I do. Oh, and that door leads into the garden. That was the architect's idea. He said if people had to come down that narrow staircase they ought to be able to get outside fast. It's usually bolted. Come upstairs.'

Loretta and Peggy followed Clara up the winding stairs, finding themselves in a light room which took up the entire upper floor. At one end, below the window in the roof, was a double bed; at the other, a picture window provided a spectacular view across the valley.

'What d'you think? Will it do?'

'It's delightful,' Loretta said sincerely.

'I knew you'd be impressed. Now, d'you want some help in bringing your things over?'

The three women returned to Baldwin's; Peggy disappeared into the spare bedroom, and Clara carried one of Loretta's bags and her typewriter over to the cottage. Loretta went down to the lay-by where she had parked her car, and drove it round to the space in front of the cottage recently vacated by Wayne's Trans-Am.

'Got everything you want? The Aga runs on oil, the instructions should be in that drawer. See you later.'

Clara departed, leaving Loretta alone with Mrs Abbott. With some difficulty, she succeeded in persuading the cleaning lady not to make a second attempt on the kitchen floor; and so at last, almost twenty-four hours later than she had expected, Loretta found herself in sole possession of Keeper's Cottage.

She was pulling on a pair of jeans, thrown into a suitcase at the last moment in reluctant recognition that conditions in the country were occasionally damp and muddy, when a voice drifted up the stairs.

'Hey, Loretta? You around?'

It was Herc's voice; she pulled a sweater over her head and ran lightly down the stairs, through the bathroom and into the kitchen, where she'd left the front door open.

'Will I do?' she asked nervously, observing that Herc was wearing jodhpurs and riding boots.

'Sure,' said Herc, leading the way out of the cottage. 'Ellie's old boots are in the car. You can borrow a hard hat at the school.'

Ten minutes later Loretta was given a leg-up on to a large horse which, although it seemed to her to be brown, was apparently bay in colour. On her head perched a white crash helmet not unlike those she'd seen in newspaper pictures of riot police.

'Don't forget your whip,' Ellie said, edging near on a black and white pony which was already displaying signs of a skittish nature.

Loretta reluctantly took the long stick Ellie was holding out to her, and pulled hard on the reins to prevent her horse from moving in front of the black and white pony. They were lined up and ready to move out of the stable-yard, Herc bringing up the rear, when a breathless figure in riding gear appeared.

'Wait for me!' It was Robert.

'Thought you weren't coming,' called Ellie.

A couple of minutes later Robert joined the tail end of the little procession as it wound slowly into open country. The late afternoon sun shone and Loretta's horse, Albert, moved forward at a gentle pace; she began to enjoy herself. Suddenly the horse veered sideways and dropped his head, pulling up a clump of grass from the hedge to Loretta's left. At once a chorus of voices offered advice.

'Pull his head *up*!'

'Don't let him eat!'

'You've got to show him who's boss!'

It was the start of an extremely uncomfortable hour. No matter how hard Loretta pulled on the reins, Albert came to a standstill whenever he espied anything edible; so often did these meal breaks occur that she began to wonder whether the animal had been fed at all in the previous week. Soon Herc's horse, a frisky brown pony, had overtaken Albert and was trotting happily into the distance. Loretta was left to endure a stream of instructions from Robert, who seemed determined that she should learn something called the rising trot. She cooperated only because it slightly alleviated the painful bumping she had to suffer every time Albert moved at more than a gentle walk, wishing that someone had had the foresight to warn her to wear a bra. By the time the horses finally wound their way back into the stable-yard she was flustered and sore, certainly in no mood to listen to Robert's assurance that she'd done rather well for a novice. When the others pressed her to accompany them to a pub in the next village – they had decided to boycott the Green Man in Flitwell, they explained, because of its refusal to serve Clara – she was reluctant to agree; but without her car, and with aching legs, she was not in a good position to argue.

In the event, she felt a little better after consuming half a pint of lemonade. She relaxed, and told herself that good neighbourliness was the sort of thing she missed out on by living in London. She even allowed herself to be talked into going back to Ellie's house for supper; Robert slipped home to change and make a telephone call, but joined them just in time to eat.

It was after eleven when Herc dropped Loretta off in the road next to the wooden gates that led to Keeper's Cottage. Closing them behind her, Loretta looked across to her right and saw that no lights were visible in Baldwin's; perhaps everyone had gone to bed. She skirted round her car, felt in the pocket of her jeans, and drew out the key. As she put it into the lock, she thought she heard a noise from inside the cottage. She waited a second, then, when it wasn't repeated, turned the key and felt inside for the light switch. As she stepped into the kitchen, she heard the unmistakable sound of footsteps overhead; she froze, looked round for the phone, and remembered there wasn't one. Panic seized her: the feet were now clattering downstairs without any attempt at concealment, the intruder would be upon her in seconds – Loretta threw back her head and screamed at the top of her voice. She went on doing so as she heard the door in the bathroom fly open, and footsteps pound across the garden; there was a confusion of voices, someone calling her name, then Clara was beside her in the kitchen.

'Loretta! Are you hurt? Loretta! Get her a drink, someone! There's brandy in the house. Come on, Loretta, it's all right now, you're safe!'

Loretta clung to Clara for a moment, then allowed herself to be guided to a chair. She bent forward, arms clasped to her chest, while her terrified sobs subsided. A glass was pushed into her hand, and she looked up to find Peggy studying her anxiously. At that moment Jeremy appeared in the kitchen, out of breath and holding his stomach as though he had a stitch.

'Bastards got away,' he gasped, stumbling forward and pulling out a chair. 'Lost them in the trees.' He shook his head despairingly. 'Hopeless. Is that brandy?'

Loretta passed the glass across, and Jeremy finished it. Quite suddenly, she took in what he'd said.

'There was more than – there were two – ?'

'I saw two,' Jeremy confirmed, wiping his face with a handkerchief. 'Christ, you look terrible. Has somebody phoned for a doctor?'

This question was directed at Clara. Loretta started to get to her feet, protesting that she would be all right in a moment.

'It's just the shock. Please don't –'

'I'm not surprised.' Clara patted Loretta on the shoulder, soothing her as she would a child with a grazed knee. 'Can you remember what happened?'

'Oh yes. But there isn't much to tell. It all happened so

quickly.' Loretta described her return to the cottage, her tears starting to flow as she reached the point where she heard footsteps upstairs.

'And then we heard you screaming blue murder and came rushing over,' Clara finished for her. 'Did either of you ring the police?' She looked from Jeremy to Peggy, who shook their heads. 'Well, one of you had better. What's been taken?'

As Jeremy left the cottage, Loretta got up and began to look around.

'It all looks much the same in here,' she said slowly, registering that her Japanese radio and cassette player was still on the kitchen table. 'I suppose I ought to look upstairs?' She didn't relish the prospect, even with Clara and Peggy for company. A friend had been burgled in London a month before and had come home to find everything from broken whisky bottles to human excreta littering her bedroom. Her nervousness apparently transmitted itself to Peggy, who gave her an understanding look.

'I'll go,' she said, heading for the door into the bathroom. Loretta and Clara waited in silence until they heard Peggy coming down the stairs; she came back into the room, shrugging her shoulders.

'Seems all right to me,' she said. 'Doesn't look like anything's been taken. It isn't a mess, if you wanna have a look.'

Loretta did, and saw that the girl was right; the room was surprisingly undisturbed. The intruders hadn't even bothered to take either of her suitcases, which she hadn't had time fully to unpack.

Shortly after this two policemen arrived and insisted on taking brief statements from them, expressing their disappointment that no one had got a good look at the burglars as they fled across the garden. Jeremy, when pressed, became irritable.

'It is dark out there, in case you hadn't noticed,' he pointed out. 'I was more concerned with trying to catch up with them than to take in where they do their shopping.'

'There's been a spate of break-ins round here lately,' Clara said accusingly. 'There was one at the Etterbekes' place in the village the other week, and someone got into Mrs Cullen's while she was away in Florida. This could be the same people – you must have *some* idea who they are.'

'*If* they were burglars, ma'am,' said the older of the two policemen. 'Did anyone know there was a young woman staying here on her own?'

'Well, of course, I told several people Loretta was moving in, there didn't seem to be any reason to keep it a secret – Good God, you're not suggesting –'

'There was a very nasty rape over in Crockham last month,' the man said, looking from Clara to Loretta. 'We have to keep our minds open ... according to the young lady here, it doesn't look as though they've nicked anything. Either they hadn't had time, or they were after something else. Just as well you screamed, miss. Sex crimes are on the increase in this area. Either way, you want to get a locksmith to look the place over while you're getting that door fixed.' He gestured towards the bathroom, where the door had been crudely forced.

His words struck deep into Loretta, producing a vivid picture of what might have happened if the inhabitants of Baldwin's had not responded to her cries. She gasped, turned an anguished face to Clara, and once again burst into tears.

3

Loretta woke to bright sunshine and an unfamiliar room; it took her a moment to recognize it as Imo's bedroom, in which she had been installed the previous evening after the break-in at the cottage. She sat up in bed, wondering if the furniture, including a pretty wash-stand in one corner, had been chosen by Imo or Clara. Her watch, sitting on a small table next to the bed, showed the time as nearly eleven o'clock.

Climbing gingerly out of bed, Loretta became aware of an unaccustomed ache in her inner thighs – the result, presumably, of yesterday's horse ride. She slipped on the dressing-gown – not hers – which was hanging on the back of the door, and went downstairs. Clara was sitting at the kitchen table, a cup of coffee in one hand and that morning's *Guardian* in the other.

'Just look at this, Loretta,' she demanded without preamble. 'Have you ever *heard* such nonsense? Coffee?' she added abruptly, as Loretta took the paper from her.

'Don't worry, Clara, I'll make some tea in a second.' She drew out a chair and lowered herself as she did so.

The paper was folded open at an inside page, and it took Loretta a moment to find what she was supposed to be reading. Then she spotted it, a story headlined 'MP SEEKS ADDED PROTECTION FOR US BASES':

A Conservative MP last night pressed the government to support a new bill designed to give added protection to American bases in Britain.

Mr Colin Kendall-Cole, whose constituency includes the

Dunstow base in east Oxfordshire, has drawn up a bill which would give the American authorities the right of veto over land use within 500 yards of the perimeter fence of any US base in England and Wales.

Mr Kendall-Cole denied that the aim of the measure was to get rid of peace camps outside US bases, saying his main concern was possible terrorist action in the light of recent threats from Libya. Five F1-11 bombers from Dunstow took part in the raid on Tripoli last month in which many people were killed and injured.

'The difficulty the Americans face is that, while the people who join these peace camps may be well-meaning, they are in fact doing the enemy's work for him,' Mr Kendall-Cole said last night. 'Their presence outside bases like Greenham Common and Dunstow is a threat to morale, not to mention public health, and may even be providing cover for *Spetsnaz* agents who are passing vital information back to the Russians.'

Spetsnaz agents are the Russian equivalent of the SAS, and there have been allegations in the past that they have infiltrated peace camps in Britain, particularly the women's camp at Greenham. These allegations have never been proved.

Referring to the attack on the Dunstow peace camp on Friday night, when masked men are alleged to have pulled down tents and set fire to a caravan, Mr Kendall-Cole said: 'I am naturally concerned for the safety of the women in this particular camp. I know that feelings are running high locally, since many of my constituents are actually employed at the base. These women need protecting from themselves but, because they happen to be on private land, nothing can be done. My bill will protect both our NATO allies and the misguided women who seek to disrupt their work.'

Mr Kendall-Cole is seeking a meeting with the government's business managers at the earliest opportunity. Without their support his bill, entitled the NATO Bases (Enhanced Security) Bill, would stand no chance of making its way on to the statute books.

Last night a spokesman at the London office of the Greenham women condemned Mr Kendall-Cole's action as 'vindictive and irrelevant'. 'You can't legislate peace camps out of existence,' she said.

Loretta put down the paper and found Clara pouring her a cup of tea.

'I shall have to have another word with Colin,' Clara said grimly. 'What does he think he's talking about? *Spetsnaz* agents indeed! It just shows what a madhouse the Commons is. Until he got elected in, um, 1979, he was a perfectly ordinary country solicitor. And now he's seeing Russian spies everywhere. He's angling for a job in the next reshuffle, that's what all this is about. He more or less admitted it when I first spoke to him about this business. But honestly, this is too much! A lot of innocent women get attacked and all he can think of is looking after the base!'

Loretta agreed the MP's action was illogical. But she couldn't help regarding it as fairly predictable, and doubted whether Clara's protest would have any effect, even if she had known Kendall-Cole for years.

'Goodness, Loretta, how rude of me,' Clara said suddenly. 'I haven't even asked how you are after that dreadful thing last night. Did you manage to sleep?'

'Like a log,' Loretta admitted. 'I can't imagine what came over me, weeping all over you like that.'

'It's hardly surprising, after what that idiot policeman said.' Clara refilled her cup with coffee. 'All that nonsense about rape being on the increase. Anyone would think the Viking hordes were sweeping across Oxfordshire. If you want my opinion, he was just trying to draw attention away from all these burglaries. It's obviously the same people, and the police are embarrassed because they still don't seem to have a clue. In either sense,' she added, smiling briefly. 'The only place round here where violent crime is on the increase is that bloody base. But the police don't seem to care what happens to the peace camp.'

'Gosh,' said Loretta, a new idea striking her. 'D'you think the break-in had something to do with the peace camp? With the letters and phone calls, I mean?'

Clara sighed. 'It did cross my mind. But somehow I can't see a connection. If it was the same people who threw the paint, you'd have expected more damage. Clothes thrown around, that sort of thing.'

'But maybe I interrupted them, like the police said.'

'Even so, I'd have expected them to have done something downstairs – more paint, slogans sprayed on the wall, that sort of thing. It wouldn't have taken long. No, I still think it was an attempted burglary. Lucky you came back when you did.'

Loretta wasn't so sure. 'Actually, it's made me a bit nervous about staying there . . . ' she began.

'Heavens, Loretta, there's no need!' Clara seemed surprised. 'I rang the locksmith first thing this morning and he's over there now. He's putting locks on the windows as well, you'll have nothing to worry about tonight. Look, whoever they were, they know now that we're keeping an eye on the cottage. You've got to be practical about these things.'

Clara's robust common sense made Loretta feel rather wimpish. 'Maybe you're right,' she said, making a mental note to double-check every lock and fastening before retiring to bed that night.

'Where's Peggy?' she asked, changing the subject.

Clara frowned. 'She insisted on going back to the camp when she got up. I wanted to keep her here another day or two, but she wouldn't hear of it. I admire her determination, of course. But I think I'll go up there this afternoon just to make sure she's all right. Want to come?'

Loretta had heard so much about the Dunstow peace camp that she readily agreed. They arranged that Loretta would come over to Baldwin's around two, and she went back upstairs to change before returning to Keeper's Cottage to inspect the locksmith's handiwork.

'Something extraordinary's just happened,' Clara said as they set off in her car that afternoon. 'A complete stranger knocked on the door and said he'd like to buy the house.'

'Is it for sale?' Loretta asked, startled.

'Good God, no. Baldwin's is about the last thing in the world I'd part with, even if I needed the money, which I frankly don't. That's what's so odd about it. He said he was in the area on business and just happened to be driving past. I told him I'd no intention of selling – my family's been here since the turn of the century – and he was so crestfallen I found myself inviting him in. He couldn't have been more complimentary about it, he kept going on about how much Rose, that's his wife apparently, would like it. They've been looking in this area for ages, he said. So I made him a cup of tea and sent him on his way. But he insisted on leaving his card in case I ever change my mind. Don't you think that's strange?'

Loretta agreed that it was; not so much because she'd never heard of such a thing before as because Baldwin's, with its forbidding frontage, didn't strike her as the sort of house with which anyone would fall in love at first sight.

'What was he like?' she asked, feeling uneasy. Although there was no obvious link between the harmless incident Clara had just described and all the other things that had happened at the house in recent days, she found it hard to dismiss this latest event as mere coincidence. But what was the connection?

'Perfectly charming,' Clara said, answering Loretta's question. 'Late forties, public-school accent, didn't say precisely what his job was but I gathered he was in the City. The number on his card was genuine, by the way, I did check.' She glanced sideways at Loretta as though she had read her mind. 'The woman who answered put me through to his secretary, and she knew all about his trip up here. So – where does that leave us?'

'But why –'

'This is the turning,' Clara interrupted, signalling right. 'The camp's just up here on the left. I'll leave the car here. There was a lot of rain a couple of weeks and it's still rather muddy.'

She parked the car at the side of the tarmac road which led up to a gate in the perimeter fence. In front of them a sign bore the name 'RAF Dunstow', and gave dire warnings about contravening the Official Secrets Act. Someone had painted over the word 'RAF' with the letters 'USAF'. A bored sentry in a box just inside the gate pretended not to see them. To their left was a belt of trees, and a track running along the side of the fence. Loretta followed Clara along the track, which was rutted by the passage of vehicles. To her right, the high wire fence had been topped with coils of the razor wire she recognized from Greenham. A hundred or so yards inside the base, huge arched structures made of concrete blotted out the light; it took Loretta a moment to recognize them as aircraft hangars, smaller than the Cruise missile silos she had seen elewhere but, to her eyes, just as sinister.

'Hideous, aren't they?' said Clara, turning to address Loretta over her shoulder. 'Hello, it's me,' she called, suddenly leaving the track and moving into a clearing in the trees to their left. At the far side an old coach had been parked, its shape and condition suggesting it was at least twenty years old. Half a dozen tents had been pitched in front of it and, in the centre of the clearing, a group of women were sitting round a pit from which a thin column of smoke drifted steadily upwards. The women were drinking from mugs, and odd pieces of clothing had been hung out to dry on a makeshift washing-line between two trees. From the branches of another tree was suspended a torn sheet which had been painted with the slogan: *Take the toys from the boys*.

Loretta was nervous. Her visits to the women's peace camp at Greenham Common had always coincided with major demonstrations, and she didn't know how these women would react to the arrival of a stranger on a quiet Monday afternoon. Especially after Friday night, she thought, spotting a caravan further into the trees; the area around the door was smoke-blackened, and she remembered someone saying that the attackers had attempted to set fire to it.

'Want some tea?' A middle-aged woman stood up, beckoning Clara and Loretta over to the ancient vinyl sofa on which she'd been sitting. Several other women glanced up at the visitors and nodded greetings. Their attitude was neither friendly nor unfriendly, Loretta thought; it was as if their minds just happened to be on other things. One was writing a letter on airmail paper, Loretta noticed, accepting the offer of a seat. Another was knitting a jumper in purple and green, presumably because they were suffragette colours.

'Oh, er, no thanks.' She realized that the middle-aged woman had repeated her question about tea.

Clara joined her on the sofa, also refusing refreshment. 'How's things?' she asked.

'Could be worse,' said the woman, who had a soft Edinburgh accent. 'Hetty and Ulrike were thrown out of the caff place on the main road this morning – the manager says we upset the other customers. Tender plants, lorry drivers.' She shrugged. 'Thanks for bringing the commodes, by the way. I've asked everyone not to go to use them alone at night, and we bought some good strong torches this morning. We had a good post, nearly thirty pounds in donations.'

She and Clara fell into conversation about the events of Friday night, giving Loretta the chance to have a good look round the camp. Most of the tents were proper canvas affairs, and there was an air of permanence about the place which contrasted sharply with conditions at Greenham, where the women were subject to repeated evictions by council bailiffs. Even so, she marvelled at the willingness of the women to give up the comforts of everyday life to live in primitive conditions next door to thousands of hostile servicemen. It wasn't just the idea of being exposed to the elements that bothered her, it was also the sheer relentless boredom of spending day after day in the same place. Much as she agreed with their convictions, Loretta admitted to herself, the life of the peace women was not for her.

'Loretta!'

She turned her head, and saw Peggy and another woman emerging from the trees, their arms full of wood. Getting to her feet, she walked across the clearing to meet them, waiting while Peggy added her haul to the stock of firewood piled under a tarpaulin next to the old coach.

'How're you feeling?' Peggy asked, straightening up.

Loretta was about to answer when she saw Peggy's expression freeze; the girl was looking past her towards the track from the road, a look of utter dismay on her features. Loretta turned and saw a young man in jeans standing on the edge of the clearing, his feet planted firmly apart as though he was preparing to resist any challenge that might be thrown at him. There was an unnatural silence in the camp, and an air of tense anticipation. When he finally spoke, his words were an anticlimax.

''Lo, Peggy. I've been looking for you.'

Peggy stayed where she was, the group of women and the fire between herself and the newcomer.

'You needn't have bothered. I'm all right where I am.'

'You must be joking! Call this a home?' He gestured towards the camp with his left hand, not even trying to conceal his contempt. 'This is no place for you, girl. The bike's down the road. Why don't you come home?' For a second he sounded unsure of himself; it was more a plea than a question.

Peggy said nothing, and another uncomfortable silence ensued. After a moment the man moved further into the clearing, stopping on the edge of the group of women. Loretta could see a complicated tattoo on his left forearm: a heart pierced by an arrow, and in its centre a woman's name, Peggy.

'You keep back, don't come any closer!' His movement had stirred Peggy into action. She looked around frantically, as if for a weapon. 'Keep away from me, Mick, I mean it! I don't want nothing to do with you any more!'

'For Christ's sake, Peggy – ' He began to advance round the circle of women, holding out his right hand as though coaxing a shy animal. 'Look, we gotta talk – for the kid's sake. What've you done with the kid?'

A squeal of rage broke from Peggy. 'Don't you mention her, you, you – ' Words seemed to fail her. 'She's in a safe place where you'll never get your hands on her, you vicious bastard! Get away from me, *get away!*'

The man had rushed forward, and Loretta began to move; Clara was quicker, posing her considerable form between Peggy and the enraged Mick.

'That's *enough!*' she cried in tones that rang across the clearing. 'Peggy's told you she doesn't want you here, whoever you are, so you can take yourself off! Go on, you heard me!' She pointed back in the direction of the road. 'Go *on.*'

The young man glowered at her for a second, then ducked suddenly under Clara's arm and made a successful grab for Peggy. The two struggled together, Peggy screaming and gasping as she tried to break free, Mick cursing as her kicks and scratches went home. Loretta and Clara flung themselves into the fray, and Loretta received a sharp blow to the side of the head as Mick let go of Peggy and grappled with his new assailants. She staggered back, as other bodies rushed past her; seconds later Mick was on the ground, shouting ineffectual obscenities at the half dozen women who had pinned him down. She saw Clara lean forward, fixing him with a fierce glare as she addressed him slowly and clearly.

'In a moment, my friends and I are going to let you go. I'm going to count to ten, and if you haven't got the sense to disappear before I get there, we'll have to do something that'll make you sorry you ever came here. Understand?'

Loretta heard the words 'you old bitch' escape the man's lips as he made another bid for freedom. Clara was unperturbed.

'That's quite enough of that, young man. You've already shown us what bad manners you have.' She went down on one knee and poked him sharply in the chest. 'This is my land and I don't want the likes of you on it. Got it?'

Mick nodded his head in sullen agreement, and Clara stood back.

'All right, eveyone, let him go. One . . . two . . . three . . .'

Mick was already on his feet and making for the edge of the clearing. When he reached the track, he turned and jabbed two fingers obscenely in Clara's direction. 'I'll be back!'

'Seven . . . eight . . .'

He disappeared down the track. Clara shook her head, and turned to Peggy, who was hugging herself with both arms, apparently oblivious to the trickle of blood running down her face from a cut over her right eye.

'My poor girl,' Clara said, moving to embrace her. 'Let's take you back to the house and clean you up. Loretta, are you all right?'

'I think so.' Loretta felt her head gingerly. 'Clara, you were magnificent.'

Clara shrugged, dismissing the incident, and began to lead Peggy along the track to the road where the car was parked. Loretta climbed in the back after Peggy, who was whimpering quietly; when Loretta took her hand, Peggy held it tightly.

'Take her in while I park the car.' Clara stopped outside the front door of Baldwin's and handed Loretta the keys. Loretta opened the door, returned the keys to Clara, and led Peggy inside. She drew a chair from under the kitchen table and helped Peggy into it. Peggy folded her arms on the table, put her head down and started to sob. Loretta placed a hand on the girl's shoulder and then, as she became calmer, went about the business of putting the kettle on. She returned to the table, took a seat opposite Peggy, and waited.

'He's me husband.' Peggy looked despairingly at Loretta.

'I guessed he was.'

'I don't know how he found me. The women at the place I was staying, the refuge, they *promised* they wouldn't tell.'

Loretta spotted a box of tissues on the windowsill and leaned across to offer them to Peggy. Now she had time to take a proper look, she could see that the cut over Peggy's eye was superficial.

'You were in a refuge?' she asked gently, wanting to know more but unwilling to press her.

'Yeah. He hit me, see. It wasn't me I minded about – well, not much. It was the kid. She's only two. I don't want her to grow up with that – seeing her dad lay into me every time he's been drinking.'

'What's her name?' Loretta asked, wondering but not daring to ask where the child was.

'Maureen,' Peggy said. 'After me mum. That's where she is now, with me mum. D'you wanna see a picture of her? Oh, you can't – it's in me bag, it's up at the camp.' She started to get up.

Loretta leaned across and placed a restraining hand on Peggy's arm. 'Don't worry, we can get it later. I'll go up there, or Clara. Just sit quietly for a while.'

Peggy sank back into her seat. 'I didn't know where else to take her,' she said, returning to the child's whereabouts. 'When I left him last month, I took her to this place for battered women, but I didn't wanna keep her there, there wasn't room to swing a cat. And I knew he'd find me somehow. So I took her to me mum. She's got a sister in –' Peggy stopped, glanced nervously at Loretta, and looked down at the table. 'Her sister lives up north. Mick won't find them there, he never took no notice of me mum. I thought he might see sense after a bit and I could have her back.' She clasped her hands together and stared blankly into space.

'So how did you – why did you come to the peace camp?' Loretta asked, wondering whether Peggy's presence at Dunstow had more to do with her need to hide from Mick than her opposition to nuclear weapons and American bases.

'Oh, I was in the refuge when they bombed that place, you

know, Libya,' Peggy said. 'When I heard it on the radio, I thought, Christ, that's the last straw. I can get the kid away from Mick, but how can I save her from these bombs? I didn't know much about it before, but in the refuge everyone was talking about it all the time. This girl Yvonne, she was one of the helpers, she'd been to that place where they have the Cruise missiles, Greenham. Then she told me there'd been a camp set up here, where the planes went from. And I thought, this is me chance, it's not the sort of place I wanna take Maureen. So when I was well enough to take her to me mum's and get her settled, I hitched here. I wasn't just hiding from him, you know.'

'Sorry,' Loretta mumbled, embarrassed at the ease with which the girl had read her thoughts. 'I'll make some tea.'

At that moment Clara breezed in and led Peggy away to the downstairs bathroom to wash the blood off her face. When they reappeared, Peggy was looking uncomfortable in a Liberty print dress several sizes too big for her.

'I've put Peggy's things in the washing-machine,' Clara announced. 'She's going to stay here for a day or two in case that man comes back. No, Peggy, you really can't go back to the camp for the moment. You'd got to be sensible about this. Look, if he doesn't show up in the next week or so, we could even have your daughter brought here. All right?'

Faced with this bait, Peggy's protests subsided, while Loretta marvelled at Clara's skill in manipulating people. 'Oh, Peggy's things are still at the peace camp,' she told Clara. 'Shall I take her up there to pick them up?'

'That's very kind of you, Loretta. Oh, there's the phone.'

Clara left the room, returning almost at once.

'It's for you, Loretta,' she said. 'Robert – Robert Herrin.'

'Oh. Did he say what he wanted?' Loretta was surprised.

'No. The phone's on the desk in the drawing room.'

Perhaps Robert wanted to arrange another ride, Loretta thought, leaving the kitchen. He'd said something about it the night before. Well, the way she was feeling today, wild horses wouldn't drag her back to that stable-yard. She smiled as she picked up the phone, realizing the aptness of the metaphor.

'Loretta? How are you? I've just heard about last night.'

'Oh, that.' The previous evening's attempted burglary had

been driven from her mind by the scene she had just witnessed at the peace camp. 'Sorry, I'd rather forgotten. Things happen so fast. I've just come from the peace camp – Peggy's husband turned up and attacked her.'

'No! Is she hurt?'

'Don't think so, just knocked about a bit. Clara sent him off with a flea in his ear.'

'Good for her!' Robert laughed. 'You have to be a brave man to tangle with Clara – you should see her in action on the parish council. Well, you *are* having an exciting time.'

It was an odd way to describe the last couple of days, but Loretta realized Robert was right at least about the latest incident; Clara's triumph over Mick had left her feeling rather elated.

'Actually, I was ringing to ask you to supper. If you're free tonight, that is. I thought you might like an uneventful evening. I've lived in this house for eight years without being burgled – in fact the only person I know who's got it in for me is a music critic on *The Times*.'

'Well, I –' Loretta began, suddenly unsure of herself. Although nothing in their brief acquaintance had suggested that Robert was attracted to her, the invitation had raised an immediate suspicion. If a single and, as far as she knew, heterosexual man asked her to supper at his place in London, she would recognize it as an oblique question and act accordingly. But here – there wasn't a restaurant for miles, and perhaps Robert simply liked her company. And why jump to the conclusion she was to be the only guest? Maybe he intended to introduce her to more people from Flitwell. It was an intriguing question.

'Loretta?'

'Yes, I'm here. I was just thinking about some work I was going to do tonight – some essays I have to mark. But they can wait. What time should I arrive? And where's your house?'

She took down directions, and promised to turn up at half past seven. Then, smiling to herself, she returned to the kitchen, and asked Peggy if she was ready to go back to the peace camp to collect her things.

Robert Herrin's house was a semi-detached three-storey

building at the opposite end of Flitwell from the cottage owned by Ellie and Herc. The front door was at the side and Loretta had to open a small wrought-iron gate to get to it. She paused at the side of the house, trying to identify the faint piano music coming from the house: Fauré, she thought, wondering if Robert was the player. He wasn't; she heard his footsteps as soon as she rang the bell, but the music continued. She straightened the grey wool suit she'd been wearing when they met on Saturday, and waited for him to open the door.

'Loretta. Right on time.' He stood back to let her in, gesturing along the low-ceilinged corridor that ran towards the front of the house.

She followed it to a half-open door, then paused.

'Go in. What would you like to drink?'

'Wine, if there's some open. Oh, and I brought this.' She handed him a bottle of Rioja, one of several she'd brought with her from London. 'What a wonderful room.'

It was low and wide, with an inglenook fireplace to her left; it was a cool evening and a couple of branches were burning on cast-iron firedogs. To her right was a Victorian sofa with mahogany armrests and legs. Behind, the remaining space in the room was almost completely taken taken up by a grand piano – not a baby, but a full-scale Broadwood. The music, she noticed, was coming from a Swedish stereo system discreetly out of the way in one corner.

'I'm glad you like it,' Robert said, handing her a glass of red wine from an open bottle standing on a low table. 'You're looking at years of work. Everything was dark brown when I moved in, even these.' He pointed upwards to the exposed ceiling beams. 'It took me ages to get all the paint off, it was a standing joke when people came up from London – Herrin's unfinished ceiling.'

Loretta looked at him blankly.

'Like Schubert's Unfinished Symphony,' he explained, amused by her incomprehension. 'Though I've got one of those lying around, too. Hungry?'

'I am, rather,' she said, wondering whether she should take a seat or continue hovering by the door. Was anyone else going to arrive? She studied Robert covertly as he crossed the room to turn over the record, which had just finished. Although she hadn't registered an attraction to him at their previous meetings, she was now aware of a *frisson* of excitement which was making her intensely conscious both of her own movements and of his. It was a long time since she'd slept with anyone – not since the disastrous affair of the previous autumn, in fact – and this stirring of interest was novel and welcome. For some months after the last affair, she'd simply been off men; then, at some point, she'd seemed to get out of the habit of noticing them. Perhaps that was why she hadn't before taken in his narrow shoulders and thin hands – now that she had, she hoped she had not read his intentions wrongly. It was as if part of her that had been dry and still as a leafless branch had suddenly felt the first intimation of spring.

'We might as well go through to the kitchen, it'll be ready in five or ten minutes,' Robert said, coming back to her side. His fingers brushed her elbow as she moved in front of him into the corridor; the contact was brief, but the signal clear.

Glad that he could not for the moment see her face, Loretta followed the corridor to the back of the house, discovering an untidy kitchen organized around an old farmhouse table. Loretta pulled out a chair and sat down, avoiding Robert's gaze in case her thoughts were written too clearly in her eyes. He moved past her to the oven and opened the door.

'We can eat now, if you like, it's taken less time than I expected.' He shut the door, came over to the table, and began laying two places.

'You travel a lot,' Loretta remarked, observing the posters that covered the walls, many of them advertising concerts at which Robert had conducted his own music.

'Yes. It gets a bit wearing in the end, living out of suitcases. One hotel room' – he used an oven glove to carry an oval dish to the table – 'is very much like another.'

'What's that? It smells heavenly.'

'A *gougère*. And there's monkfish to follow. I suppose we ought to be drinking white – or are you happy with red?'

'I'm always happy with red. Where do you get monkfish round here?'

'Oh, the fish van comes round every Monday. We're not

completely cut off from civilization, you know. Is that enough? You can always come back for more.'

Dinner seemed to last for hours. Robert was a good cook, and they lingered over each of the four courses. Loretta was careful to drink enough to loosen her inhibitions without getting drunk. Robert, she guessed, was doing the same. Eventually, around ten, the conversation came to a natural pause. They sat in silence for a moment.

'How d'you feel about going back to the cottage, after last night?' Robert asked suddenly, giving her a direct look.

She returned it unwaveringly. 'Clara's fitted it up with enough locks for Fort Knox,' she said lightly. 'But I'm not all that enthusiastic.'

'Stay here, then.'

'All right.'

It was admirably simple. The only thing Loretta felt guilty about, as Robert undressed her upstairs a few minutes later, was the amount of money Clara had wasted on all those security devices.

Loretta didn't bother with lunch, having enjoyed a leisurely cooked breakfast with Robert before returning to Keeper's Cottage next morning. As she let herself in, she noted with relief that the antiseptic smell had begun to fade. Around three she walked over to Baldwin's, intending to ask Clara if she could use her phone; she'd promised to let her mother know she'd settled in safely. Clara was out, but she found Peggy in the kitchen eating a bowl of soup.

''Lo, Loretta,' Peggy said cheerfully. She was back in her old jeans, and looked much more comfortable then she had in Clara's print dress. 'D'you want Clara? She's out, I dunno where. Want some soup?'

Loretta refused the offer politely, explaining she'd come to use the phone.

'Go on,' Peggy advised her, 'she won't mind. I used it to phone my little girl last night, and she wouldn't take no money.'

Loretta's mother, who lived in Gillingham, answered the phone at the third ring. She was in the middle of icing a cake, she said, and couldn't talk for long. Satisfied that she'd done her duty, Loretta returned to the kitchen.

'You look well,' she told Peggy, observing the rosy colour in the girl's cheeks. Even the cut over her eye now looked insignificant.

'Yeah, I feel it,' Peggy confirmed. 'You know, Clara's great. I thought she was dead bossy first time I met her, but it's just her way. I feel dead . . .' – she groped for the right word – 'dead *safe* here. Mind you, she's hopping mad today.'

'Who is? Clara?'

'Yeah. You should have seen her this morning when she read the paper. They've put something in about the peace camp, and she was . . . ooh, her eyes really sparkled. She rang up and gave them what for.'

'What did it say?' asked Loretta.

'Oh, I didn't read all of it. But it was by that MP bloke she knows, Colin something. He's got a posh name. It was about how all the girls at the camp are lezzies, and they should go home to their husbands. That's what he says. Just shows what he knows,' she added, raising her eyebrows to show her contempt for this assertion of traditional values. 'He oughta go to a refuge, one of them places I was in. That'd teach him a few things about why women leave their fellas.'

'And this was in the *Guardian*?' Loretta asked, surprised. This was the only paper she'd seen delivered to Baldwin's the previous day, but it didn't sound like a *Guardian* feature.

'Nah, it was in that other one, the *Daily Telegraph*,' Peggy told her. 'Jeremy, he went down to the village shop this morning and bought it. He took it with him to London.'

Loretta was disappointed, and wondered whether she'd be able to get a copy at the shop in Flitwell. She had to go into the village some time that afternoon – Robert was coming over for a late supper, and she needed to buy food.

'Oh well, I'll be off,' she said, thinking that she might as well do this errand next. 'Tell Clara I used the phone, and I'll give her some money when I see her.'

'OK.' Peggy lifted a hand in farewell. Loretta left her struggling to open a packet of ginger biscuits.

Robert arrived earlier than expected that evening and Loretta met him with a half-peeled peach in one hand and a kitchen knife in the other.

'Did you think I was another intruder?' he asked, shutting the front door and putting his arms round her. 'Mmm, you taste of peaches.'

'They're supposed to go in with the lamb, but I can't resist eating them,' she said, kissing him again. 'I hope it'll be all right.' She moved back to the Aga and stirred something in a battered Le Creuset casserole. 'It's supposed to be lamb with apricots, but they didn't have any in the village shop. I'm having to make do with peaches instead – I brought some with me from London. Flitwell isn't *that* civilized, I couldn't get any fresh coriander, either. What would you like to drink?'

'This'll do.' He picked up the open bottle of red wine standing on the table and filled the empty glass Loretta had put out for him. Then he leaned across to turn up the volume of Loretta's cassette player, which was in the middle of a recording of highlights from *Turandot*. 'Listen to that,' he said above the noise. 'Perfect – just perfect.' He drew out a chair and sat down at the table, idly turning the pages of a magazine Loretta had left lying there.

Loretta smiled and carried on slicing peaches. When she'd tipped all the pieces into the casserole she put on the lid and looked round for the potatoes she'd put out to scrub. She cleaned them, dropped them in boiling water, and began topping and tailing a heap of green beans.

'It'll be ready soon,' she said, turning to look at Robert.

He raised his eyebrows, unable to hear her over the music. Loretta shook her head, hoping they weren't disturbing Clara. She went back to the Aga, wondering if the lamb was cooking too fast. Behind her, Robert turned the volume of the music down to its previous level.

'I could listen to that for hours,' he said, getting up and coming to peer over her shoulder. 'Smells good.' He ran a finger lightly down her back from the nape of her neck to her waist. 'Oh, about the coriander. If you really can't do without it, you could try Clara. She grows it herself, she's very proud of it. I'm sure she'll let you have some.'

Loretta untied the apron that was protecting her linen trousers and silk shirt and hung it on the back of a chair.

'Won't be long.' She stopped at the front door and blew a

kiss to Robert. Leaving the door ajar, she began picking her way round her parked car.

She followed the path through the gap in the hedge, pausing on the other side to enjoy the scene that lay before her. To her left, the wood on the far side of the valley was a dense mass, the sky above it deep and brilliant blue. There was a faint perfume on the night air, roses perhaps, or some other flower she didn't recognize. Loretta took a deep breath, savouring a moment of unalloyed happiness; she would have lingered longer had it not been for her eagerness to complete her errand and return to Robert in the cottage.

As she passed the bay window of the drawing room she noticed that light was showing through the crack where the curtains hadn't quite been drawn together; someone was in although, when she went through the conservatory to the back door, there was no light in the hall. She tried the back door which was, as usual, unlocked – Clara had laughed off Loretta's suggestion that it might be sensible to keep it secured after dark. Loretta stepped into the hall, felt for the light switch, and called Clara's name. There was no reply.

'Clara!' She tried again, louder this time.

It occurred to her that Clara might be using the phone in the drawing room. She moved to her right, and rapped with her fingers on the half-open door. There was still no response, nor could she hear anyone talking. Loretta pushed the door gently. It swung wider, revealing a chair lying on its side on the floor. The realization that something was wrong froze Loretta for a second, then, gathering her courage, she moved further into the room.

Clara was lying in an armchair on the far side of the fire-place, sprawled back as though thrown into position with considerable force. Her legs were apart at an ungainly angle, and one arm was flung back above her head. But what hor-rified Loretta most of all was the way in which Clara's eyes were fixed on a point in the ceiling; it was this detail, the rolled-up, bulging, *unnatural* eyes, that forced the truth upon her. Clara Wolstonecroft was dead, quite dead – before the fact had begun to sink in, and certainly without conscious thought, Loretta was stumbling out of the room, across the hall, into the conservatory. Her breath coming in strangled

73

gasps, she plunged headlong into the dark garden, one thought and only one hammering in her head: she must get away, away from this place of death, before the thing that had happened to Clara happened to her, too.

4

A dark shape shot past, causing Loretta to fall; she was up on her feet in seconds, but incoherent with fear and horror by the time she reached the front door of the cottage. It gave at her touch, propelling her into the kitchen. Robert leapt to his feet as she crashed into the table, the smile on his face fading into astonishment as he registered the state she was in. Loretta tried to speak, failed to get out more than Clara's name, and gave up the attempt. Instead, she caught Robert's arm and began dragging him towards the dark garden. To her relief he didn't argue, and it was only when they reached the open back door of Baldwin's that he stopped to ask questions.

'Where is she? Downstairs?'

Loretta nodded.

'Which room?'

She pointed wordlessly to the door of the drawing room. Robert was already striding across the hall when she lunged after him, grabbing his arm again.

'She's *dead*,' she said incredulously.

Robert stared at her for a moment, gently removed her hand, then moved towards the open door. He paused on the threshold, looked back at her, and went inside. Almost at once she heard a wail, and Clara's cat appeared round the door. He took a few steps towards her, danced back, and then returned to brush up against her legs in a state of extreme agitation. Absent-mindedly, Loretta bent to stroke his head; it was his form, she realized, that she'd stumbled over in the garden. The cat permitted her caress for a second, then darted away into the drawing room. Loretta stood up too quickly, and her head began to spin; she looked round, spotted a chair by the back door, and lowered herself on to it, gripping the upright back tightly with one hand. She realized she had been taking quick, shallow breaths, and forced herself to draw air into her lungs and hold it for a count of five. The dizziness receded and she looked up, gazing round the hall as if puzzled by its very ordinariness. Her glance took in her hand, still clutching the back of the seat, and a new thought struck her: fingerprints, she shouldn't be touching *anything* in case there were fingerprints. She drew her hand away, staring at it as though it had been invisibly contaminated, even though there was no reason at all why the murderer should have . . . her mind stopped there, for the first time making conscious acknowledgement of what she had half-known all the time, that Clara had been murdered. Why else had she fled from Clara's body instead of ringing for an ambulance? She let out a soft 'oh' of despair, letting her head drop forward as though, by closing her eyes, she could transport herself elsewhere. To no avail: the practical part of her mind immediately presented her with an image of the drawing room as she had seen it a few moments before, and she was aware of a nagging question. How? How had it been done? She concentrated hard, trying to make her inner eye travel dispassionately over the body in an attempt to recall whether she had seen signs of violence. It was no good, all she remembered clearly were the protruding eyes, the horribly sprawled limbs. Blood, she asked herself, had she seen blood? She had only the vaguest recollection of what Clara had been wearing – something flowery and pink, probably one of her Liberty print dresses – and she simply couldn't remember blood stains. All right, what about the neck, did her mental picture include marks of strangulation? Loretta gasped and clenched her fists, frustrated by her inability to recall the scene in detail. She was still engaged in this fruitless exercise – it didn't at any point occur to her to go back and take a second look at the dead woman – when Robert returned to the hall.

'I phoned the police.'

He was ashen, distracted. The cat appeared again, this time making straight for Loretta. She picked him up, murmuring soothing noises and wishing she could do the same for Robert; she didn't know him well enough to know which words might soothe, which merely irritate. The shock had been bad enough for her, who had met Clara only three days before; what must it be like for an old friend like Robert? They waited in anguished silence, neither knowing what to do. Eventually Loretta got up, letting the cat slip to the floor.

'Robert –'

Crash!

Loretta jumped backwards, colliding with the chair. Her nerves were so stretched that it was only when the sound was repeated, a double-rap this time, that she realized it was the door-knocker, its impact magnified by the previous silence in the hall. Before she had fully gathered her senses, Robert was moving towards the front door.

'Oh . . . I was expecting Clara. Is she in?' A smartly dressed middle-aged man was standing on the doorstep, apparently taken aback by their presence. Loretta wondered if the shock of Clara's murder was still visible on their faces.

'I –' he began.

'She –' said Robert.

They stopped and looked at each other. Loretta swallowed, unequal to the task of telling this unsuspecting visitor that the woman he had come to see was dead.

Robert cleared his throat. 'Look, you'd better come in.'

The man paused on the threshold, looking from Robert to Loretta and back again.

'Is something wrong? Oh, no, she hasn't – don't tell me she's not here? I know I'm a bit late, but this is the limit. I mean, it was *her* idea I should come tonight. I had to leave a meeting early to get here –'

'No, no, you don't understand! Clara's –' Loretta couldn't bring herself to finish.

'I'm sorry, but she's dead.' Robert spoke flatly.

'Dead? Dead?'

Loretta saw the shock hit the man's eyes, like a mask slipping. His face went very white; he looked, she supposed, as she had directly after discovering the body.

'But how can she – I don't understand. I talked to her this

afternoon, she didn't say – she sounded – look, this isn't some sort of joke?'

'Of course not! She's in there if you want to see for yourself!' Loretta pointed at the door of the sitting room.

The man stared at her for a moment, then turned abruptly and strode into the room. It suddenly hit Loretta that she'd done the wrong thing – surely the fewer people who went near the body the better? She cast an agonized glance at Robert, who seemed to grasp her meaning. He moved towards the door but, as he did so, there was a gasp from within and the stranger reappeared.

'You didn't tell me she was – like that!' He glared accusingly at Loretta.

'You didn't give us a chance!' Tears welled up in her eyes again; this scene was more than she could take. She felt Robert move to her side, and his arm went round her.

'It hardly makes any difference,' he said coldly. 'The main thing is she's dead. We can stand here arguing all night but it won't bring her back. Excuse me.' He went to where the front door was still standing open and shut it.

The newcomer sighed and shook his head. 'I'm sorry. It's just – so unexpected. I've known Clara since we were children. Have you called the police?'

'They're on their way. I don't think we should do anything till they get here. I'm Robert Herrin, by the way. We met once at dinner.'

The man stared at Robert for a second. 'Yes, of course. I remember now. And you're . . . ?' He looked at Loretta.

'Loretta Lawson. I'm staying in Clara's cottage.' For some reason, she was unwilling to extend her hand.

'Colin Kendall-Cole. I came to see Clara about something. She – she rang me this afternoon.' His hand went to his collar, feeling underneath the plain grey tie to loosen the top button of his shirt.

Loretta took in his dark, slicked-back hair and expensive, faintly striped suit. He looked exactly what he was, she thought: a country solicitor turned Conservative MP. She felt justified in her instinctive reluctance to shake hands. Then, her eyes moving briefly across his shocked face, she was overcome with guilt; he was a human being, and one who had just witnessed the corpse of an old friend.

'Perhaps we could go and wait in the cottage?' she suggested, looking from Colin to Robert.

'Wait a minute.' Robert held his head to one side, as though he had heard something. The noise was faint, but at this moment Loretta heard it too; a police car was approaching. The siren got louder, then abruptly cut off. Car doors slammed, and there was a pounding on the front door.

The first contingent was a uniformed patrol which happened to be the area on other business at the time of Robert's phone call. They viewed the body briefly, then returned to the hall.

'Which of you people found her?' asked the older man.

'I did,' Loretta said hesitantly, wondering whether to embark on the whole story or wait until someone more senior arrived.

'What time was that, miss?'

Loretta realized she didn't know, and looked at Robert for help.

'I got to the cottage about ten past nine, maybe quarter past,' Robert said consideringly. 'I suppose I'd been there – what, twenty minutes? – when you came over here?'

'Which means you found her between nine thirty and nine thirty-five,' the older policeman said, turning back to Loretta. 'Then what happened?'

'I went back to the cottage for Robert . . . I suppose I was frightened,' she said lamely.

'So then you came and had a look, sir?'

'Yes. And dialled nine-nine-nine.'

'And you, sir, when did you arrive on the scene?'

Loretta felt Colin stiffen. 'I arrived on the scene, as you put it, officer, five or ten minutes ago. I'm afraid I can't be more precise. It's been a great shock.'

'And I suppose you went to have a dekko as well?'

'I did, officer.' Colin was feeling in an inside pocket of his suit jacket. When his hand emerged, it was holding a wallet. 'Perhaps you'd like to take my card?'

The policeman took it, and Loretta watched a flush travel up his neck and on to his cheeks.

'Sorry, sir,' he mumbled. 'Have to make these inquiries –

sure you understand.' He paused, then turned to Loretta. 'Sorry, miss – I don't think I got your name.'

After he'd written down Loretta's and Robert's names, the policeman made a show of going to the stairs and peering up them. His foot was on the first step when there was the sound of more cars drawing up; moments later, reinforcements arrived in the shape of a man who introduced himself as Chief Inspector Bailey. He was accompanied by a group of people whose functions seemed to be mainly technical, including a couple of men with fingerprint equipment and a woman detective. A few minutes later a doctor arrived. After consulting with the uniformed PCs who were already on the scene, Bailey went into action.

'OK, start in there,' he said, directing his team into the sitting room. Then he turned to where Loretta, Robert and Colin were silently waiting. 'I'll just take a look at the – deceased, and then I'd be grateful if you'd all accompany me to the station.' He gave a cool nod and began to move towards the door.

'Wait a minute, Chief Inspector.' Colin's voice succeeded in being at once smooth yet insistent. 'Will that really be necessary? I think I'd better introduce myself – Colin Kendall-Cole, MP for Oxfordshire South-East. I don't want to be a nuisance, but can't we get the formalities over here?'

The detective gave him a measuring look; Loretta had the feeling he was personally unimpressed by Colin's status, but aware of its potential as a complicating factor.

'Well, sir, it's usual to get everyone away from the scene of the crime, as I'm sure you know. My men have a job to do, and I'm sure this young lady' – he glanced at Loretta – 'would feel happier down at the station.' Loretta looked at Bailey in surprise, disconcerted by this unexpected concern for her welfare. Or was it merely a clever ploy on Bailey's part?

'I understand all that, Chief Inspector.' Colin's tone was equally reasonable, but it was clear a battle of wills was taking place. 'But these are not normal circumstances. We're nowhere near the station – I take it you mean Headington – and it's getting late. Can't you take our statements here? I'm sure Miss – er – wouldn't mind.' He glanced at Loretta in a manner that commanded her agreement. She hadn't time to protest before he played his trump card. 'Look, Chief Inspector, I don't want you to think I'm pulling rank. My problem is that I've got a meeting with the . . . ' – he glanced round the hall and lowered his voice – 'the minister in the morning, first thing. You know how busy these people are.' His tone suggested that the detective was a colleague, as familiar as he with the schedules of government ministers. He looked briefly at his watch. 'It's well after ten already. I've got to be in Whitehall at eight. This has been the most terrible shock – Mrs Wolstonecroft was a very old friend. If you *could* relax the rules for once . . . I'd be most grateful.'

Bailey looked at his own watch for a moment, his face impassive. Then: 'As you wish, sir. We'll use the kitchen. But I'll have to get it dusted for fingerprints first. *If* that's all right with you?' It was impossible to tell whether the final sentence was intended to be deferential or sarcastic.

Colin chose to believe the former. 'Of course. Go ahead.'

The small group waited in the hall while one of Bailey's men, recalled from the sitting room, made an examination of the kitchen.

'Right, then,' Bailey said as his man reappeared. He addressed Loretta. 'You found the body, Miss . . . ' – he glanced at his notes – 'Miss Lawson. Better have you first. On your own, were you?'

Afterwards, Loretta couldn't imagine why it was only at this point that the most obvious and terrifying part of the puzzle became clear to her. As she moved obediently towards the kitchen door, her mind went through a series of logical steps: yes, she had been alone when she entered the sitting room; no, she hadn't seen or heard anyone else in the house; and in that case –

'Where's Peggy?'

She stood stock still in front of the kitchen door, her words cutting across the various low-voiced conversations taking place in the hall and sitting room. Bailey, Robert, Colin, the woman detective, they all stared at her.

'Where's Peggy?' She spoke on a rising note of panic: in her imagination, she could already see the girl's body sprawled across a bed, her dyed blonde hair matted with blood. Or was she in one of the bathrooms, senseless on the floor while the very people who should be helping her wasted time looking for minute clues? Loretta started for the stairs, only to find her way blocked by the detective.

'Wait a minute, miss. Who's this Peggy?'

Loretta could have cried with frustration. 'She was here, I saw her –'

'When? Tonight?' Bailey was suddenly alert.

'No, no, not tonight, that's the *point*. She should be here and she isn't. She –'

'You mean someone is staying here? Clara didn't mention her when she spoke to me this afternoon.'

'Why should she?' Loretta turned on Colin angrily. 'You're the last person she'd tell – you and your stupid bill!' She turned and cast Bailey a pleading look. 'She's from the peace camp. She was staying here for a few days because . . .' Loretta paused, wondering whether she should tell Bailey about Mick.

'Has anyone checked whether anything's missing?' Colin asked abruptly. Loretta stared at him, not immediately taking in his meaning.

'Well, it's the obvious thing, isn't it? Wouldn't you say, Chief Inspector?' He appealed to the policeman, man to man. 'I had a brief chat with Mrs Wolstonecroft this afternoon about these so-called peace women. I didn't like her involvement with them, didn't like it at all. I tried to make her see what a risk she was taking – after all, nobody knows a thing about these women, I gather a lot of them don't use their real names. Aliases by the dozen. Isn't that so, Chief Inspector? And now Mrs Wolstonecroft's dead, and one of them is missing. I'm simply making the obvious inference.'

'You're not suggesting *Peggy* had anything to do with this?' Loretta was wide-eyed with astonishment. 'Of all the –'

'Wait a minute, this is getting us nowhere,' Bailey interrupted, looking from Loretta to Colin as if to make plain he wasn't taking sides. 'What we *have* established – correct me if I'm wrong – is that a young woman from the, er, camp has been staying in this house and hasn't been seen since this afternoon. Right?'

'*Yes*,' said Loretta, in an agony of impatience.

'So the logical thing is to have a thorough search of the

house – I assume PC Wilkins had a quick look round before I got here?'

'No, he didn't!' Loretta took a deep breath.

'I don't think he had time,' Robert said, coming to the man's defence.

'OK, I'll deal with that later. Wise, you take downstairs.' The woman detective headed for the door of the downstairs bathroom. 'Lucas!' A uniformed constable appeared from the sitting room. 'You come with me.'

Loretta watched the two men climb the stairs, her fists clenched so tightly that her nails dug into her palms. She forced herself to take deep, calming breaths, but her heart went racing on nevertheless. DC Wise came out of the bathroom, shaking her head. Loretta watched her make for the long corridor at the front of the house which, she remembered, led to the music room.

'Heard one of your pieces on the car radio the other day,' Colin remarked to Robert. 'Radio Three. Short piano piece, now which one would that have been?'

Loretta's nerve snapped.

'How can you stand there talking about *music*? With all this going on.' She waved a hand towards the stairwell, from which echoed the sounds of cupboards being opened and closed. 'After what you've said about Peggy! How could you? You don't even *know* her! The idea that she – oh, it's just ridiculous! What do you know about peace camps? I bet you've never been near one in your life! Or if you have, it'll be on some Ministry of Defence briefing!'

'I –'

'And if it comes to that, what were *you* doing here tonight? Clara was furious about your stupid article! Don't tell me you were making a social call!'

The MP stiffened. 'As a matter of fact, Clara asked me to come round. I've already told you that. It wasn't very convenient, but I felt I owed it to her – as an old friend. She wanted to talk to me about the peace camp, on which, as you so rightly say, our views differed. I believe she had got into an emotional state about the base, and hadn't thought through the consequences of what she was doing. No doubt she was hoping to change my mind. The discussion would have almost certainly been fruitless, but I felt I had a duty.'

'And that, m'Lud, closes the case for the prosecution!'

'Loretta!' Robert placed a restraining hand on her arm, his shocked tone showing he thought she'd gone too far.

'It's all right, Herrin, I can see she's overwrought. Oh, and by the way, I'm a solicitor, not a barrister.'

'Miss Lawson, can you come up here for a moment?'

Bailey was standing at the top of the stairs. Loretta's entire body was suddenly cold as stone. She climbed the stairs slowly, as if preparing for the worst.

'You've found her?' Her words were little more than a whisper.

'No. Do you know which room she was staying in?'

'That one.' Loretta pointed to the door half-way down the corridor that led to Clara's study.

'I thought so. There's a pair of trousers and a shirt rolled up under the bed, and the bed's obviously been slept in. But nothing else. She must have had a bag – something to keep her things in?'

'Oh yes.' Loretta cast her mind back to the previous evening, when she'd taken Peggy up to the peace camp to collect her belongings. 'A barrel bag, you couldn't miss it, it was bright pink.'

'What's a barrel bag?'

'One of those long round ones, like a tube. About this long.' Loretta held her hands about three feet apart.

'All right, miss. If Wise hasn't found anything downstairs, I'll send her up to the – the peace camp. It's conceivable your friend's gone back there. And I'll organize a search of the garden.'

He stood back so she could lead the way downstairs. Instead, Loretta moved closer to him and spoke rapidly in a low voice.

'Look, Inspector. What he suggested, Kendall-Cole I mean, it just isn't possible. I *know* Peggy. She would never have hurt Clara. She was grateful to her for taking her in. Her husband beat her up, that's why she was staying here. He followed her to the peace camp and tried to make her go home. It was Clara who stopped him. I was there when it happened.' She willed the policeman to believe her.

Bailey thought for a moment, head sunk on chest. Then he looked up.

'All right, I'll bear that in mind. But there's another way of looking at it, you must see that?'

Loretta stared at him, not understanding.

'Your Peggy may have been *in league* with her husband, have you considered that?' He paused, then went on. 'They set up the scene at the camp, hoping Mrs Wolstonecroft would bring Peggy back to the house. Then tonight he comes here, she lets him in. He starts helping himself – there's a lot of nice stuff in the house – and Mrs Wolstonecroft disturbs him. He panics, kills her, and they take off together.'

'But there's no evidence – nothing's been taken!' Loretta protested.

'Oh, but it has,' said Bailey, moving past her down the stairs. He turned half-way down, and looked back at her. 'From the state of Mrs Wolstonecroft's bedroom, it's a fair bet that someone – and I'm not saying it's this Peggy – has made off with the best part of her jewellery. Excuse me, I've got a search to organize.'

The next hour was a nightmare for Loretta. More police arrived and began searching the garden; she was asked to provide keys to the cottage and to her car. Colin, who had parked in the lay-by in the lane next to the house, surrendered his car keys with a surprising lack of fuss. One by one they were searched, Loretta by a specially summoned WPC. Shortly after this DC Wise returned from the peace camp with the news, overheard by everyone in the hall, that Peggy had not been seen there since the previous day. Then Bailey, who had been here, there and everywhere during these grim proceedings, came to a halt before Loretta and said he was ready to interview her.

'Sorry we couldn't get this over earlier,' he said, as he and the WPC followed her into the kitchen. 'Your information about this woman Peggy gave us a lot to do. Have a seat.'

They settled themselves at the kitchen table, the WPC ready to write on a clipboard in front of her.

'Now, can we start with the routine stuff – name, address, that sort of thing? WPC Baker here will take down what you say, and we'll ask you to read it through and sign it afterwards.'

Loretta complied, supplying in answer to Bailey's questions a brief account of how she came to be staying in Keeper's Cottage. Then he took her through a minute-by-minute account of how and when she'd found Clara's body, ending with the arrival of the first police car. The detective, who had been making odd notes of his own, sat back and chewed the end of his pen. Then he put it down and leaned towards her across the table, his hands clasped in front of him.

'That was admirably clear, Miss Lawson. You're an excellent witness. What I don't understand is why you, and Mr Herrin, presumably, didn't hear anything.'

'You mean . . . anyone arriving at the house? Or leaving? But the cottage – there aren't any downstairs windows facing the house.'

'I didn't mean that so much,' Bailey said, leaning back and tapping his pen on the table. 'No, I was wondering about the shots.'

'*Shots?*'

'Why, yes. As you were the one who discovered the body, I assumed you knew Mrs Wolstonecroft had been shot. Twice, as a matter of fact. Through the heart.'

Loretta swallowed several times, suddenly feeling sick.

'But there wasn't any blood . . . '

'Wouldn't be. Small-bore gun, close range. Just two neat holes, with a bit of blackening round them. You're not telling me you didn't see them?' His tone was disbelieving.

Loretta felt a cold anger.

'Inspector, I haven't seen many dead bodies in my lifetime. Finding the body was – the most dreadful shock. I didn't know Clara well, but I liked her very much. I could see she was dead, but I didn't stop to think about how or who'd done it. You may think that's – inadequate. Perhaps it is. But it's the truth.'

The detective bowed his head.

'I'm sorry, I have to ask these questions. But you're sure you didn't hear the shots? The doctor can't be certain yet, of course, but he thinks Mrs Wolstonecroft was killed not long before you found her.' He sounded less accusing, and Loretta had the impression her little speech had impressed him. Or perhaps he was just relieved that she hadn't started to cry. She gave his question her full attention.

'I really can't – oh! I know what must have happened! I was listening to some music when Robert arrived – some Puccini. *Turandot*. It's very noisy in places.'

'I know it,' Bailey said.

'Robert turned it up for a while towards the end. I remember wondering if we were disturbing Clara . . . I don't think we'd have heard anything from outside while it was turned up.' She sighed, feeling she'd somehow let Clara down. Though by the time the shots had been fired, Clara had almost certainly been beyond help.

'Where did the gun come from?' she asked suddenly, trying to summon up her mental picture of the scene in the drawing room and wondering why she hadn't spotted it.

'We won't know much till we get the ballistics report,' Bailey said, 'the gun itself being missing. We don't even know what type it was yet. I'm glad to say we didn't find it when we searched your cottage,' he added, a fleeting smile passing across his austere features. 'Which inclines me to think you and Mr Herrin are probably in the clear.'

Loretta looked blankly at him; it hadn't occurred to her that she and Robert were suspects.

'Don't worry, miss, at the moment you're well down my list. Now, what can you tell me about your friend Peggy?'

Loretta was about to protest Peggy's innocence again but decided it might antagonize Bailey; she was also very tired. She told the detective what she knew, which didn't really amount to much – she realized she didn't even know Peggy's surname or where she had lived in London. But she was able to give full descriptions of both the girl and her husband, not forgetting the tattoo on Mick's forearm; Bailey cheered up considerably on hearing this detail, and said something about getting the Met on to it.

'Right, then . . . if you'll just read through your statement and sign each page at the bottom – if you agree with it, that is . . .'

Loretta took the long, hand-written statement and examined it page by page. The sentences were short, inelegant; even so, she had to admire the way in which the policewoman had succeeded in reducing Loretta's occasionally disjointed narrative into a concise account of her part in that evening's events. She signed her name half a dozen times, and returned the clipboard to WPC Baker.

'You can go.'

Loretta started to get up. Bailey held up a hand.

'No, I meant WPC Baker.'

Loretta sat down again, wondering what was coming next. Bailey waited until the other woman had left the room, then leaned back with his hands behind his head.

'So – who d'you think did it?'

Loretta blinked. Until this moment the detective's manner had been neutral, occasionally accusing, not one to invite confidences. She remembered the exchange at the top of the stairs and, without further thought, rapped out two words.

'Not Peggy!'

'That's why I'm asking you. You're obviously convinced this girl's innocent – why?'

'I – it's just . . . not in character. I told you – she was grateful to Clara for taking her in . . . It's just – impossible.'

'So we go back to my original question. Who d'you think did it?'

Loretta sat in silence, unable to think of anything to say. She realized, surprised, that she'd hardly considered the question. It was as if, from the moment she discovered Clara's body, she had taken to living in the present tense. The evening seemed to have stretched backwards in time until it occupied most of her recent life; she was aware of a protective numbness in her brain which had excluded all but the demands of each long moment. She shook her head slightly, seeking to dislodge the film that seemed to have grown over her mind. Bailey, observing her, appeared to understand the process.

'Take your time,' he said quietly.

Loretta looked up, taking in the detective's features for the first time. He had fair hair and skin, grey eyes which lacked expression; it was a face she found impossible to read. But – he seemed genuinely interested in what she had to say.

'Since Peggy's missing,' she said slowly, 'the obvious person is Mick. She wouldn't have gone with him voluntarily,

I'm sure of that. But what if he came here to get her back, and Clara tried to stop him? He might have taken the jewellery to make it look like a robbery. But – ' she stopped, realizing she had been thinking aloud.

'But?' Bailey prompted her.

'I was just thinking about the gun,' she said reluctantly. 'Somehow . . . well, I just can't see Mick as the sort of person who'd carry a gun. He was violent, yes. But with his fists, or maybe a knife . . . not a gun. Though these days . . . ' She trailed off. She had a nagging feeling that she'd forgotten something, and it didn't feel as if it had anything to do with Mick. What was it? She cast her mind back over the last few days, trying to pin down something that was floating just beyond reach of her conscious mind. Then, 'Oh! How could I forget . . . Inspector, Clara was being threatened! Phone calls, letters, they started as soon as she allowed the peace women on to her land. Look' – she had seen a momentary flicker in Bailey's light eyes – 'I don't know what your feelings are about the peace camp, and I don't want to know. What I'm telling you is fact. Clara was getting anonymous letters and phone calls – most of them were silent, the phone calls, I mean, but she said someone read the burial service to her once. And someone threw paint at the house on Saturday night – you know about that, of course?'

Bailey nodded. Loretta wondered whether to tell him about the voices she and Clara had heard in the night, but something held her back.

'She showed you these letters?'

'No.'

'You hear any of the phone calls?'

'No, but I haven't been here very long . . . She was keeping a list of them somewhere, a sort of log. I expect you'll find the letters when you search the house.'

'So you're suggesting that the people behind these letters and phone calls are responsible for Mrs Wolstonecroft's death?'

'*I* don't know! You asked me a question, and I'm doing my best to answer it. You must admit, it's a very odd coincidence that Clara got all these threats and now she's been killed.'

'Miss Lawson, there's a world of difference between

sending anonymous letters and shooting someone. Crime statistics show that the sort of people who make threats very rarely carry them out –'

'But what about Saturday night – the paint? That was real enough! What if that was a warning, and now –'

'Sorry, you're way off beam there. We charged three eighteen-year-olds with criminal damage' – he looked at his watch – 'several hours ago. They left the station just before we got your – Mr Herrin's call. I don't think any of them's likely to have nipped straight back here and shot Mrs Wolstonecroft on the way home. The time's wrong, for one thing, and two of them had their dads with them.'

'I didn't know that.' Loretta felt cheated; she had more or less decided to trust Bailey, and he'd been holding out on her.

'No, and I think you've been reading too many spy novels, Miss Lawson.'

'And you've been watching too many gangster movies! You seem to think Peggy's some sort of moll, sucking up to Clara just so she could let her husband into the house. And it's *Dr* Lawson, I told you at the start.' She was sick of people who couldn't remember her name or get her title right; as soon as the words left her lips, she regretted them, but it was too late. Bailey's expression – hostility – was for once all too easy to read, and she knew she'd blown any chance she'd had of persuading him of Peggy's innocence. He opened his mouth to speak but was interrupted by a knock at the door.

'Come in!'

A young PC appeared, edging into the room in a state of suppressed excitement.

'Excuse me, sir – sorry to bother you – but I found this.' He whisked something pink from behind his back and placed it triumphantly on the table in front of them. Loretta gasped; it was a barrel bag identical to the one she had described to Bailey earlier.

'It was in the bushes at the side of the garden, just before you get into the trees.'

'Well done.' Bailey was on his feet, drawing on gloves. Holding the very tip of the zip fastener, he slowly eased the bag open. His hand darted inside, and reappeared holding a small square object in a gilt frame. Loretta recognized it at once as one of the paintings from Clara's sitting room.

'Probably realized it was too easily identified,' Bailey said, putting the picture down next to the bag. 'Looks like your friend Peggy's got some explaining to do,' he went on, turning to Loretta. 'I take it this *is* her bag – the one you were telling me about?'

Loretta nodded miserably.

'You can go now, *Dr* Lawson. Thank you for your coopera-tion. We'll be in touch if we need to speak to you in the next day or two.'

She was being dismissed, and the detective was already building up a case against Peggy.

'Look, Inspector Bailey –'

'*Chief* Inspector.'

'All right, Chief Inspector. I really don't want to quarrel with you. I'm sure you want the person who did this caught as much as I do.' She wasn't expressing herself very well; shock and exhaustion had taken their toll. 'I just think you should –'

'Thank you, Dr Lawson, I can assure you I know how to do my job.'

His gaze had dropped from her to the bag on the table in front of him. He picked it up and shook it; it seemed to be empty.

She turned unhappily to leave the room.

'Oh, I forgot.'

The sound of Bailey's voice made her turn. 'One of my men found this on the floor in your bathroom.' He tossed a cassette tape on to the table. 'Don't want you to accuse us of holding on to your property unnecessarily.'

Loretta reached across and took the cassette, wondering when she'd dropped it. She remembered carrying a shoebox containing tapes up to the bedroom – perhaps it had fallen out then. She put it in a trouser pocket, too tired to think. Bailey hardly acknowledged her goodbye, and she returned down-cast to the hall.

She decided to wait for Robert, a decision she later regretted since it meant she was still sitting on the bottom stair when Clara's body was removed from the house. The corpse was carried to a waiting van on a stretcher, covered up, of course, but its awkward contours impressed her as an indelible image of lifelessness. It wasn't Robert's fault that Loretta was present at this unhappy juncture, but Colin Kendall-Cole's; Bailey had asked to see Robert after Loretta, but Colin had made a great show of looking at his watch and muttering about his important appointment.

'Sorry, old chap – sure you understand,' he had said, looking from Robert to Bailey with an apologetic shrug.

Robert hadn't bothered to argue, telling Loretta afterwards that he simply hadn't the energy. In fact, as she drove him back to Flitwell just before one in the morning, he seemed even more exhausted and dispirited than she. As she drew up, he shook himself out of a reverie and gave her a bleak look.

'I can't – it seems unreal.'

Loretta was once again oppressed by an uncertainty as to how she should respond. Was Robert the sort of man who'd welcome physical closeness in grief, as she would? Or would he prefer to face his thoughts and feelings alone? She placed her hand tentatively on his, and read her answer in his lack of response.

'I'd better get back to the cottage,' she said in a low voice, making it clear she didn't expected an invitation to stay.

'Sure you'll be all right?' He squeezed her hand at last, as though grateful for the space she had established between them.

'Oh yes. It's probably the safest place in Oxfordshire tonight,' she said with a determined attempt at lightness. 'There must be more police per square foot than anywhere else in the county.'

'See you tomorrow.' Robert opened the door and climbed out.

She drove quickly back to the cottage, observing as she parked the car that Baldwin's was still ablaze with light, and that dark shapes were moving about the garden.

She put her key into the lock and let herself into the cottage, finding that the light had been left on in the kitchen. Sitting on the table was the Le Creuset casserole in which she had been cooking the lamb; its contents were blackened and stuck to the sides and bottom. Whoever had moved it from the hob – a policeman, she presumed – had been too late to save the food. It hardly mattered; her appetite had long ago disappeared.

She bolted the front door and went into the bathroom, pausing to check that the door in there was locked before climbing the spiral staircase to the bedroom. It was still a warm night, and she opened the small window in the roof, letting in the faint scent of flowers she had noticed hours before. She dropped her clothes on to a chair, pulled on a night-shirt, and lay on top of the bed cover, her eyes fixed on the sloping ceiling. After a moment, she leaned across and turned off the bedside lamp. Her first night in Keeper's Cottage and Clara's last on earth: the thought, sentimental, uselessly melodramatic, refused to be banished from her head as she lay in the imperfect darkness. She tensed her body and tried to relax it limb by limb, at the same time taking long, slow breaths. Even so, sleep remained elusive; for what seemed like hours she lay restless, occasionally disturbed by voices in the garden, despairing of ever getting to sleep.

5

Loretta awoke next morning to a pounding on the front door. Running downstairs in her night-shirt, she found Ellie and Herc on the doorstep. Herc's expression was grave; Ellie was flushed and voluble.

'Loretta, is it true? The police won't tell us anything, they won't let us near the house. Is it true?'

Loretta was borne back into the kitchen by the force of Ellie's anxiety. She pushed her hair back from her eyes, which were puffy and sore after a night of, at best, fitful sleep, and braced herself for another interrogation.

'Loretta, *please* – Betty in the post office says Clara's dead – I just can't believe it! Say it isn't true!'

Ellie was gripping the back of a chair with both hands, her eyes wide with fear. Loretta was trying to think of the right words with which to confirm the news when Herc intervened.

'Wait a minute, lovely.' He placed a restraining hand on his wife's arm. 'Loretta looks all in.'

'Oh, don't worry about me,' Loretta said distractedly. 'Let me make you some tea.' If she was going to have to go through the whole dreadful story, she would need something to sustain her. She peered round the room, noticing again the charred remnants of the previous night's meal.

'Leave it to me,' said Herc, pulling up a chair and guiding Loretta into it. 'Take it easy.'

A sob broke from Ellie, who fumbled in her jeans and brought out a large, crumpled handkerchief. 'It *is* true, isn't it? Clara's dead.' She sat down suddenly, blowing her nose hard. Herc went to her side and helplessly stroked her hair.

After a moment he moved away and got on with the job of making tea. The brief silence in the room was broken by a wail from outside, followed by a scratching noise on the other side of the front door. Loretta got up and opened it, whereupon Clara's cat started forward and wound in and out of her legs.

'Bertie, you poor boy,' she said, guessing that the animal hadn't been fed since the previous day. She went to the fridge, took out a carton of milk, and poured some on to a saucer. The cat's loud purr began before the saucer reached the floor, and he lapped it eagerly. When he'd finished, he went to Loretta's chair, jumped on to her knees and curled himself up in a ball. Herc placed three mugs on the table and filled them with tea.

'OK. Loretta, you up to telling us what's happened?'

Loretta nodded and sipped her tea. It was too hot, and she put the mug back on the table. Speaking in a low voice, she gave a concise and unadorned account of the events of the previous evening, leaving out distressing details like the body's sprawling posture.

'Jesus Christ.' Herc shook his head from side to side. 'Jesus Christ.'

'Do *you* think Peggy did it?' Ellie asked abruptly.

'Of course not!' Loretta was horrified' 'But I *am* afraid she's been taken away against her will. By her husband.'

'Where was Jeremy Frere last night?' Ellie's second question was as sudden as her first.

'Now wait a minute –' Herc began, but Ellie ignored him.

'Don't they say most murders are committed by members of the family? I wouldn't put anything past that cocky little bugger,' she said viciously. 'D'you know where he was?' She looked fiercely at Loretta.

'In London, I suppose?' Loretta said vaguely.

'You *suppose*?' Ellie pounced on her like prosecuting counsel.

'Honey, Loretta can't be expected to know his exact movements,' Herc protested.

'Sorry.' Ellie sighed and wiped her nose. 'It's no good glaring at me, darling, I'm upset.'

Loretta returned to the point. 'Peggy said something about

Jeremy going to London when I saw her yesterday afternoon. The police wanted to know how to get hold of him, and Robert thought he was in the London phone book. He's got a flat over the gallery or something?'

'Or something,' Ellie said grimly. 'What the papers like to call a love nest, I think. He never spends a night alone if he can help it. Poor Clara.' Her resentment against Jeremy was clearly a long-standing one.

'OK, no one's denying he gave Clara a rough time. But that ain't the same as bumping her off. Anyway, say he is involved, why steal his own wife's jewellery? He's her next of kin, right?' Herc's tone was quietly reasonable.

'To make it look like a burglary. That's what people do, isn't it?' Ellie appealed to Loretta. She thought for a moment, then drew her breath in sharply. 'Oh God, what about Imogen? Has anyone told her?'

'The police were going to send someone to see her at Sussex,' Loretta said. 'They said they'd go first thing this morning.'

'Right. *That's* why there was nothing on the news,' Herc said. 'They inform the relatives first. Christ, what a thing.'

'She'd better come and stay with us,' Ellie said firmly. 'She won't want to be over there' – she nodded in the direction of Baldwin's – 'on her own. Or with that creep.'

'Sure.'

They lapsed into silence. Loretta shifted awkwardly in her chair, anxious not to disturb the cat.

'You got a radio?' Herc was looking at his watch. 'There might be something on the twelve o'clock news.'

Loretta pointed across the room and Herc got up to turn it on. They listened to a Central Office of Information announcement about the danger of forest fires in the current spell of good weather, followed by a warning that it was illegal to pick certain types of wild flowers. Then the news began, with Clara's murder the second item.

'Detectives in Oxfordshire have launched a murder hunt after the body of Mrs Clara Wolstonecroft, the well-known author and illustrator of children's books, was found at her home in the village of Flitwell.

'Mrs Wolstonecroft's body was found around ten o'clock

last night by a neighbour. Police say she'd been shot. Mrs Wolstonecroft, who was fifty-one, was the winner of last year's Beatrix Potter Award for services to children's literature. A police spokesman said several leads were being followed.'

'No mention of Peggy,' Loretta said, relieved. Perhaps Bailey really was keeping an open mind?

'She was so proud of that,' Ellie said. 'The award,' she explained, seeing Loretta's blank look. 'They don't give it every year, it's not like the Booker Prize. It only goes to people who are really good.'

She thought for a minute, then spoke again.

'What now?'

'I guess we wait,' Herc said resignedly. 'Well, hell, what *else* can we do?' He got up and turned the radio off.

Both women were staring accusingly at him. Ellie made an impatient gesture with her hand.

'*I* don't know. It just seems wrong to – to sit around and do nothing when –'

'OK, but what do you suggest? We don't have the resources of the cops. I don't see we have any choice.'

'I suppose you're right. Oh! What if Imo's trying to contact us? We should be at home!'

Ellie swallowed the last of her tea and headed towards the door. Herc followed, turning to speak to Loretta.

'You all right here on your own? Want to come back with us?'

'Thanks, Herc, but I won't. I've got things to do here. I'm fine, really.' She needed time to think, and she might as well tidy up the cottage while she was doing so. She got up, letting the cat slip gently to the floor, and saw them out.

Ten minutes later she was lying in a hot bath waiting for the warmth of the water to relax her muscles. From a chair on the other side of the small room Clara's cat stared intently at her, occasionally blinking his deep yellow eyes. He seemed to expect her to do something.

'What *can* I do?' she asked, half to herself and half to the cat. She was bitterly aware of the irony of her situation; less than a year before she'd stumbled on evidence of a violent crime in a borrowed flat in Paris and, for reasons which seemed compelling at the time, had failed to go to the police. The results of that decision had been so disconcerting, and so painful, that Loretta had resolved to waste no time in alerting the authorities in the unlikely event of ever again finding herself in a remotely similar position. This time she'd cooperated fully – apart from the business of the midnight voices, and she could imagine Bailey's reaction to *that* little revelation – and where had it got her? She couldn't help worrying about his attitude to Peggy; the fact that the girl hadn't been mentioned on the news didn't amount to much when she came to think about it.

Loretta sat up and added more water to the bath. Lying back, she tried to think the thing through logically. If Peggy wasn't the killer, or in cahoots with that shadowy entity – and Loretta considered herself a sufficiently good judge of character to be sure she wasn't – what were the other possibilities? A vision of Peggy dragged protesting from the scene of the crime by her husband was so uncomfortable that Loretta sat up and reached for the soap to dispel it. But wasn't she jumping the gun? Wasn't it just as likely that Peggy had left the house of her own accord in the afternoon or early evening? Perhaps she had gone back to London, or set off for her mother's house in – no, Loretta remembered that Peggy had been careful not to mention where her mother lived. Or was it her mother's sister? But, if that was the case, surely Peggy would come forward as soon as she heard about the murder? Much as Loretta distrusted Chief Inspector Bailey, he'd done nothing so far to frighten Peggy off. Unless – unless Peggy suspected Mick had had something to do with the killing . . . Loretta leaned over the side of the bath and pulled a towel from the mahogany towel rail. She dried herself briskly and pulled on trousers and a T-shirt. It was all so *frustrating*.

She returned to the kitchen, made another cup of tea, and half-heartedly opened a packet of biscuits. She ought to eat something, but her appetite had completely deserted her. She nibbled a chocolate digestive, still trying to make sense of what had happened. The most obvious suspect, surely, was Mick. He had reason to hate Clara – Loretta vividly recalled the loathing in his eyes as he lay pinned to the ground at the peace camp on Monday – and was known to be violent. But how did that tie up with the sustained campaign of intimidation against Clara in the days before her death? The idea that the threats had nothing to do with the murder was something Loretta couldn't bring herself to accept. And yet – she now knew the identity of the perpetrators of at least the paint-throwing incident, and she had to agree with Bailey that the three youths he'd mentioned were unlikely to have popped round to kill Clara immediately after being bailed. On the other hand, even Bailey hadn't suggested the boys were responsible for all the hostile acts directed against Clara and the peace camp; Clara's decision to invite the peace women on to her land had upset an extraordinary number of people, ranging from the landlord of the Green Man to the local police chief to Colin Kendall-Cole. Now there was a thought: what had the MP been doing at Baldwin's last night? He *said* he'd come to reason with Clara about the camp but, if he knew her as well as he claimed, he must have known he was embarking on a futile exercise. And he'd certainly been on the scene very soon after the murder. Loretta was beginning to get excited when several points struck her. Kendall-Cole had been searched by the police in her presence, he'd even handed over his car keys without a protest, and there'd been no sign of the murder weapon or the missing jewellery. Nor did he have an obvious motive. Was it really plausible that a Conservative MP, right-wing though he was, would up and shoot one of his constituents because he had a political disagreement with her? It was certainly a new twist to the concept of extra-parliamentary activity. Now she came to think of it, there was even some indirect evidence to support Colin's story that he'd been summoned to the house by Clara; according to Peggy, Clara had been so infuriated by Colin's article in the *Telegraph* that she'd phoned the paper to complain. It was perfectly possible that, getting no satisfaction from that quarter, she'd rung up the MP and demanded to see him. Reluctantly, Loretta moved Colin down her list of suspects. It was a pity; remembering his high-handed behaviour, and the way he hadn't even bothered to register her name, she'd rather relished the idea of his being cautioned and led away.

She got up, threw a half-eaten biscuit into the bin, and began to stack dirty dishes in the sink. The question of motive was troubling her. If Clara's death really was connected with the threats against her, and therefore with her role as protector of the peace camp, shouldn't Loretta consider the possibility of some sort of conspiracy against her? But by whom? She recalled Clara's suspicions about the involvement in the attack on the camp of the local residents' group – what was it called? RALF, that was it. Somehow she couldn't visualize an alliance of local estate agents and farmers sitting in the back room of the Green Man, orchestrating Clara's removal. What about the Americans? Didn't they have the most obvious motive to get rid of Clara? Loretta turned off the taps and dried her hands. Conspiracy theories made her uneasy. In spite of her hostility to the presence of American bases on British soil, she couldn't really believe they'd go as far as murder to get rid of the peace camp. Yes, they were sometimes brutal; she remembered reading a leaked memo in the newspapers in which an American division at Greenham had boasted about running over a peace protestor outside one of the gates. And they were certainly abnormally sensitive at the moment in the wake of the barrage of criticism of their raid on Libya. But an actual murder? In any case, killing Clara wouldn't necessarily bring about the eviction of the peace camp at Dunstow – that would depend, presumably, on who inherited the land. Loretta was sure Imo's attitude to the peace camp would be far more sympathetic than Jeremy's. She wondered how she could discover the contents of Clara's will, if it existed. Ask Imo? That seemed the simplest thing, although Loretta was anxious not to add to the girl's distress. She made a mental note to inquire if a suitable opportunity presented itself.

She wandered aimlessly round the kitchen, pausing to straighten the towel and drying-up cloths hanging on the rail in front of the Aga. What *was* she thinking of? Clara as the victim of political assassination? Her imagination was too vivid. Wasn't it just as likely that Clara had disturbed a common or garden burglar who, in line with the general trend towards more violent crime, had reacted with unexpected savagery? Loretta considered for a moment, then sighed. This line of reasoning, instead of cutting down the number of suspects, made it impossibly wide. Anyone could have walked quietly across the garden, unobserved by herself and Robert in the cottage. Herself and Robert? Had she any grounds for excluding him from her list of candidates? Had Robert slipped into Baldwin's, shot Clara twice, then sauntered casually over to Keeper's Cottage? After all, it was on his prompting that she had gone to the house to speak to Clara. Was this a daring ploy on his part to ensure that she, and not he, would discover the body?

Loretta smiled uneasily and pushed her hair back from her forehead. It was preposterous! Robert, cool, intelligent Robert – he couldn't possibly be Clara's killer. But – was that why she had drawn back from spending the previous night with him? Had the suspicion already been there, ticking away in her brain since then? No, of course not. Her decision to return to the cottage had been due solely to her anxiety not to intrude upon his grief. In any case, he hadn't got a motive. She had no more reason to suspect Robert than she had Jeremy. And she was inclined to dismiss Ellie's remarks about the latter on the grounds of her obvious prejudice against him; he, like Robert, had no obvious motive, especially as he was a successful art dealer in his own right. On top of which, there was no evidence that he was anywhere near Baldwin's at the time of the murder. It was hopeless.

As Loretta reached this conclusion, there was a loud knocking at the front door. She opened it, and was startled to be addressed in the warmest tones by a complete stranger.

'Loretta! My poor love, *what* you must have gone through!' The woman lunged forward and kissed her on both cheeks. 'I absolutely *had* to come straight over and make sure you're all right!' She lowered her voice conspiratorially. 'Shh, don't say a word. It's the only way I could get past the law.' She pulled a face and jerked her head backwards in the direction of Clara's garden, where two uniformed PCs were regarding her suspiciously from just beyond the hedge. 'Can I come in? Thanks.' Her voice rose again as she bore Loretta before her into the room. 'Darling, what a *thing* to happen!' She turned, gave a cheery wave to the observers outside, and closed the front door. She advanced on Loretta, right hand outstretched.

'Adela L'Estrange, *Daily Mail*. Well, freelance really, but that's who sent me. Sorry about that, those *beasts* won't let anyone from the press get near you.'

Loretta took in her visitor's swept-back blonde hair, her earrings which resembled gilded birds' nests, and her expensive black linen suit.

'How did you –'

Ms L'Estrange was putting her handbag on the kitchen table. 'I was in the area – friends have a cottage down the road, well, it's not a cottage really, not like *this*.' She glanced round the kitchen, conveying an unspoken message of surprise that anyone could live in such cramped conditions. 'Yes, I was in the area, and obviously I *had* to come. I was on the phone to the newsdesk as soon as I heard about it. Such a loss, such a loss. Now why don't we sit down and you can tell me all about it?'

By this time Loretta had collected her wits. Pointedly, she remained standing.

'How did you know my name?'

'Your name? Oh, I made a few inquiries on my way here, always pays to do your homework, you know.' She gave a rich laugh, which set the earrings shaking madly. Loretta watched fascinated, half-expecting a baby bird to tumble out. Then the woman's smile faded and she leaned across the table to clasp Loretta's hand again. 'I know – I *know* what you're going through.' Her tone was low and vibrant. 'Losing a friend – it's, oh, it's the *worst* thing. Last year I . . . I lost a dear friend – someone I'd been at school with.' She lifted her head and gazed liquidly at Loretta, groping for a chair with her free hand and sinking into it.

'Actually, I didn't know Clara very well. What did your friend die of?'

'Oh – it was cancer.'

Adela looked taken aback; Loretta was about to ask her to leave when a thought occurred to her.

'I suppose you've talked to the police?' she asked. It would be useful to know what sort of line Bailey was giving out.

'Of course. I had a long chat with Inspector . . . Bradley this morning. But what our readers want is the personal touch – what Clara was really *like*, as a woman, that is.' She paused, and Loretta forbore to point out that she could hardly say what Clara had been like as a man. 'The personal touch, that's what I'm after. I want our readers to feel as if they've met her, as if they've lost a *friend*. That's where you can help me, Loretta. Don't you want to do that? For her?'

Loretta sat down and gave what she hoped was a brave smile.

'I'll help you as much as I can,' she said. 'But what did Inspector Bailey tell you?'

'Oh, just the outline,' Adele said, brushing aside the correction. 'I gather there's some jewellery missing from the house, and they haven't found the weapon. But tell me, Loretta, what was she really like?'

Loretta considered. It looked as though Adela wasn't going to be much use to her, but she couldn't see any harm in answering the question.

'She was marvellous,' she began, watching as Adela made marks in an otherwise empty notebook. 'Kind, intelligent, independent – an admirable person, if you know what I mean. Take this business of the peace camp. A lot of people were –'

'Peace camp?' Adela looked startled.

'Yes, it's just up the road. Hasn't anyone told you about that? You should go up there and talk to some of the women, I'm sure they'd have something to say about Clara. It's outside the base, RAF Dunstow. Though it's really American. In fact, some of the planes that bombed Libya flew from it. That's why Clara was so against it. She felt passionately about it.'

'And she – I don't understand. What was her connection with this – peace camp?'

'It was on her land,' Loretta explained.

'I see. Actually, it wasn't so much that sort of thing I was after – politics and all that. I mean, one person votes Labour and another Tory, but it doesn't tell you about them as *people*, does it? Now, am I right in thinking there's a daughter?'

'Yes.'

'Name? Age.'

Loretta told her; the information was readily available and Adela might as well get it right.

'And the husband? It's her second marriage, I gather?'

'Yes.'

'And . . . *not* a very happy one?'

Loretta looked up sharply. 'What makes you say that?'

'Oh, I expect it's just gossip, you know how these things get inflated out of all proportion . . . '

'I don't think I do.'

'Well, it's common knowledge that they don't – sorry, didn't – get on. There isn't a party in London that Jeremy Frere isn't at, and he usually *accompanied*, if you know what I mean.'

Loretta stared at the journalist, wondering what she was getting at. Was this an attempt to needle Loretta into revealing that Clara had enjoyed a lurid secret love life? She began to get up.

'I'm sorry, I can't help you. As I said, I didn't know Clara very well.'

'If you're sure . . . ' Adela tailed off, not at all put out. If she made a habit of asking questions like this, Loretta thought, she must be used to being rebuffed. 'While I'm here, there is *one* more thing . . . ' She stopped, her hand on the catch of the front door. 'D'you happen to know the truth about all those rumours?'

'Rumours?'

'About Jeremy Frere's *gallery*.' She spoke as though Loretta was a wilfully stupid child. 'You must have heard. They say it's in a lot of trouble, last two exhibitions didn't go very well. In fact' – lowering her voice – 'I've heard the Larry Schmidt stuff absolutely *bombed*. I mean, I'm not surprised. No one really goes for that brutal realism stuff any more, do they? You haven't heard – aah! Get it off! *Get it off!*'

Loretta bent down and detached Bertie's claws from the skirt of Adela's suit. The cat wriggled and tried to regain his foothold, but Loretta held him tight.

'Take it away, I can't stand cats! Look what the wretched creature's done to my dress! You ought to do something about it, it's obviously dangerous!'

'No, he isn't,' Loretta objected, picking up Bertie and

hugging him. 'He's just choosy about his friends.'

Adela L'Estrange stared at her for a moment, then pulled open the door with a 'hmmph' of displeasure.

'Sorry to have troubled you, I'm sure,' she said, retreating down the path towards Baldwin's. Loretta watched her pick her way across the lawn in her stilettos, pondering the remarks Adela had just made about Jeremy Frere's financial situation. Only half an hour ago she had more or less ruled him out as a suspect on the grounds that he had money of his own. But if Adela's information was correct, the situation now looked rather different.

Except – except that, if Jeremy Frere was involved in his wife's murder, what had happened to Peggy? Loretta let the cat slip to the floor and returned to the chair she'd been sitting in. That Mick might have forced Peggy to leave with him was one thing; Jeremy Frere, on the other hand, had no reason to abduct her. If he had killed his own wife, why stop at someone else's? Unless he was intending to use her as a hostage in the event of the police tracking him down? Loretta shook her head, embarrassed by these ridiculous thoughts. Casting Jeremy as a crazed kidnapper was just as ludicrous as her earlier theory that Clara was the victim of a political assassination. No, if Jeremy Frere was the killer – and there wasn't a shred of evidence to suggest he was – then Peggy's absence from the house must be coincidence.

Loretta suddenly felt very weak, and sat down. The sour smell of last night's ruined meal was making her feel sick, and the walls of the small room seemed to be pressing in upon her. The feeling that she had to get out of the cottage was overwhelming, and her hand was on the catch of the front door before she stopped to consider where she might be going. What she needed, she told herself, was other people – somewhere she could blend in with the mass of humanity as it went about its everyday business. That, and food; lacking though her appetite was, it was now well over twenty-four hours since she'd eaten. Although the rest she'd come to Oxfordshire to find was plainly out of the question, there was no point in neglecting her other bodily needs. Oxford couldn't be more than six or seven miles away, and she'd certainly find plenty of people there – the city was notoriously over-crowded. And there was bound to be some sort of place where she could get food, even though it was getting towards the end of the lunch hour. She slipped briefly upstairs to pick up a jacket and returned to the kitchen to find her bag; a miaow from Bertie, who had positioned himself in front of the Aga just as he used to in Clara's house, reminded her that she ought to stock up on cat food. It seemed unlikely that the police over in Baldwin's would realize that the cat needed feeding.

She opened the front door, and immediately became aware of raised voices outside. She looked across in the direction of Baldwin's and spotted a figure in the midst of an angry confrontation with a uniformed policeman. It took her only a moment to recognize Jeremy; seconds later he glanced towards the cottage and caught sight of her.

'Can you believe it?' He strode up the path towards her and stopped on the far side of her car. 'They won't let me into the house – *my* house, I might add, as Clara's next of kin. What is this, a police state? I thought this was supposed to be a free country! They won't even tell me how long they intend to lounge about in there, drinking my Laphroaig, I don't doubt!'

He glared at her, spots of colour on his pale cheeks. It occurred to Loretta that he might have been drinking. Her initial feeling of guilt on being confronted with the object of her recent suspicions instantly evaporated; there had been no word from Jeremy about Clara, nothing about Loretta's unhappy role in the previous night's events, only this selfish tirade against people who were, after all, getting on with a rather unpleasant job.

'I'm sure they won't keep you out any longer than necessary,' Loretta said coolly. 'Is there anything in the house you need urgently? You could try asking them to bring it out to you.'

'What, ask that bunch of twopenny ha'penny fascists? You must be joking!' He glanced viciously over his left shoulder, then turned back to Loretta. 'Anyway, what I came to say was, I assume you're moving out now all this's happened? Since Stalin over there won't let me into my own home, it would suit me pretty well to stay here for a day or two. D'you think you'll be out by this evening?'

Loretta regarded him open-mouthed. Even though Jeremy was probably within his rights in asking her to leave, it seemed a bit much to do it without any notice at all. And what was his motive for trying to hustle her out of the way? If Jeremy needed to be in Flitwell, he could jolly well put up at the Green Man for a few days – the ban on Clara hadn't extended to him as far as Loretta knew. Why the rush? Loretta examined Jeremy's bad-tempered face, and all her suspicions came rushing back. She decided to dig her heels in.

'I'm sorry,' she said, 'but that's *quite* out of the question. My arrangement with Clara was that I'd be here for a few weeks, and I can't just go back to London at the drop of a hat. I'll have to speak to the people who are renting my flat, for a start.' Her righteous indignation on the part of her mythical tenants was so strong that she completely forgot that, only three days before, she'd been offering to return to London and leave the cottage free for Jeremy. Fortunately for her, he failed to notice the discrepancy, although his colour was rising by the minute. 'Look,' she said firmly, holding up her hand to forestall whatever he might be going to say, 'I don't want to quarrel with you. I had a pretty rotten time last night, what with finding Clara's body and giving a statement to the police, and I'm feeling shattered. I'll ring the people in my flat and explain what's happened, and I'm sure they'll do their best to find alternative accommodation. That's the most I can do. I'm sorry if it *inconveniences* you' – she put a sarcastic stress on the word to convey her contempt for his behaviour – 'but that's the way it is. Now, is there anything else?'

To her astonishment, Jeremy Frere sighed and looked away.

'I'm sorry,' he mumbled, avoiding her gaze. 'I know what you must think . . . I'm – in rather a state. I hardly know what I'm saying . . . ' He paused. 'Of course you must stay, I don't know what I was thinking of – that stupid bloody policeman upset me . . . I'm sorry.'

His confusion seemed to be genuine, and Loretta remembered that he'd capitulated in exactly the same way during the original row over the cottage. Perhaps she was doing him an injustice – he was an impulsive man, apparently unable to control his emotions, but that didn't mean he was unmoved by his wife's death. Grief affected people in different ways.

'That's all right,' she said awkwardly, wishing he'd meet her eye. It was off-putting, talking to someone without being able to see his expression. 'I tell you what, I'm just off to Oxford to get something to eat. Why don't you make yourself a cup of tea in the cottage while I'm gone? I'm afraid it's rather a mess – I haven't had time to clear up since last night.'

'Great,' said Jeremy, with the air of someone making a tremendous effort to be friendly. 'Got the keys? I'll pull the door shut behind me when I leave.'

Loretta moved to open the tall wooden gates to the road, but Jeremy was there before her.

'Let me.'

She got into the car, started the engine, and pulled forward until she could see the road was clear. As she moved away she looked in her driving-mirror; Jeremy Frere was standing just outside the gates watching her. Then he turned and went in.

'Hello, can I speak to Dr Bennett? Oh, right, I'll try again in a minute.'

Loretta sighed, anxious to get her conversation with Bridget over. Presumably her friend had heard of Clara's death by now, but she might welcome the chance to talk about it with someone who'd been so closely involved. Reluctant as she was to go through it all again, Loretta felt she ought to offer Bridget what information she had. She had called the college number as soon as she arrived in Oxford, only to be told that Bridget was out. Now, after Loretta's late lunch in an arts centre in George Street, the switchboard said that the extension was engaged. Loretta looked at her watch and pressed the buttons for a London number. The *Sunday Herald* answered and she asked for John Tracey.

'Hello, stranger! Where are you? You went off without telling me how to contact you.'

'I'm in Oxford, in a phone box. Well, one of those horrid modern things without a door, actually. Can you take the number in case I run out of money?'

As Tracey wrote the figures down she wondered how to

begin; seeing the money she'd put in disappear at an alarming rate, she decided to be direct.

'John, there's been a murder!'

'Not *again*. What's that saying? One could be an accident but two looks like carelessness? Who is it this time?'

'Honestly, John – you might be a bit more sympathetic. I don't know why I bothered ringing you. I couldn't help finding the body, even if it is the second time it's happened. Anyway, last year doesn't count, it wasn't really a body.'

'No need to bite my head off. What happened?'

'I've been staying in a cottage near Oxford –'

'The one you didn't tell me about.'

Loretta sighed; Tracey was obviously still peeved about the way she'd ushered him out of her flat the previous week. He could be so insensitive at times, she thought. No wonder their marriage hadn't lasted.

'It's a village called Flitwell –' The rest of the sentence was cut off by the signal to put in more money. 'Ring me back!' she cried, and then the line went dead. Loretta waited impatiently for a couple of minutes, pretending she hadn't seen the angry looks directed at her by the people queueing behind her to use the phone. When it finally rang she snatched it up.

'Loretta? Sorry, the news editor wanted to check something with me. You were saying?'

'I was saying I've been staying in a cottage belonging to a woman called Clara Wolstonecroft –'

'Oh yes, now I'm with you, it came up on Ceefax this morning. That was bad luck, after you'd just moved in. Looks like a burglary that went wrong, not much in it for us.'

'I didn't ring because of your wretched paper! What did you think I was after, a fiver for the tip-off? John, I've just had a *terrible* experience!'

'Well, yes, I can see that. Are you all right now?'

His tone expressed polite interest, as though Loretta had told him she'd sprained her wrist playing squash or been involved in a minor car accident.

'I suppose so – I mean, as well you'd expect. I still feel fairly shaken up by it . . .'

'Well, of course, you would be. Listen, Loretta, I'll have to go – I've got a meeting in five minutes. Why don't you give me a ring when you get back to London and I'll buy you a nice lunch? You can tell me all about it then.'

If I can get a word in edgeways, Loretta thought sulkily, remembering how all her recent conversations with Tracey had been dominated by the subject of his love life.

'Um . . . I'm not sure when I'll be back, I've got one or two things to do here . . . ' She trailed off, hardly knowing herself why she was so reluctant to return to Islington.

'Hang on a minute, Loretta.' She seemed to have Tracey's full attention for the first time. 'You're not up to anything, are you? You know what happened last time! You had us both running round like blue-arsed flies, and it was a complete waste of time. Leave it to the police, that's their job. Loretta?'

'Yes, I'm here. Do I take it the *Herald* isn't interested in the murder?'

'I thought you said you weren't ringing with a story?'

'I'm not. I just thought – well, Clara's quite famous. I though you'd be doing *something* about it.' Loretta didn't want to admit that, as well as expecting sympathy from Tracey, she'd also hoped he might have some inside information to offer her.

'I expect there'll be something on the literary pages, some kind of obituary,' Tracey said. 'But it doesn't look like much of a news story – like I said, sounds straightforward. You haven't answered my question. You're not up to your old tricks, are you?'

'Of course not.' Loretta crossed her fingers. 'It's just that I've got to do . . . How's Rita?' She changed the subject abruptly, sure the question would divert him from inquiring too closely into her plans.

'Oh. All right.' He paused. 'Well, that is – actually, we've decided to call it a day. By mutual consent. Absolutely for the best, no hard feelings on either side. But – I'd rather not talk about it if you don't mind.'

Loretta had to admire the cheek of it, after all the time she'd spent listening to Rita this and Rita that. It also explained Tracey's perfunctory interest in her welfare; he was obviously preoccupied with thoughts of the athletic Rita.

'I'm sorry,' she said formally. Underneath her irritation she really did feel sorry for him – this affair had been the most significant he'd had for years. 'I'll give you a ring at home some time. You can't call me – the cottage isn't on the phone.'

They said their goodbyes and Loretta inserted her remaining change into the coin-box.

'Just one more call, I won't be long,' she assured the woman who was next in the queue. If only the cottage had a telephone, she thought to herself. There was still her mother to ring, but that would have to wait . . . She hit the buttons for Bridget's college number.

'Bridget . . . it's Loretta.' She paused, signalling to her friend that she was ready for almost any reaction.

'Oh, Loretta! I've been trying to get you all morning, but the police kept answering the phone in the house . . . Are you all right?' Bridget's voice was tremulous and Loretta guessed she was near to tears.

'Oh, I'll survive,' Loretta said diffidently. 'How are you feeling? I thought you might like to know what happened – I was there, I mean. But not if it would make things worse . . .'

'Oh, no, I'd rather know! It'll be in all the papers tomorrow, I suppose, and I'd rather hear it from you. If it won't upset you, that is.'

'Don't worry about that. Listen, I'm in Oxford now. Shall I come over to your office? Or would you like to meet somewhere in town? As long as I get back to the cottage this evening . . . ' She hadn't made a firm arrangement to see Robert, but she'd wondered about calling at his house later on. She had no idea whether their brief relationship could survive the shock of Clara's death, but she had a feeling it would be wise not to delay their meeting for too long.

'Come over here, if you're sure you've got time. D'you remember how to get here?'

'You'd better give me directions again,' Loretta said. 'I'm in the middle of town, I don't know what the street's called. There's a big Boots and W. H. Smith's.'

'Cornmarket.' Bridget gave Loretta directions and said she'd expect her in five or ten minutes.

'I just can't believe it. I've known Clara since – it must be at least ten years. I can't imagine her – dead.'

Loretta had just finished her account of the previous evening. She sat in silence, thinking it would do Bridget good to talk.

'And in her own house, too. It's – well, it's not what you expect of a place like Flitwell. Did you know, Clara's family has lived in that house since Queen Victoria? I wonder what'll happen to it now? I can't imagine Imo wanting to stay . . .'

'But won't it go to Jeremy Frere'

'Jeremy! I'd forgotten him! Funny, I never remember Clara's married again. Her folly, that's what we used to call him – Imo and I.' She smiled slightly. 'I can't think of anyone more unsuitable for Clara to marry. She met him on a cruise, you know.'

'A cruise?' Loretta was startled.

'Yes, odd, isn't it? It was three or four years ago when Clara had her big depression. The menopause, her doctor said, which just shows what an old fool he is. She just hadn't got over Charles's death – her first husband, Imo's father. He died very suddenly, he had a heart attack. He hadn't been ill or anything, even though he was a lot older than Clara. 1980 or thereabouts, it must have been. Clara seemed to be getting over it, as far as that's possible, but it turned out she'd just been stuffed with tranquillizers. When she tried to come off them – that's why her doctor blamed it on the menopause, of course. Doctors never like to admit to iatrogenic illness. Anyway, she got worse and worse, and all her GP could suggest was more drugs or a holiday. And she announced quite suddenly she was going on a cruise to the West Indies. Jeremy was on it. His gallery was doing a lot better in those days, as far as I can gather. She rang me up when she got back. Bridget, she said, you're not going to believe this – I can hardly believe it myself. I'm engaged. I was flabbergasted, all her friends were. But I thought, if it makes her happy . . . and she'd started working again. Having Jeremy to talk to seemed to make all the difference. She'd hardly been able to pick up a brush since Charles's death, and then suddenly, when she met him . . .'

'So when did things go wrong?'

Bridget pulled a face. 'Not long after they got married.

Clara came back to Baldwin's a day early – she'd been up in Scotland for some reason – and found him in bed with the woman who did the publicity for the gallery. Twenty years younger than Clara, of course. You can imagine how she felt.'

'Why didn't she just throw him out?'

'That was her first thought, but then – she said she still needed him in a funny sort of way. They came to an arrangement – she turned a blind eye as long as he kept his girl-friends well away from Baldwin's.'

'No wonder Imo doesn't like him. Or Ellie. You know Ellie?'

'Mmm.' Bridget nodded. 'Though I don't dislike him as much as they do. I always thought he was rather . . . pathetic. But he does know about art. And as Clara said, she didn't marry him for sex. I think she looked on him as a child – tiresome a lot of the time, and given to whingeing, but she was less lonely. Oh!'

Bridget started to cry, fumbling in her pocket for a hand-kerchief. Loretta leaned across and took her friend's hand; she had been on the verge of asking whether Bridget con-sidered Jeremy capable of killing his wife, but the question would have to wait. After a while Bridget's sobs began to subside. Loretta looked out of the window and saw it was still a sunny day.

'How about a walk?' she suggested. 'Fresh air might do you good.'

Bridget looked surprised, but agreed. The two women went downstairs, across the quad, and into the small college garden. They walked arm in arm under the trees, Loretta listening patiently while Bridget talked disjointedly about Clara. After a while Loretta looked at her watch.

'Nearly five,' she said. 'I ought to go. I wanted to pick up some food before setting off.'

'You'd better hurry,' Bridget agreed. 'Most of the shops close at half past.'

She accompanied Loretta to the main gate. 'Thanks,' she said, kissing her friend on both cheeks.

As Loretta walked quickly back towards the main shopping centre, it occurred to her that Bridget hadn't once speculated on the identity of Clara's killer. Perhaps she assumed it was a break-in, Loretta thought. Then she recalled how taken aback she'd been when Chief Inspector Bailey put a direct question to her the previous evening. Bridget was clearly in a state of shock; perhaps the impact of grief was so great that questions were put aside until later.

Loretta hesitated for a moment outside Keeper's Cottage, wondering whether Jeremy Frere was still inside. She couldn't hear anyone moving about so she unlocked the front door and called his name. There was no reply, but the grey cat appeared from the bathroom and wailed softly. She put her box of shopping on the kitchen table, noticing as she did so a folded piece of paper under a cup. She picked it up warily, hoping that Jeremy hadn't changed his mind about evicting her from the cottage forthwith.

'My dear L,' she read, 'I came over this afternoon in the hope of seeing you – suddenly remembered I have to be in London this evening. Jeremy was here, sd he thought you'd gone shopping. Sorry to have missed you – will be back tomorrow tea time. See you then?' The next couple of words had been scored out and the message ended: 'Love, Robert.' What had he originally written? Loretta wondered. She picked up the note and held it to the light but was unable to decipher the words.

She sighed and let the note fall on to the table. She had been looking forward to seeing Robert. It wasn't his fault, of course; they hadn't made a proper arrangement, and he couldn't help having business in London. Even so . . . she picked up the note and read it again. The tone was friendly enough, and he had gone to the trouble of coming over to see her. But she felt bereft: she was on her own, with no one to talk to, she couldn't even ring any of her friends in London unless she went to the bother of finding a phone box. Looking up, she caught sight of the dirty dishes, still stacked in the sink. Instead of feeling sorry for herself, she should clear those out of the way and think about what she was going to have for supper. She took off her jacket, rolled up her sleeves, and began running hot water into the sink.

As she scraped burnt meat from the bottom of the cas-serole, her thoughts returned to the problem that had been in the back of her mind all day: why hadn't there been any news of Peggy? The copy of the *Oxford Mail* she'd bought on her way back to the car had contained full and rather lurid coverage of the murder, but the missing girl hadn't been mentioned. Loretta wasn't sufficiently *au fait* with the way the police worked to know whether this fact was significant. If Peggy had come forward and been eliminated from the inquiry, would the police have mentioned it to reporters? Presumably not, unless she had been able to give them some leads. But if Peggy had left Baldwin's well before the murder took place, it was a fair bet that she wouldn't know anything. On the other hand, if she was still missing, why hadn't the police asked for help in finding her? It was very puzzling.

To her relief, the casserole was coming clean; Loretta finished it off and put it on the draining-board with the other dishes. She went to the fridge, took out one of the fresh trout she'd bought in the covered market in Oxford, and began cleaning it. Bertie leapt down from the chair on which he'd been sleeping after demolishing half a can of Whiskas and started dancing round her feet. As she fended him off with her right foot, an idea came to her: why not pay a visit to the peace camp? It was a long shot, but there was just a chance that someone there would remember something about Peggy – her surname, or where in London she came from. Loretta paused; what would she do with this information if she got it? She recalled Tracey's warning not to meddle and shrugged it off. What harm was there in trying to track down Peggy? Even if there wasn't anything sinister about the girl's disappearance, Loretta would like to be sure. Pleased that she'd thought of something constructive to do, she made herself a simple supper of trout and almonds with new potatoes, followed by some seedless grapes.

It was around eight thirty when Loretta set off in her car for the peace camp. She parked and headed for the track that ran beside the fence, wishing she'd had the foresight to make the trip before it started to get dark. When she came to the clearing the fire was still smoking in its pit, this time with a kettle suspended over it from a crude device constructed of branches, but there was no one in sight. She looked around and decided her best bet was the old coach; she picked her way across the clearing and knocked hard on the closed door. It was opened almost at once by a woman she hadn't seen before who gave her an unfriendly stare.

'What d'you want?'

Loretta paused. 'I've been here before, I'm a friend of Clara Wolstonecroft, the woman who was killed last night. Can I talk to you for a moment?'

'Yeah.' The woman didn't move.

'Can we go inside? I think it's starting to rain.' Loretta could feel the first drops on her face.

'You a cop?'

'No. Honestly. Look, this is important. Can I come in? It'll only take five minutes.'

The woman moved backwards with obvious reluctance and Loretta climbed up the steps, pushing the door shut behind her. The seats had been removed from inside the coach to create a surprisingly large living area, and a curtain suspended from a piece of twine divided the space into two. A couple of women were sitting on orange boxes, drinking from mugs. Loretta recognized them from her earlier visits to the camp but there was no sign of the friendly Scot she'd talked to on Monday. The woman who'd opened the door resumed her seat on a pile of grubby cushions, and all three women stared at her expectantly. No one invited her to sit down.

'Look, I –' The hostile atmosphere was making Loretta nervous. She was also self-conscious, aware of the contrast between her own clean clothes and the generally down-at-heel air of the camp. 'I was here two days ago, with Clara – the woman who's been murdered. I was here when that man came, Peggy's husband. There was a fight, remember?'

One of the women nodded.

'The thing is, I'm trying to find Peggy.' She thought she saw a flicker in the eyes of the woman nearest to her, then another of them spoke.

'We haven't seen her.'

'Not since Monday.' The woman who'd answered the door joined in.

'OK, OK.' Loretta knew they didn't trust her, and battled to break down their hostility. 'I'm nothing to do with the police, really. I'm just worried about Peggy. She was supposed to be staying at Clara's, but nobody's seen her. I just want to make sure she's all right.' She looked at each woman in turn, a pleading expression on her face. 'Won't you help me?'

'We can't. Like Karen says, we haven't seen her.'

'Yes, but one of you might know her last name? Or where she comes from? Her address in London . . . ?' She trailed off, seeing it was useless. 'Is anyone else here? In the camp, I mean?'

The woman called Karen shook her head. 'They've gone to a meeting. At Greenham. They won't be back for hours.'

'When they get back, will you ask them? Tell them I'm trying to find her?' Loretta was clutching at straws. She found a scrap of paper and a pen in her bag and wrote rapidly. Then she held out her hand; for a moment she thought no one was going to take what she'd written. But one of the women stood up, took the paper without looking at it, and pushed it deep into her jeans pocket.

'That's my name and address,' Loretta said, dismayed by their lack of curiosity. 'I'm not on the phone, but I'll be there for the next few days. Thanks.'

She hesitated; when no one spoke, she moved back towards the door of the coach and climbed down the steps. Once outside she closed the door behind her, thinking that the visit had been a waste of time. Even if one of the absent women happened to know Peggy's surname, Loretta was sure they wouldn't contact her. She made her way back to the car, wondering why the women were so hostile. Had the woman detective upset them the night before, or had frequent contact at demonstrations rendered them automatically suspicious of anything connected with the law? Not that there was any reason why they should think she, Loretta, was in league with the police . . . It was a pity: another avenue closed. She drove thoughtfully back to the cottage.

She passed a restless evening half-listening to Radio Four, flicking the pages of the Margaret Atwood, drifting from one room to another. She couldn't resist looking at her watch every few minutes, indulging the fruitless game of what-was-I-doing-this-time-last-night? As a result, she ran the events before and after the murder as a series of vivid and distressing pictures in her mind. By eleven o'clock she'd had enough; she let out the cat, picked up the radio-cassette player, and went upstairs. She slipped into her night-shirt and began putting away the clothes that were beginning to mount up on a chair. As she folded the linen trousers she'd been wearing the previous evening, something fell out of a pocket; she picked it up and recognized the cassette tape she'd been handed by Chief Inspector Bailey the previous evening.

It was a new-looking cassette, without its box; she turned it over to see if there was a hand-written note of its contents – it wasn't one of the pre-recorded sort – but found no clue. She had brought a couple of clean tapes with her, in case she wanted to record something on the radio, but had they been this make? She didn't think so. In fact, she was beginning to think the tape wasn't hers after all; perhaps it belonged to Wayne and he'd dropped it on his way out?

She went over to her cassette player, removed the tape of *Turandot* which was still inside it, and put in the mystery tape. Then she lay back on the bed and waited, wondering about Wayne's taste in music. Country and western? Or perhaps he was an Elvis fan?

A minute or so passed, then she heard a click. It was followed by voices, and she didn't immediately recognize what she was hearing.

'That, my lords, ladies and gentlemen, is the last will and testament of the late Herbert George Fellows.'

'Good God – the man must have been out of his mind!'

'I should remind you, my Lord, that you are speaking of my dearest friend.'

'My brother was always penny-pinching but it did not occur to me that even he – '

'God be thanked that his poor dear sister is not alive to hear such words.'

'His own flesh and blood.'

'Poor, poor Cousin Maude.'

Loretta sat bolt upright, staring into space. These were the voices – the voices she had heard in the night. That meant – that meant there *was* a plot against Clara. Someone was so anxious to frighten her that they'd gone to the trouble of making this tape and rigging up the apparatus needed to play it. And yet – Bailey's man had found the tape in the bathroom of Keeper's Cottage. Why there? Why not somewhere in Baldwin's? Loretta's heart race as her mind tried to grapple with all these questions. Wait a minute – hadn't Clara said she'd had a good look round the house without finding anything that might be the source of the disembodied voices? What if the tape player or whatever it was had been hidden not in Baldwin's but in Keeper's Cottage? Did that mean that Wayne was in on the trick? Suddenly Loretta remembered the two men who had fled from the cottage on Sunday night – the very day Wayne moved out. Perhaps they weren't burglars at all but – who? The campaign against Clara was now beginning to look like a very professional job. Threatening letters, sinister phone calls, eerie voices – someone had been making a pretty systematic attempt to terrify Clara Wolstonecroft into evicting the peace camp. Or perhaps the aim had been to drive her away altogether, in the hope that her house and land would pass to a new owner with a more reliable attitude on the subject of anti-nuclear protesters. Either way they'd mis-calculated. Clara wasn't the sort of woman to be intimidated, and her determination to protect the peace camp had never wavered. Was that why it had been necessary to kill her?

Aghast at the thought, Loretta got off the bed and walked the length of the room to the far window. She pulled up the blind and looked out on to the dark valley; dozens of brilliant stars were twinkling overhead. She realized the voices had ceased and went back to the tape player, pressing the *rewind* button briefly. Then she pressed *play*; at once she heard the voices again. She stopped the tape, took it out and examined it. It was a widely available make, and there were definitely no distinguishing marks. How had it been done? Even if a tape player had been concealed in the cottage rather than in Clara's house, how had the voices been beamed across to the study? She cast her mind back to Saturday night: the voices hadn't sounded as though they were coming from the direction of Keeper's Cottage.

Loretta sighed, frustrated by her lack of technical know-ledge. A new thought occurred to her: if only she'd told Bailey about the voices last night. If she had, and he'd then produced his find, what a strong position she'd have been in. Presumably he or one of his men had listened to the tape and dismissed its contents as irrelevant. But, combined with her story . . .

Loretta pulled off her night-shirt and began dressing clumsily. It wasn't too late – even though she hadn't mentioned the voices last night, this was evidence. Clutching the tape she ran down the spiral staircase, through the bathroom and into the kitchen. She pulled open the front door without bothering to turn on the light, then paused on the threshold. Beyond the hedge Baldwin's stood silent and unlit, its windows dark blanks in a grey façade. The police had gone. Loretta hesitated, racked by indecision. She was desperate to present her evidence to Bailey, and yet she could not bring herself to step out into the shadowy garden. And unless she did, she was stranded without a phone. She took a pace forward, heard a rustle in the low bushes to her left, and jumped back. There was a plaintive cry, and Clara's cat appeared. His yellow eyes glinted up at Loretta for a second, then he bolted past her into the kitchen.

Loretta took a deep breath to control her pounding heart. What were the choices open to her? Even if she made her way to the house, it was unlikely that the police had left it unsecured. If she wanted to phone Bailey, she would have to get into her car and drive until she found a call box. A vision of herself pulling open a heavy red door in a dark country lane, visible to anyone who passed but unable herself to penetrate the darkness because of the faint light from over her head, made her shudder. These people are professionals, she told herself, retreating into the cottage as her stomach churned with fear. She closed the front door and stood with her back to it, peering across the moonlit kitchen as though she expected a burst of machine-gun fire to pepper the old stone walls at any moment. Intensely aware that she was alone, without a phone, only yards from where a murder had been committed, she turned and slammed home the shiny new bolt on the front door. Then she sped into the bathroom, checking that the door in there was securely fastened. A minute later, doors and windows as fast as she could make them, she began to climb the wrought-iron stairs, ready to spend the night in a state of siege.

6

Loretta heaved open the door of the phone box and peered inside, wrinkling up her nose as the smell of stale urine assailed her. She was glad she hadn't come on this errand the night before; the kiosk was in a lonely spot on the main road past the air base. Propping open the door with one foot so she could breathe fresh air, she looked to see what coins she needed. The box was an old-fashioned one – although she had several twenty-pence pieces and one fifty in her purse, the only slot that hadn't been blocked up was for tens. Loretta had four of these, and hoped Bailey would be in his office. Or should she wait a little longer? She looked at her watch: nine fifteen. Surely he'd be there by now, she thought impatiently. He was in charge of a murder inquiry, after all. She decided to risk it.

'Hello, can I speak to Chief Inspector Bailey?'

She waited a moment while the switchboard operator tried an extension. A man's voice answered.

'Sergeant Gorringe.'

'Is Chief Inspector Bailey there? It's about the murder. The Wolstonecroft murder,' she added, suddenly realizing Bailey might be dealing with more than one.

'Mr Bailey's in London today, miss. Can I help you?'

'Oh.' Loretta was crestfallen. During a restless night she had cheered herself up by imagining the expression on Bailey's face as he listened to the tape recording which was at present sitting safely in her shoulder-bag. Now she had been robbed – if only temporarily – of her triumph. She wondered whether to explain the whole business to the sergeant, and decided against it.

'No. Can I leave a message? That Dr Lawson would like to speak to him.'

'OK, miss. Does he know where to contact him?'

'Who?'

'Dr Lawson.'

'*I'm* Dr Lawson.'

'Oh, *you're –* ' The sergeant's voice was cut off by the pips. Loretta's hand hovered over the coin slot, then drew back. Why waste her last couple of coins on this ridiculous conversation? She pressed down the rest, listened for the change in tone, and dialled a London number. After a couple of rings she heard a click.

'Hi, this is John Tracey's answering machine. I'm not here at the moment, so why not leave a message and I'll call you back as soon as – ' The rest was cut off by the signal for more money. Exasperated, Loretta put the phone down. Then, having second thoughts, she picked it up again and dialled 100 for the operator. A man's voice answered and she asked to make a transferred charge call to the *Sunday Herald*. When she got through, Tracey's extension rang and rang without reply. Loretta was about to put the phone down when someone picked it up. To her relief, she heard Tracey's voice.

'Thank God! You can't imagine the trouble I'm having with phones this morning –'

'Well, you're lucky to get me at all this time in the morning. I'm only in early 'cause I've got to go through a pile of documents before I see someone for lunch. Where are you speaking from?' Arriving early at the office obviously wasn't good for Tracey's temper.

'Haven't a clue,' Loretta said quickly. 'I'm on a country road near Clara's house. Listen, have you got a moment?'

'You'll have to make it quick. I've got a stack of documents a mile high . . . Is it important?'

'I think so.' Making her account as concise as possible, Loretta told Tracey how the tape had come into her possession and she'd recognized its contents.

'You all right, Loretta? You're not making this up?'

'Of course not!'

'OK, but it does sound a bit far-fetched. People are always ringing up with stories about their houses being burgled and their phones tapped, and the next thing you know they're telling you it's because they're personal friends of Queen Victoria.'

'I don't think that's very funny.'

'It's not – ' Tracey's words became inaudible as two fighters roared overhead in close formation. 'Christ, what was that?'

'Planes from the base, F1-11s I should think. At least you know I haven't made them up!'

'All right, but what d'you expect me to do? I've told you, you shouldn't get involved. Why not take this tape to the police?'

Loretta explained that Bailey was in London for the day. 'And I can't just do nothing. I thought you could make a few inquiries for me – you've got contacts with those sort of people.'

'What sort?'

'You know, spies.' Tracey had pulled off a considerable journalistic coup the year before when he'd exposed several Eastern bloc agents working in sensitive positions in West Germany. At that time, and since, he'd conveyed the impression he was really rather well connected in the intelligence world. 'You could ask around for me, see whether anyone knows about the Americans doing this sort of thing.'

'I thought you disapproved. You weren't very complimentary about my story from Berlin last year.'

'All right, but that doesn't mean I don't want to find out what's going on here. Please, John.'

Tracey gave a deep sigh. 'I'm not promising anything. The guys I know are Brits, not American. I can't just ring up Five and ask if they know what covert ops the Yanks have been running near their own bases.'

'Sorry, you've lost me. What's Five? And what are ops?' Loretta was irritated; Tracey habitually adopted this type of jargon when talking about his intelligence contacts.

'Come on, Loretta.' Tracey had dropped his voice and sounded ill at ease. 'It doesn't do to discuss these things over the phone.'

'You just told me that people who think their phones are tapped are loonies.'

'I didn't mean my end – look, leave it with me and I'll make a few inquiries. But I don't hold out much hope. Even if you're right and the Yanks are up to something, I very much doubt whether anyone'll admit it.'

'Thanks, John.' In spite of his short temper, Tracey could usually be relied on. 'When shall I call back? This afternoon?'

'I shouldn't think there's a snowball's chance in hell that I'll know anything by then. But if you like. If it keeps you out of mischief.'

Loretta put down the phone and stepped out of the box, glad to leave its lavatory stench behind her. She got into her car and headed back towards Keeper's Cottage, cheered by the thought that she hadn't just let things lie. She stopped the car in the road next to the cottage, got out and opened the wooden gates, then parked neatly in front of the cottage. She locked the driver's door, turning towards Baldwin's to see if anyone had returned to the house – the police making more checks, or Jeremy Frere. As she did so, she caught sight of someone on the lawn below the house. Shading her eyes against the morning sun, she knew the man was familiar without first realizing who he was. Then, as he walked towards her, she recognized Colin Kendall-Cole. He was dressed much more casually than on the occasion of their first meeting, in an old sports jacket with worn leather patches on the elbows.

'Morning. It's Dr Lawson, isn't it?'

Loretta stared at him. 'That's right.' She was taken aback by his recollecting her name. Since Tuesday night she'd built him up into an ogre in her mind – the sort of man who'd deliberately serve South African wine at his dinner parties. Now they were unexpectedly face to face again, and he was regarding her with a questioning smile, she found herself nonplussed.

'I hope you're feeling better. Terrible business, Tuesday night.'

'Yes. Yes, it was.'

'By the way.' He paused. 'I gather I upset you a bit. I wanted to apologize – tongue was a bit unguarded. Just goes to show – one thinks one's in control all the time, but a thing like that . . . ' He sighed and shook his head. 'I can't imagine what came over me, flinging accusations about like that. I'm sorry.' He gave her an open, frank look and Loretta felt even more uncomfortable.

'I – well, I suppose we were all rather upset. Did you get to your meeting? Yesterday morning?'

'Meeting? Oh yes, yes I did. Don't think I contributed much, but at least I didn't let the old man down. I'm afraid you wouldn't approve, it was about the base. The minister wanted to discuss this bill of mine.' He gave her an apologetic smile and looked back towards Baldwin's. 'I actually called to see Jeremy,' he added, changing the subject. 'Wanted to offer my condolences. But there's no one in.'

'The police were there till quite late last night,' Loretta explained. 'I think he's staying somewhere in the village, the Green Man maybe. He'll probably be back soon – the police seem to have finished.'

Colin looked at the gold watch on his left wrist. 'I wonder if I should hang on for half an hour? I'd like to see him, poor chap.'

Loretta hesitated, wondering if she'd detected a hint that Colin would like to wait in the cottage. Extending an invitation was much against her inclination, but his apology had left her feeling guilty. As the silence between them lengthened, she decided she had no choice.

'Would you like to come in for a coffee? I was just going to make some.'

'That's very kind.' He responded with alacrity. 'You're sure I'm not disturbing you?'

'No, don't worry.' Resigned to making small talk for the next half hour, Loretta unlocked the front door and led the way inside. Colin followed, then stopped on the threshold.

'Well, well! This is rather a change! Joe and I used to play here when we were kids, this place was falling to pieces then. They've made a pretty good job of it, I must say. Joe's Clara's elder brother,' he added, seeing the question in Loretta's eyes. 'I haven't been inside since it was done up. Didn't that Aga used to be in Baldwin's?'

'I've no idea, I'm sorry. Take a seat. Would you rather have tea?'

'What?' Colin pulled out a kitchen chair and sat down, settling the battered old briefcase he was carrying by his feet. 'Oh, whatever you're having. Don't go to any trouble. Poor old Joe, this must have hit him hard. D'you know him?'

'No, but then I hardly knew Clara. She's a friend of a friend. I just happened to borrow the cottage for a few weeks.' She poured a handful of beans into the coffee grinder.

'I see. When did you move in?'

'Saturday. Four – no, five days ago. Though it feels like ages.' She decided against explaining that she hadn't spent many nights in the cottage.

'And your friend – Peggy. How long had she been staying with Clara?'

'The same. But that was a coincidence. Clara brought her over from the . . . peace camp, after what happened on Friday night.'

'And there's been no news of her?'

'Not as far as I know,' Loretta said stiffly, wishing Colin would change the subject. The peace camp, and Peggy, were subjects on which they were unlikely to agree, so why keep picking at them like a scab?

'And you didn't know –'

Colin's next question, whatever it might have been, was interrupted by a knock on the front door. Relieved, Loretta went to open it and found Jeremy Frere standing outside.

'Oh, hello, I just came to let you know I've finally – Colin! What are you doing here?'

Behind her, Colin was getting to his feet.

'I'm truly, truly sorry.' Colin clasped Jeremy's right hand in both of his for a moment. 'Such a loss . . . I came over to offer my condolences on the off-chance you were here. Connie sends hers, too. Not that words are much use at a time like this . . . '

'That's very decent of you, Colin. And Connie, too. Tell her I was asking after her, won't you?'

'Dr Lawson here very kindly offered to make some coffee,' Colin said, turning to Loretta.

Her heart sank. She had been hoping that Jeremy would take Colin off to Baldwin's, but now it looked as though she would be stuck with both of them. Colin's mention of Peggy had started an idea in her mind, and she wanted time to think it over. But good manners required her to extend her offer of refreshment to Jeremy. He accepted with alacrity, and settled himself into a chair.

Loretta transferred the ground coffee to the *cafetière*, and waited for the kettle to boil. Colin was asking Jeremy about the funeral arrangements for Clara, which gave her a moment's grace. Why had Chief Inspector Bailey gone to London? At the time of her phone call to the police station, she had been so anxious to speak to Bailey about the tape that his absence for the day had struck her only as inconvenient. But as soon as Colin raised the subject of Peggy the obvious question had occurred to her: was the detective's trip connected with the missing girl? Or was she missing? Had Bailey gone to London because Peggy had turned up, safe and sound, to announce that she'd left the house on Tuesday afternoon, hours before the murder? But in that case, Bailey would hardly have gone to the trouble of interviewing her himself. Perhaps there'd been a sighting of Mick? Or even an identification, because of his singular tattoo?

'Sorry?' She realized both men were looking at her.

'I was just asking if you need any help,' said Colin, gesturing to a point behind her. She turned, and found the kettle boiling fiercely. She filled the *cafetière*, carried it to the table, and set out three cups and saucers.

'Any biscuits?' Jeremy asked hopefully, watching her pour out. She went silently to a cupboard, took out the opened packet of chocolate digestives, and plonked them on the table in front of Jeremy. She was about to sit down when there was another knock at the front door.

'You're popular this morning,' Jeremy said facetiously.

Loretta skirted the table and opened the door again. Two men she didn't recognize were waiting outside.

'Sorry to trouble you, miss.' One of them flashed a warrant card towards her. 'I wondered if you'd seen Mr Frere this morning. We tried the pub, and they said he was coming back to the house.'

Loretta turned and saw Jeremy get up, his face even paler than usual. 'Well, he's here, as a matter of fact . . . ' she said slowly.

'Don't tell me you want to search the house *again*.' Jeremy clearly knew they were police officers. 'I'll have to start charging rent if this goes on much longer!' His attempt at a joke failed to disguise his sudden nervousness.

'We may need further access later today, sir. But we haven't come about that. Is there somewhere we can talk privately?' He glanced meaningfully at Loretta and Colin.

'Privately? Is there really any need – oh, if we must. Shall we go over to the house?'

'Well, sir, my instructions are to ask you to accompany me to the station.'

'The station? What for? You're not arresting me, are you?' Jeremy's voice was shrill.

'No, sir. At this stage, I'm just asking you for help with our inquiries. Voluntarily, of course.'

'Do I have to go?' The question was directed at Colin, and Loretta remembered he was a solicitor. Colin got to his feet and put a restraining hand on Jeremy's arm.

'Look, old chap, you don't *have* to go. But is there any reason not to? After all – '

Jeremy shook the hand off. 'All right, all right. What happens now? Handcuffs?' He thrust his wrists belligerently in the direction of the detective who'd done the talking.

'That won't be necessary, sir. I'm grateful for your cooperation.' This last was said with heavy irony.

Jeremy paused for a moment, looked as if he was about to say something, then thought better of it. He moved towards the door, turned, and attempted a cheerful wave. 'See you later, then! Soon as I escape from Alcatraz!' He strode off across the garden, the two detectives in his wake.

There was an awkward silence in the kitchen, broken eventually by Colin, 'Surely they don't think – ' He stopped.

Loretta shrugged. It certainly looked as though the police suspected Jeremy of involvement in his wife's murder, but why? How did that tie in with the evidence of the cassette tape? Surely he wasn't in league with the Americans – if it was they who'd made the tape – against his own wife? None of these was a thought she wanted to share with Colin; she shook her head, wishing he would go. 'I don't know what it means.'

Colin moved to the table, picked up his cup, and drank some of the coffee in it. 'Well, I must be off – bit of constituency business to see to. Thanks for the coffee.'

'You're welcome.'

He picked up his bag, inclined his head in her direction, and left by the open door. Loretta closed it and collected up the cups, rinsing them in the sink as she tried, and failed, to make sense of the morning's developments.

Around four, she decided she could no longer bear sitting in the cottage trying to write letters. Frequent trips to the front door had revealed no sign that Jeremy had returned; she wondered if he was still being questioned. Had he even been charged? She looked at the clock, realized she'd just missed the news on Radio Four, and ran lightly up the stairs. She took off her trousers and changed into a summer dress; Robert should be back from London any time now, and she could make a detour to ring Tracey on her way to see him. In the kitchen she checked that the tape was still in her bag, pulled the front door shut behind her, and set off in her car for the phone box she'd used that morning.

Tracey picked up his extension as soon as it rang.

'Loretta? Sorry, no luck.'

'What d'you mean?'

'I spoke to a chap who does a bit of liaison work from time to time, and he says the Yanks aren't talking.'

'You mean – they won't say whether they made the tape?'

'No, I mean they won't say anything at all. The point is, and I was told this quite forcefully, that Anglo-American relations are at an all-time low. Or as my friend actually put it, those fuckers wouldn't spell the president's name without an official request in writing from the DG. He says it's not even worth asking them.'

'But if they aren't involved, why wouldn't they say so?'

'Look, as I understand it, the Yanks don't want the Brits to know *anything* at the moment – what they're doing or what they aren't doing.'

'Oh.' Loretta was disappointed. Even though Tracey hadn't been optimistic about his chances of success, she had placed great faith in him. 'In other words, they've stopped speaking to each other,' she said sarcastically. 'Just like a bunch of schoolgirls.'

'You don't understand, Loretta.' Tracey was being patient. 'It's all because of Libya. Reagan wasn't prepared for all the flak he's got in the last few weeks, and he wants to know why nobody warned him. The Yanks feel let down –'

'*They* feel let down –'

'Let's not get into a political discussion. I agree with you, as it happens. I'm no more in favour of Reagan using British bases to bomb Tripoli than you are. But I'm not a fan of Colonel Gadaffi, either.'

'Neither am I. Now who's starting a discussion?'

'All right, I'm just telling you the score.'

'OK, where does that leave us?'

'Us? Listen, there's nothing else I can do. Or you, for that matter. Take your tape to the police and let them deal with it.'

'Oh yeah. A long way they'll get. Someone'll put a quiet word in somewhere, and it'll all be dropped.'

'Maybe. Maybe not. At least give them a chance. They'll get further than either of us could.'

'Oh, all right. Thanks for your help.'

'Don't mention it. When are you coming back to London? There's nothing for you to do up there. And I don't like the thought of you hanging round a place where a woman's just been murdered.'

'Is that a warning? Did your friend in MI5 –'

'Shhh! I don't want to talk about it on the phone! And no, he didn't say anything about warning you off. Stop being melodramatic. It's just common sense.'

'Well, I'll come back after I've seen the police. And I must go, I promised to go and have tea with some people in the village.' It was half true, she thought, crossing her fingers. 'I'll give you a ring when I get back to London. Bye.'

'Loretta –'

She put down the phone, anxious to avoid questions from Tracey about the identity of the people she was about to visit. Although they had been separated, though not divorced, for years, she still didn't like discussing her lovers with Tracey. He, feeling no such inhibition, had a highly developed sense about when to ask searching questions about the very private side of her life. It wasn't until she was getting into her car that it occurred to her that she'd forgotten to mention Jeremy Frere's summons to the police station; she hesitated, wondering whether to ring back and ask Tracey to do a bit of digging on her behalf, then decided against. She intended to see Bailey as early as possible next day, and she'd find some way of raising the subject then. She closed the door, fastened her safety belt, and set off for Flitwell.

Loretta parked the car in the road outside Robert's house and walked through the side gate. The faint sound of music from the drawing room told her Robert was at home, and she was immediately nervous. She paused before ringing the bell, trying to analyse what she was feeling; it was more than the mingled sense of anticipation and fear of disappointment that usually accompanied meetings with a new and unfamiliar lover. Her mind had flown back to the brief suspicions she'd harboured the day before as to Robert's possible involvement in Clara's death: there was guilt, yes. And there was anxiety, the knowledge that she might say or do the wrong thing at this delicate point in their relationship. The only thing to do, she decided, was to stop anticipating and get on with it. She pressed the door-bell.

At once the music stopped; this time, it seemed, the player had been Robert. She heard footsteps, then the door opened.

'Loretta!' He seemed genuinely pleased to see her, stepping forward to embrace her. 'Come in. I didn't hear your car draw up.'

He stood back, allowing her to precede him into the drawing room.

'I'm sorry about yesterday, missing you, I mean. I had to do an interview with a Japanese TV company, they're over here making a film about British composers. It was arranged weeks ago, and I couldn't put them off. Do sit down.'

Loretta took a seat at the end of the sofa.

'I'm sorry I wasn't there when you came over. I suddenly couldn't stand being in the cottage any more – I went racing off to Oxford to do some shopping and get something to eat.'

Robert sat down next to her.

'Poor old thing,' he said, taking her hand. 'Probably did

you good to get away. Were you all right on Tuesday night? I feel rather bad about letting you go back there after what happened. Did you get any sleep?'

'A bit,' she said, relieved that they were able to talk about the murder as easily as this. 'I wasn't scared. As I said, the place was crawling with police. Are those today's papers?'

'Yes, have you seen them? Dreadful stuff. I don't know what the press is coming to in this country.'

'No, I haven't seen any of them. I didn't want to go to the village shop in case anyone realized who I was and started asking for all the gory details. Can I have a look?'

'Of course. Drink?'

It was a bit early in the day for Loretta, but she was beginning to relax and thought that one drink would do her no harm.

'Yes please – gin and tonic?'

'Coming up.' Robert got up and left the room, leaving her to look through the pile of papers lying on the floor. She quickly found what she was looking for: the *Daily Mail*. Although the murder was front-page news, she had to turn to an inside page to find Adela L'Estrange's contribution. It took up most of page five, and was lavishly illustrated. There was a picture of Clara, unsmiling and rather fierce; one of the exterior of Baldwin's, taken from the front; another showing double glass doors with *Frere Fine Arts* painted across them in imitation handwriting; and one of Jeremy himself. This last was a blurred snapshot taken in what looked like semi-darkness – Jeremy, champagne glass in one hand, had thrown his other arm across the shoulders of a woman whose cleavage threatened to burst the fragile restraint provided by her plunging neckline. 'When the wife's away . . . the husband used to play', the caption read, adding unnecessarily that the photograph showed Jeremy and a blonde friend at a recent nightclub opening.

Loretta winced and turned her attention to the main text, wondering nervously if she would find herself featured in it. The article began unpromisingly: Clara's surname was misspelt, allowing Adela to claim an entirely fictional link between the dead woman and the author of 'the famous sixteenth-century women's lib manifesto, *A Violation of the*

Rights of Woman'. It went on to describe Clara as the mother of one daughter, 'a brilliant student at Brighton University', whose name was given, inexplicably, as Eileen. Worse followed. Clara, who had apparently won something called the 'Beatrice Potter Prize for Children's Books',

> was adored by kiddies all over the world. Little did they know –
> they would not, Thank God, have understood – that the
> motherly, grey-haired woman who wrote innocent stories
> about Burmese cats called Bertie and Lettice, was in fact an
> extreme feminist.
> 'She was one of those peace women, a real fanatic,' said one
> of the dead woman's neighbours, a pretty blonde school-
> teacher, yesterday.

It took Loretta a moment to recognize herself from this description; she read it twice, gasped, and carried on.

> Last month, after Mrs Thatcher gave President Reagan permis-
> sion to use US bases in Britain to wipe out terrorist strongholds
> in Libya, Mrs Wollstonecraft allowed a breakaway group from
> the notorious women's 'peace' camp at Greenham Common to
> set up shop on land she owned next to RAF Dunstow. In spite
> of protests from the base commander, who fears the camp
> could be used by terrorists disguised as 'peace' women, and
> from local shopkeepers, who have reported a spate of petty
> thefts since the arrival of the women, Mrs Wollstonecraft
> refused to make them leave.
> Meanwhile her husband, Mayfair socialite and gallery owner
> Jeremy Frere, 36 – Mrs Wollstonecraft refused to change her
> name at the time of her second marriage – has been increasingly
> seen at parties in London without his 55-year-old wife (see
> picture, right).
> Mr Frere, who was too upset yesterday to talk about his
> marriage, is said by friends to have been driven to despair by
> his wife's association with left-wing political agitators and what
> one close friend described yesterday as 'the hard-line, pro-
> Russian, anti-men brigade'.
> The shock of his wife's murder could not have come at a
> worse time for Mr Frere, whose art business has been hit by the
> failure of two recent shows and the withdrawal from the busi-
> ness of his long-time business partner, Mr Sam 'Sonny' Moss,
> the American entrepreneur. Friends say Mr Frere has been
> pinning his hopes on the success of his next venture, the first

posthumous exhibition of the work of the recently discovered
American depressive artist, Peter Eddy.

'Have you got to the bit about the depressive artist?' Robert
had come back into the room and was holding out her drink.
'Makes me think of Van Gogh. Perhaps someone should
invent a Depressive School – lots of artists who have nothing
in common except the fact that they committed suicide. Sorry
I took so long – I couldn't remember where I'd put the tonic
water.' He sat down beside her.

Loretta sipped her drink. 'What a dreadful piece,' she said.
'Why didn't she just come straight out and say Clara was a
mad lesbian who drove her husband into the arms of other
women?'

'They're almost an art form in themselves, pieces like that,'
Robert observed, moving closer to take another look at the
story. 'Para-realism, you could call it – every fact distantly
related to the truth but with a new and ingenious inter-
pretation.'

'But she's got everything wrong,' Loretta protested, feeling
Robert was taking the whole thing much too calmly. 'Imo's
name, where she's a student –'

'Clara's age, how you spell her surname. And all that
nonsense about Mary Wollstonecraft.'

'Oh, it makes me so *angry*. Isn't there anything we can do
about it?'

'I doubt it. I've been complaining to newspapers about
unfair reviews for years, and you never get anywhere.'

'But she's misquoted me! And she's got my job wrong, not
that that matters.'

Robert took the paper from her and skimmed the article
again. Then he burst out laughing.

'Don't tell me you're the "pretty blonde schoolteacher"! But
you're not at all *pretty*!'

Loretta stared at him, disconcerted. He laughed again,
leaned across and ruffled her hair.

'Don't glare at me like that, I was paying you a compliment!
Pretty women tend to be ... indistinguishable from one
another. There's something unusual about you – interesting.
That's much better than pretty.' He tossed the paper to the

floor and his expression suddenly became grave. 'It's bad luck on us, meeting in circumstances like this. I told Clara she shouldn't keep that gun loaded –'

'What gun?' Loretta sat up straight, astonished.

'The one I told you about – the one that was missing on Tuesday night.'

'You didn't mention any gun.'

'I'm sure I did. I certainly told that policeman, Bailey. I remember thinking, as soon as I realized she'd been shot – I wonder if the gun's still there. She kept it in the top drawer of the bureau in the sitting room. Are you sure I didn't tell you this?'

'Positive. It's not the sort of thing I'd forget.'

'That's odd.' Robert appeared to be genuinely puzzled. He put his arm round her and hugged her to him. 'I'm sorry, Loretta, I could have sworn I told you . . . I must have been in even more of a state than I thought.'

Loretta moved away slightly; he, feeling her withdrawal, let her go. She turned to look at him, trying to evaluate this turn of events. Clara killed with her own gun – and Robert hadn't even told her of its existence. She could hardly believe it. The suspicions she'd entertained the previous day came rushing back, all the more uncomfortably as she was sitting so close to their object. But – surely Robert couldn't be involved in Clara's death? Common sense came to her rescue: if Robert was the killer, what did he have to hide by concealing his knowledge of the gun from her but revealing it to the police? Or was he lying when he said he'd told them?

'Loretta, don't read anything into it.' He gave her a searching look, leaving her with the clear impression that he'd read her mind. 'If I really didn't tell you, I'm sorry. Maybe Colin turning up took my mind off it.' He shifted sideways in his seat, away from her.

Anxious to retrieve the situation, she took his hand. 'I'm sorry,' she said, forcing a smile, 'I was just a bit – surprised. I suppose I'd assumed that whoever . . . did it brought the gun with him. Or her. Anyway, tell me about it. How do they know it was the same gun? If it's still missing, I mean. Or has it turned up?'

'Not as far as I know.' Robert seemed to have relaxed a

little, his hand was no longer unyielding in hers. 'I told them to ask Gilbert about it, I thought he'd know the make. He used to clean it now and again, make sure it was working. According to him – he phoned just before you arrived – the tests they did on the bullets matched what he'd told them. He feels terrible about it, he blames himself. I told him not to – Clara should never have kept it in the house.'

'Why did she?'

'It's been around for years, I think her father had it when he was in the army. When Charles died, he was Clara's first husband, she was nervous about being alone in the house. Apart from Imo, of course, and she was away at school a lot of the time. So she got Gilbert to have a look at it.'

'It's hard to imagine, Clara being frightened of anything.'

'That's because you only met her recently. She went through a bad patch after Charles died, more or less a break-down. Even so, I told her it was madness, keeping a loaded gun in the house. That's the trouble with weapons – it's just as likely a burglar will get his hands on them and use them on you. I said she should get a good alarm system. When she found out how much it would cost, she decided to stick to the gun. She had her little quirks, Clara, and not spending money on herself was one of them.'

They sat in silence for a moment, Loretta trying to think of a way to change the subject. They had been getting on so well until the gun came up . . . Her gaze travelled round the room, lighting at last on the window overlooking the street; to her surprise, she saw that someone was standing looking in.

'Who's that?'

It was too late; as Robert turned, the figure drew back and disappeared. They heard footsteps going rapidly away from the house.

'I'll go and see.'

Robert left the room, and Loretta went to the window hoping to catch a glimpse of the retreating visitor. The window catch resisted her hand, and she saw that it had been painted shut. She was still trying to open it when she heard voices at the side of the house; one was Robert's, the other she couldn't catch. She turned, waited, and a minute later Imo appeared in the doorway with Robert just behind her.

'Look who's here,' Robert said in kindly tones.

'Imo!' Loretta went forward, hands outstretched, intending to embrace the girl. Then she stopped, repelled by Imo's hostile expression. She wondered whether she'd imagined it, misled by the girl's drawn features, but the tone of Imo's voice when she spoke left her in no doubt she was right.

'It's all right, I'm not going to stay. I just came to see Robert.' She turned to look at him. 'But I don't want to *interrupt* anything. I can come back later.' Her glance went to Loretta, and returned to Robert.

'When did you get back from Sussex?' Robert asked, either unaware of the atmosphere in the room or hoping it would disappear.

'This morning. Look, I'll come another time. All right?' She moved towards the door.

'Imo –' Robert stopped, clearly at a loss.

At that moment, light dawned on Loretta and she crossed the room to the sofa where she'd left her bag.

'Time I was going,' she said calmly, smiling at them both. 'Imo, I'm terribly sorry about your mother. Perhaps we can talk when you're feeling a bit better? You're staying with Ellie?'

Imo nodded dumbly.

'Robert, where's that book I was going to borrow? I must have left it in the kitchen.'

Robert stared at her in surprise and followed her as she went down the corridor to the back of the house.

'What on earth's going on?' he asked, watching her close the kitchen door.

Loretta pulled a face. 'I'd forgotten Imo's got a crush on you,' she said. 'She must have seen my car, looked through the window, and there we were holding hands on the sofa. Poor kid, no wonder she's upset.'

'Are you sure?' Robert was flabbergasted. 'I've always been fond of her, but she's just a kid. I've never –'

'I'm sure you haven't. I noticed it on Saturday during dinner, but of course the last couple of days drove it out of my mind. Just think how she feels – first her mother's murdered, then she comes to you for sympathy and finds me here. She must feel completely *excluded*.'

'Wait a minute, Loretta, I should have thought sex was the last thing on her mind at the moment.'

'Oh, I didn't mean she's going to throw herself into your arms. It's more to do with – well, a dream, or a fantasy. Look, there's no need to worry.' She put a comforting hand on Robert's arm. 'Just go back in there as though nothing's happened. What she needs is to talk, and if you can get her to do that this other business will go out of her mind.'

'You don't think I should explain about . . . ?'

'No, I don't. Think you can cope?'

'I sup-pose so,' Robert said uncertainly. 'I'm sorry you've got to go. Shall I see you later?'

'I'd better ring, in case she's still here. I don't want to upset her more than I have already.'

'Or I could come to the cottage?'

'Yes, why don't you do that? About eight?'

'I'll look forward to it.' He followed her down the corridor to the front door. Loretta opened it, hesitated, then called in the direction of the drawing room, 'Bye, Imo!'

There was no answer. Loretta shrugged, smiled at Robert, and went to her car.

She sat still for a moment, one hand on the steering wheel, wondering how to pass the time between now and eight. It occurred to her that she wouldn't mind a drink, non-alcoholic this time, but then she remembered that she was supposed to be boycotting the village pub. She started the engine and was about to drive home when she thought of calling in on Ellie and Herc. She turned the car and drove slowly up the street to their cottage, parking outside.

'Hi there.' Herc stood in the doorway, a welcoming smile on his face. 'Come in, we've just been watching the news.'

He led the way into the small front room of the cottage where Ellie was sitting in front of the television mending a pair of jeans.

'Loretta! What's all this about Jeremy? Has he really been arrested?' As usual, Ellie was direct.

'Why, was it on the news?'

'No, they don't seem to know *anything*. I heard it from Flo two doors down. Her son-in-law's lost his dog, and he was in the police station this morning reporting it when Jeremy was brought in. By *two* policemen, he said.'

Loretta had been waiting for an invitation to sit down; when none was forthcoming, she settled herself into an old armchair with wooden arms.

'They didn't actually arrest him,' she said guardedly. 'They just asked him to go with them to the station.'

'You were there?'

'Yes. He'd just come over to the cottage when they arrived.'

'There you are!' Ellie was looking in triumph at Herc, who had moved a pile of books to the floor so he could sit on a sofa.

'Now wait a minute, lovely. Could be they want to clear a few things up – about what was stolen, maybe?' Herc sounded unconvinced.

Ellie turned back to Loretta. 'Has he come back?'

'Not as far as I know.' Loretta was about to explain that she'd been away from Keeper's Cottage since just after four, but Ellie forestalled her.

'So he's been there *all day*? Well, what more do you want?'

'But he may have come back by –'

'I doubt it. Darling, why don't you turn the telly off? I'm sure Loretta doesn't want to watch it. D'you want some cake? I made one this afternoon.'

Confused, Loretta waited for Herc to answer. When he didn't, but silently got up to turn the television off, she turned to Ellie and said she'd love some. Ellie and Herc disappeared to the kitchen together, returning some ten minutes later with two trays loaded with seed cake, scones, and a huge brown teapot.

'Tuck in,' Ellie urged, heaping two scones and a thick slice of cake on to a plate and passing it to Loretta. 'You could do with a bit more weight.'

Loretta obediently cut a corner piece off the cake and began to eat, hoping her appetite wouldn't be ruined for later. She'd been thinking of cooking Robert a light supper.

'How's Imo?' she asked, wiping crumbs from her mouth. 'I saw her for a few minutes at Robert's – she looked very drawn.'

'Too early to tell,' Herc said. 'Oftentimes these things take a while to sink in.'

'She's staying here, did she tell you?'

Loretta nodded.

'I don't know *what* Clara was thinking of, leaving the house to her and Jeremy together.' Ellie sighed and shook her head. 'That's why I want Jeremy to have done it – then Imo'll get the lot!'

'You sure about that, lovely?'

'Course, darling! This is England! We don't let people enjoy the fruits of their ill-gotten gains, do we, Loretta?'

Loretta had to admit that she didn't know. She was still turning over in her mind this confirmation that Jeremy stood to gain by his wife's death – if Ellie was a reliable witness, and Loretta wasn't sure she was. She remembered the tape, still tucked safely in her bag, and wondered if she should mention it; the cassette, with its implication of an organized conspiracy against Clara, was to some extent evidence in Jeremy's favour. But she held back, fearing that the story would be round the village in a matter of hours if she entrusted it to Ellie. If the Americans had been involved in Clara's death, the last thing she wanted was that they should be tipped off about her possession of a vital piece of evidence through local gossip.

'Wonderful cake,' she said, pleased that she'd managed to finish the huge helping Ellie had given her.

'More?' Ellie asked eagerly, getting up and going to the table on which she had placed the trays.

'No, really, I couldn't,' protested Loretta, alarmed. There was a short wrangle; in the end, Loretta was excused a second helping only after she'd promised to take a hunk of cake back to the cottage in a plastic bag 'for later'.

Ellie and Herc seemed so pleased to have her company that Loretta wasn't able to escape until well after seven. There was just time to start preparing some food for Robert, Loretta thought, heading back to Keeper's Cottage with Ellie's cake sitting beside her on the passenger seat. She'd found some buffalo mozzarella in Oxford the previous day which she could use in a salad, and there were a couple of chicken breasts in the fridge. Of course, Robert might not be hungry; she hadn't liked to mention supper earlier, in case it brought back memories of Tuesday night. She would make the salad, which she was hungry enough to eat herself if he wasn't interested, but hold the chicken until he arrived. She would also, she decided, find a moment to tell him about the tape – she might even play it to him. She had intended to mention it before, while she was at his house, but his casual revelation about the gun had shocked her out of it. That had been the only sticky moment of her visit, looking back on it; she was sure he'd sensed her flash of suspicion, and had been momentarily offended by it. By telling him about the tape, she would be making a tacit gesture of her trust in him.

She had just arrived at this satisfying conclusion when she reached the gates to Keeper's Cottage. She got out of the car, opened them, and spotted the Burmese cat sitting on the doorstep of the cottage. He waited while she parked the car and closed the gates, then followed her inside with a pro-longed wail.

'I suppose you're hungry,' she said, putting the cake down on the table. 'Well, you'll just have to wait – what on earth?'

She was looking at something on the table, and a prickling sensation ran down the back of her neck. She put out a hand, pulled it back, and turned to make sure she'd closed the front door. She looked nervously round the room straining her ears for the slightest indication that she wasn't alone in the cottage. The cat miaowed impatiently; she bent and picked him up, stroking his head and telling him to be quiet. She looked back to the front door again, checking there was no sign of a forced entry. But, if there had been, she would have noticed it on her way in. She walked silently into the bath-room, where everything was just as she'd left it. Still holding Bertie, she climbed the spiral staircase to the bedroom. Sud-denly the cat started and leapt from her arms; she glanced anxiously round the room but, seeing nothing untoward, went back down the stairs.

Someone had been inside the cottage in her absence, in spite of all the evidence to the contrary: how else had that single sheet of paper come to be lying on the table? She drew closer to it, taking in that the words on it were few and printed in neat writing she didn't recognize. Jeremy's? That had been her first thought on seeing the piece of paper lying so neatly positioned in the centre of the table. She rejected the possibility now, just as she had unconsciously a minute before; she was sure that Clara had given her all the keys to the cottage, and she certainly hadn't returned any of them to Jeremy since the murder.

She was now close enough to read the writing, which began with her name; underneath this was another, one which meant nothing to her: Fanny Fudge. The next line was simply the name and address of a church, St Michael's, Church Lane, Steeple Barford. Finally there was a time, eight fifteen, followed by the word 'tonight', heavily underlined.

Scrutinizing this enigmatic document in the vain hope that its meaning would suddenly be made clear to her, Loretta felt with one hand for the back of a chair and sat down. The woman's name, Fanny Fudge, sounded made up; was it some sort of joke? Yet who would bother gaining entry to the cottage in so professional a fashion if the object of the visit was merely to play a prank? Presumably she was supposed to set off for this place, Steeple Barford, in time for the rendezvous in – she looked at her watch – forty minutes' time. And there she would meet – who? Clara's killer? That seemed the obvious inference. But if the letter was a trap, a ruse to lure her to some deserted place where she could be disposed of, why go to all this trouble? Since the person who delivered the note had access to the cottage, why not simply wait in the bathroom for her return and beat her over the head? The cottage was relatively isolated; she could think of few safer locations in which to commit a second murder. She shivered, got up, and went to the fridge, taking out an opened tin of cat food in an attempt to banish this unpleasant reflection. She scraped the remaining food on to a saucer and put it down for the now ecstatic cat.

But if the note wasn't from the killer, who else might be its author? Loretta sat down, picked up the sheet of paper with the tips of her fingers, and turned it over. The other side was blank. She put it down, unwilling to prolong her contact with it. A new theory came to her, and her heart beat more rapidly. As far as she knew, Peggy was still missing – was the note in some way linked with her? But why would Peggy use this melodramatic means of communicating with her? Unless Peggy knew the police suspected her at least of being an accomplice in Clara's murder, and was afraid to use her own name? Loretta looked at her watch again. She had never heard of Steeple Barford, and time was getting short. She went warily out to her car and felt in one of the door pockets for a map of the area. She went back indoors, taking care to shut the front door behind her, and spread the map on the table. She quickly located Steeple Barford, a small hamlet about ten miles north-west of Flitwell. She folded up the map, picked up her bag, and left the cottage. She would need to phone Robert to let him know she had to go out; it crossed her mind to tell him about the note, to ask him to accompany her even, but she decided against it. Whoever was waiting for her might be scared off if she didn't appear alone.

She drove quickly to the phone box she'd used earlier in the day, stepped inside and dialled Robert's number. It rang and rang, but there was no reply. Loretta let out an 'oh' of impatience, and wondered if there was time to make a detour into Flitwell and leave a note at his house. There wasn't; she would just have to hope he'd wait outside the cottage or return home where she could reach him later.

She set off, driving along unfamiliar country lanes, her body becoming more and more tense as the small white car covered the miles to Steeple Barford. A bit to her left the sky was streaked with pink; soon she needed her lights on. It occurred to her that she hadn't brought any sort of weapon, but then she remembered Robert's unheeded warning to Clara about the gun and decided it was just as well.

Steeple Barford turned out to be no more than a dozen stone houses straggling along a winding lane: Loretta would have missed the left turning to the church if it hadn't been signposted. She drove slowly down a gentle slope, the banks on either side becoming higher and more overgrown by the minute. At the bottom of the hill the lane curved suddenly to the right, while a second sign to the church pointed along what was little more than a cart track to her left. She paused, checked that the track was wide enough for the car, and began to drive carefully along it. To her right was an untidy hedge and fields; to her left was a drystone wall and behind it, bathed in the golden light of the setting sun, a low, wide church. She stopped the car beside a five-barred gate and took in the scene. Instead of the steeple she'd expected, the church boasted a squat, crenellated tower. On its far side, stretching for a couple of hundred yards, Loretta could see the tumbled gravestones of an ancient churchyard. It was a scene of bucolic splendour, reminiscent of various fragments of poetry; Loretta could hardly believe someone had summoned her here with any sinister purpose. And yet – she sat on in the car, reluctant to get out in spite of the fact that she was already a few minutes late.

What was she supposed to do? Hers was the only vehicle in sight, and it crossed her mind that the whole thing was a hoax. And, if it wasn't, what should be her next move? Should she go into the church? She felt a prickle of fear at the thought of leaving the open air for the gloomy interior of the building. Stand outside and shout that ridiculous name, Fanny Fudge? Perhaps her unknown correspondent had never intended to meet her here but had concealed a message – where? It was a daunting prospect. Loretta decided she was achieving nothing by staying where she was, and opened the car door purposefully, just in case anyone was watching; she was determined not to show she was afraid. Glancing round, she saw no sign of movement and turned to lock the door. Then she stopped, thinking she might need to make a quick getaway. Leaving the car unlocked she unhooked the catch of the gate, lifting it away from the post just far enough to squeeze through. The dark porch of the church was to her left; she walked unhurriedly towards it, doing her best to conceal her fear as she stepped into its unwelcoming shadows. She turned the heavy iron ring set into the wooden door, realizing at once that the church was locked. So – whoever or whatever she was looking for was not to be found inside. She saw a noticeboard on the wall to the right of the door and paused to study it, wishing she had brought a torch; she could make out nothing more sinister than the names and addresses of the churchwardens, an appeal for famine relief in Ethiopia, and that month's flower rota. She moved gratefully into the twilight again and turned to look back. There were no obvious hiding places to the exterior of the building, and she began to walk in the direction of the graveyard.

Apart from a small area to her right, close to the gate, where half a dozen fresh graves had been heaped with flowers, the headstones were worn and the burials in disrepair. Several had fallen to the ground; directly in front of her a headless angel, its hands streaked with birdlime, presided over a stone table tomb whose horizontal surface had buckled under a concealing shroud of ivy. She shivered, reminded no longer of Gray's *Elegy* but of the late-night horror films she avoided unless there was someone present to hold her hand. She moved on, stopping before an unadorned stone slab with four or five names carved into it. *Edgar Elijah Bliss*, she read, *1782–1844*. The second name was that of a woman, *Bertha Bliss*. Presumably his wife, Loretta thought, though this information did not follow the woman's dates. Then a new idea struck her. Bertha Bliss, Fanny Fudge – she was supposed to be looking for a headstone. Thinking that whoever had written the note possessed a very odd sense of humour, Loretta began to pick her way along the row with a new sense of purpose. *Rankine, Moore, Littlejohn, Nicolson* – she came to the end and doubled back on herself. When she found the grave, what then? Would she discover a second note, this time attached to the headstone in some way, or nestling at its foot? She hoped she wasn't about to be faced with further instructions, as though she was taking part in a macabre treasure hunt. She reached the end of the row, again without luck, and started the next.

It wasn't easy work; the light was failing fast and in this part of the churchyard the ground was choked with weeds, the inscriptions hard to decipher. But she kept going, assuring herself that the author of the note must have played fair to the extent of picking a headstone that was at least legible. Soon she was down in the far corner, with a tangle of bushes beyond the graves leading to the bottom of a valley where she guessed there was a stream. A high hedge marked the side of the churchyard, making this part of it seem gloomier and more confined than the rest. She picked her way along the last set of graves, a row of nineteenth-century burials, wishing again that she'd brought a torch, and all of a sudden there it was: *Fanny Fudge, 1815–1845, Her Soul Is With The Lord.*

Loretta knelt down, a mixture of excitement and relief making her pulse race. Then she sat back on her heels, puzzled. There was no note, no sign that anyone had visited this grave in the last twenty years. She glanced up, uneasily aware of how quickly the graveyard was being swallowed up in darkness. A little to her right the sun had gone down, leaving only a vivid red glow along the horizon as a reminder of its presence; she had to fight off the idea that the sky itself was smouldering, about to burst into flame. She turned her head a little further, and saw that the church had become a secret, shadowy mass against the thick blue of the night sky. And there was silence, an absence of noise so profound that, when a twig suddenly cracked behind her, she knew without a shadow of doubt that someone was approaching.

For a second she remained where she was, crouching at the foot of the grave, rooted to the spot with horror. Was this why she had been lured to this desolate place, to fall victim to a cowardly attack from the shadows by an unseen assailant? Well, she wouldn't give up without a fight. In a single swift movement she was up on her feet facing the dark figure advancing unhurriedly towards her up the slight slope, her terror increasing as she realized how tall he was. Her only hope – assuming he didn't have a knife or a gun – was surprise: if she ducked under the first blow, she might be able to wind him long enough to make a run for the car – thank God she'd left the door unlocked. She balanced herself on the balls of her feet, her eyes fixed on the stranger's hands–

'Thirty.' He came to a halt before her, hunching his shoulders and digging his hands deep into the pockets of his quilted bomber jacket. 'Thirty don't seem so old these days.'

'What?' Loretta was so astounded by his words and laconic delivery that she took a step backwards, colliding with the stone edging around the grave of Fanny Fudge.

'Careful,' the stranger said, putting out a gloved hand to steady her and withdrawing it when she flinched away. 'I was just remarking about that lady – the one whose remains you're standing on – that she only got to thirty. Seems pretty young these days. I guess you're hoping to do better?'

'Who are you?' Her voice was hoarse, afraid; his cropped hair and light American accent had already suggested an answer to her question.

The stranger shifted his weight from one foot to the other in the manner of a man comfortably aware of his own strength.

'Let's forget the introductions. You've been asking questions – I've got the answers, some of them. Fire away.'

'What questions?' Her voice was stronger now; if he was going to kill her, surely he'd have done it by now?

'Don't mess around. I know a whole lot about you, Ms Lawson – *Dr* Lawson, I should say. Laura Anne Lawson, known as Loretta. Like the singer, huh? And you're a bit more than thirty, though I don't like to mention a lady's age.'

'How did you ... ?' She stopped, chilled by his knowledge of her. It was frightening confirmation of her earlier hypothesis, that he had some sort of intelligence connection. But why had he summoned her here? She glanced sideways across the churchyard, trying to estimate the distance to her car.

'Don't try it!' He had seen the movement of her head. 'We've got things to talk about.'

'So you're responsible for the tape?' she asked. It was a shot in the dark; she couldn't think of any other reason why he'd be interested in her.

'Not me personally. I knew nothing about it till you started asking questions today. We're talking unauthorized operations here.' He paused. 'Turns out I've got a couple of cowboys on my team, couple of guys who just got moved out of Managua. They don't know the difference between operating here and what we do in hostile territory.' He pronounced it *hostel*, Loretta noticed. 'They've been trying to throw a scare into your friend in the big house, trying to make her sell up and move on out.' He paused again.

'And when she didn't ... they killed her?' Loretta was surprised to find her voice was steady, in spite of the audacity of the question.

'No, they did *not*.' For the first time his tone had ceased to be conversational, matter-of-fact; the dark hollows of his eye sockets mesmerized Loretta. She felt threatened, menaced, but stood her ground.

'You expect me to believe that? When you've admitted bugging the house, all that nonsense with the tape recorder?'

'Not me, I just told you –'

She interrupted him, reckless now. 'So why did they call it off before she was killed – tell me that! They did, didn't they? They got into my cottage on Sunday night and removed the evidence, then they –'

'Because they got scared! All that stuff going on at the camp, those guys firing the trailer Friday night, it got too hot.'

'Oh, come on –'

'Look, this is a friendly country. We don't mess with murder. You better believe it – if you don't want to end up like Fanny down there.' He nodded towards the grave behind her.

Loretta felt a shiver run down her spine and decided it wasn't the moment to point out the inconsistency in the American's last speech.

'How did they do it?' she asked, trying to sound merely curious. 'The voices, I mean. You might as well tell me.'

He appeared to consider for a while, then shrugged his shoulders. 'OK. Tape recorder in the shack in the garden, place where the American lived. Speakers hidden in the house, miniature ones with receivers in back of them. Kids' stuff.'

'So they're still there, the speakers?' As soon as it was out Loretta regretted the remark; she'd been thinking aloud, pouncing on the chance to find more evidence of the plot against Clara.

The American laughed. 'You're not so bright after all. I thought you'd spotted that as well. Or didn't she tell you?'

'Tell me what? I don't know what you're talking about.'

'Guy turns up, says he wants to buy the house. Gets inside, has a look round. Smartest bit of the operation, and it's down to your guys, not mine.'

Loretta stared at him open-mouthed, remembering one of her conversations with Clara. 'You mean he was . . . ?'

'You got it.'

There was silence. The man's gaze wandered across the dark churchyard, then returned to Loretta. 'Any more questions?'

'Yes.' She took a deep breath, more afraid now than at any time in the last fifteen minutes. 'What happens now?'

'Now . . . we do a deal.'

'A deal?'

He nodded, slowly and emphatically. 'You hand over the tape, and you go home. The calls, the voices, they never happened. You forget the whole thing.'

'And if I don't go along with this deal?'

He lifted a hand and drew it sideways across his neck. 'What do you think?'

Loretta swallowed. 'What if I haven't got the tape with me?'

'But you do, don't you? After all those break-ins at that place you're living in, there's no way you'd leave it behind. Hand it over.'

'Can I ask one last question?'

'Make it quick.'

'You say your men had nothing to do with the murder – all right, I believe you!' She felt him relax again. 'But – do you know who did do it?'

'Nope.' He shook his head.

'And you don't know what's happened to Peggy – the woman from the peace camp?'

'No. That's two questions. The tape.' He held out a gloved hand.

Loretta reached reluctantly into her bag. She took out the cassette and dropped it into his hand, taking care not to touch even his glove.

'Thank *you*.' The tape disappeared into a pocket. 'Now walk. You're going to get into your little car and drive away. You say nothing, got it?'

Loretta nodded.

'OK. *Walk*.'

Her eyes fixed on his face, trying to memorize at least the shape of his head, Loretta began moving sideways towards the church.

'Faster. Move!'

She turned and walked as quickly as she could, given the rough ground and darkness. Every muscle in her body tensed as she tried to fight off the notion that a bullet was about to rip through her back. She tripped once and, panting, looked back to where she had left the American. He raised one arm in a threatening gesture and she forced herself up and on. She fumbled with the heavy gate, letting it slip from her grasp. Too afraid to go back and shut it, she threw herself into her car and turned the key in the ignition, pressing the accelerator so hard that it roared into sudden life. Then she swung the car round to face the road, without lights, desperate not to present a target; the brakes squealed as she took off much too fast for the dusty surface.

7

It occurred to Loretta afterwards that she remembered nothing of the ten-mile drive back to Flitwell. As fear was replaced by relief that she'd got out of the churchyard alive, a stream of unpleasant thoughts passed through her mind, preventing her giving full consideration to any of them. Chief among them was that she'd lost her evidence – the only concrete proof that people from the USAF base had been waging a campaign of intimidation against Clara. She could just imagine Chief Inspector Bailey's face if she went to him next morning with her unsupported story. And what would happen to her if she did tell? The American in Steeple Barford seemed pretty well informed about her movements, and the threats he'd uttered were unequivocal. But was she going to allow her course of action to be influenced by concern for her own safety? Theoretically, the answer was a resounding no: bringing Clara's killer to justice was the single most important thing. On the other hand, the American had been adamant that his men weren't involved in the murder – but then he *would* say that, wouldn't he? Surely she should tell Bailey the whole story and to hell with the consequences! Wait a minute, said the small, seductive voice of self-interest, what will that achieve? How will your death help Clara? Loretta swallowed, her throat dry, and argued back. Revealing what she knew was obviously her best means of protection – the Americans wouldn't *dare* kill her then! Oh no? the small voice persisted. Don't you think they're capable of making it look like an accident? And what if they really were innocent of Clara's death? She was still grappling with this appalling dilemma when she remembered Robert. She looked at her watch and made out that it was just after nine o'clock. A whole hour late! Should she go straight to his house on the assumption that he'd long ago returned home, or check the cottage first? And what was she going to tell him? She'd have to think up a pretty good excuse if she wasn't going to reveal the whole story – but was it wise to confide what had happened to anyone other than the police? And in any case, would he believe her? She hadn't shown him the tape earlier in the day when she'd had the opportunity. The only decision she came to was to try the cottage first, in case he'd left a note. She'd have to decide everything else as she went along.

She slowed in the road as she reached the wooden gates that led to the front door. She was half out of the car before she realized that the gates were already open and a car was parked in her space; she saw the glowing tip of a cigarette bobbing its way towards her.

'Loretta! Is that you? Christ, where have you been? I've been worried to death!'

'John! What are you doing here?' Loretta stood in the road, astonished to hear Tracey's voice.

'Come on, let us inside, there's no point in us all standing out here in the dark.'

The cigarette end retreated and Loretta heard another voice in the garden. Her heart sank; she was fairly sure it belonged to Robert, and she could think of few people in the world she'd rather have kept apart. She sighed, went back to her car and locked it. Then she made her way round what she now recognized as Tracey's black Golf to the front door. Robert was standing several feet away, his face a pale, unreadable shape in the darkness. She put her key in the door and, as it opened, felt inside for the light switch.

'Nice place you've got here,' Tracey said conversationally, following her in. 'Bit small.'

Loretta turned to Robert, who was staring at her grimly from the doorway.

'Robert, I'm *so* sorry. I tried to ring you but you were out. I can tell you the whole story –'

'Yes, where *have* you been?' Tracey demanded shortly, stubbing his cigarette out in the sink. 'Roger here –'

'Robert,' interrupted Loretta, casting an anguished glance in his direction.

'OK, Robert. He says you were supposed to be here at eight o'clock, that's over an hour ago. What's going on?'

'Look, I – ' Loretta stopped, looking from one angry face to the other.

'Come on, what've you been up to? I *know* you, Loretta, you're up to no good! I've driven all the way from London – '

'Yes, what *are* you doing here? I don't remember giving you my address.'

'For Christ's sake, Loretta, credit me with *some* intelligence. The name of Clara's house is all over the newspapers. You were hardly difficult to find.'

Loretta closed her eyes, completely drained. The scene in the churchyard had exhausted her, she had no resources to cope with this.

'Um, have you introduced yourselves?' she asked, unable to think of anything else to say.

'Oh yes,' said Robert, speaking for the first time. 'John's explained that he's your husband.'

'*Ex*-husband,' Loretta said viciously, glaring at Tracey as he lit another cigarette.

'Well, we're not actually divorced,' Tracey said, inhaling deeply.

'Either way, I think I'll be off,' Robert said coldly, moving away from the door-frame on which he'd been leaning. 'I only hung around to make sure you were safe – that you hadn't had a car accident or anything.' He lifted a hand in farewell and stepped into the garden.

'Robert, wait!' Loretta started to follow him and got to the door in time to see his narrow frame disappear into the darkness beyond the hedge.

'Now look what you've done,' she cried, whirling round to face Tracey. Tears started in her eyes, she felt for a chair, and collapsed weeping. She heard Tracey shut the front door, then he rested a hand on her shoulder.

'Loretta, what's the matter? It's not just that creep, is it?'

'He isn't a creep . . . ' She sat up, took the handkerchief he was holding out, and blew her nose. 'No, it isn't just that. But why did you have to upset him, all that stuff about being my husband? Couldn't you have been a bit more discreet?'

'OK, I'm sorry. But how was I to know you and he were . . . you know how you keep these things to yourself. I was banging on the door when he appeared and wanted to know who I was – I didn't like his manner so I said I was your husband. I'm sorry. Can I get you something?'

'Yes, please – some tea.'

'A nice cup of tea coming up. Then you'll tell me what's got you into this state?'

Loretta nodded, wiping away a few last tears with Tracey's handkerchief. What was she to do – about the sinister American in the churchyard, about Robert? He could at least have waited, allowed her to explain about her relationship with Tracey, instead of going off in a huff like that. She watched Tracey move across the small kitchen, peering at the range as though he'd never seen anything like it before, complaining about the lack of an electric kettle. Eventually he placed two cups of tea on the table and took a seat opposite her. She took a sip, decided it was too hot, and put the cup down.

'OK – begin.'

'I don't know if you're going to believe this –'

'Oh, I am.' Tracey helped himself to a biscuit from the packet he'd put on the table. 'That's why I'm here – I knew you were up to something. Biscuit?' He pushed the packet towards her.

Loretta hesitated, then took one. This domestic scene – teacups, biscuits – was making her wonder if she'd dreamed the entire episode in Steeple Barford. But she knew she hadn't; she only had to look in her bag to find the tape was no longer there.

'What would you say if I told you the Americans *were* involved? In trying to frighten Clara, I mean?'

Tracey thought for a moment. 'Who d'you mean by the Americans? And what's your evidence?'

Loretta sighed, wishing he wouldn't adopt this courtroom manner. '*I* don't know who they are. People from the base – the CIA, I expect.'

'Unlikely, if they're from the base. The CIA tends to work out of –'

'Does it matter?'

'Not a great deal, no. I was about to say – well, let's not get into that. It's never easy to get to the bottom of who's working for who. Go on.'

Loretta paused, then told Tracey everything that had happened since she arrived back at the cottage and found the anonymous note. When she finished he got up and lifted the kettle back on to the hob.

'More tea?'

'Is that all you can say?'

'I'm thinking.' He waited in silence for the kettle to boil, added more water to the teapot, and held it over her cup.

'Oh, all right. As you've made it.'

Tracey refilled both cups and sat down.

'Well – *do* you believe me?'

'Oh yes. I'm not sure anyone else would.'

'I'd worked that much out myself.'

'OK, OK, I'm trying to think about what we can do.' He picked up his cigarette packet, took one out and lit it. 'What it comes down to is this. Clara told you she was getting threatening phone calls and letters. She hadn't told the police. You both heard voices in the middle of the night. Neither of you told the police, you didn't even mention it after she was murdered. D'you know if they found any of the letters when they searched the house?'

'I don't know – I suppose so.'

'But they were anonymous, anyway. And maybe they were nothing to do with the base. Could have been someone in the village, those lads who chucked paint at the house. Then you found the tape –'

'One of Bailey's men found it. He gave it to me at the end of the interview.'

'Did he know what was on it?'

'He didn't say. I assume so.'

'I bet they listened to it. Wouldn't have given it back otherwise.'

'In that case –'

'In that case – nothing. You said yourself it sounded like a play. Look, Loretta. I think you're setting too much store by this tape, even if you still had it. Which you don't. And if you go to what's his name –'

'Bailey.'

'If you go to Bailey and say it was part of a plot to scare Clara, but you don't happen to have it any more because this Rambo character took it off you in a churchyard at dusk –'

'He wasn't anything like Rambo. More a young Clint Eastwood.' Loretta started to giggle.

Tracey smiled briefly, then became serious.

'I'm sorry, Loretta, I shouldn't have said that – it isn't a laughing matter. If word did get back to this guy that you'd talked to the police – well, I don't like to think what might happen.' He got up, stubbed his cigarette out in the sink again, and gave her a stern look. 'This is *exactly* what I was afraid of when you rang off this afternoon – that you'd dash off and get yourself involved in something like this! Honestly, Loretta! You shouldn't be allowed out alone! You've got about as much sense as – as that teapot!'

'I like that! Just because you –'

'Loretta!' He came back to his seat and faced her earnestly across the table. 'You're out of your depth and so am I. These guys aren't joking. Come back to London – forget the whole thing!'

'I *can't*!' Her tone was anguished.

Tracey reached out and squeezed her hand.

'I know how you feel. It's tough. But I don't want to be rung up in few days and asked to identify your body. Look, I'm not good at conversations like this – you know that. But I care about you. I really do.'

Loretta sat in silence, her head averted. Tracey's talking in this uncharacteristic way had deeply impressed her. Suddenly there was a scratching noise at the front door, followed by a familiar wail.

'What's that?' Tracey was startled.

'Only Bertie. Clara's cat.' Loretta got up to let the animal in. He followed her to her chair, waited while she sat down, then jumped up on her lap.

'God, Loretta, you're a real sucker! Don't tell me you've adopted a *cat*! You live in an upstairs flat. What are you going to do with a cat in Islington?'

'Lots of cats live in Islington. Anyway, I haven't adopted him – I'm just looking after him. Someone's got to!' She didn't want to admit that the possibility that she'd have to take Bertie back to London had already crossed her mind; Jeremy hadn't shown the slightest interest in the cat's welfare and Imo, though back in the village, hadn't come to collect him either. She brushed this thought aside for the moment.

'John, isn't there anything you can do? In the paper?'

'What, run it as a story?'

'Yes.' She looked at him hopefully.

'It's – it's *impossible*, Loretta.' Tracey groped for words. 'All you've got is unsupported allegations. Even if the *Herald* was prepared to run it, which I frankly doubt, we'd be a laughing stock. And more to the point, so would you. How would you look after it'd been denied by everyone from the Home Secretary downwards? Not to mention the American ambassador. You'd be walking round with an invisible label saying "loony" round your neck. People don't like conspiracy theories. Think of your –'

'Wait a minute, what about that woman in the west country – what was her name? The one who grew roses. You remember, she was writing a paper about Sizewell and then she was found murdered. There was lots in the papers about her.'

'Hilda – Hilda something. I know who you mean. But that was all pretty inconclusive in the end. No one ever proved anything. What I was going to say was, what about your career? Just think of the effect it could have, a story like this. You haven't even got tenure. Or have I missed something?'

Loretta shook her head. 'No, you're quite right. I'm eminently sackable. But it's so bloody *unfair*. Can't you get your contacts to confirm it? Those people you know in MI5?'

Tracey lit his third cigarette. 'I know you don't like it, but I need them when I'm under stress.' He inhaled deeply. 'Loretta, how d'you think your friend with the funny sense of humour knew you'd got the tape? Why leave you a note today? Why not yesterday? You've had it since Tuesday night.'

'Oh, Good God – of course! I remember now – he said something about me asking questions. That means – that means your man tipped him off?'

'It's a possibility. Though I didn't actually say you'd got the tape, I just asked if he knew of any operations of that kind around Dunstow. I think I said I knew someone up here, and there'd been funny goings-on. Anyway, it looks as if all that stuff about bad relations with the Yanks was so much guff. Either that, or – well, there is another possibility.'

'Which is?'

'That someone was tapping the line you used to call me.'

'The line *I* used? Who on earth'd go to the bother of tapping a telephone kiosk?'

'Well, it has been done.' Tracey shifted uncomfortably in his chair. 'I mean, it's never been admitted, but the evidence is quite good. Think about it, Loretta. This box you used is pretty near the base, right – those planes I heard went over very low. And the women from the peace camp, they don't have phones sitting in the trees. Tap a few local phone boxes, and you've got a good chance of finding out what their plans are – demonstrations, blockades, that sort of thing. Fore-warned is forearmed.'

'Gosh.' Loretta let it sink in. 'But – say it was your contact? Would he really do that to you? I thought you were on good terms with MI5 or MI6 or whatever they call themselves. Isn't that where your Berlin story came from last year?'

Tracey pulled a face, giving the impression he was finding their conversation excruciatingly painful.

'Yes, all right, it did. But the thing you've got to under-stand about the intelligence service . . . look, telling a journal-ist what the other side is up to is one thing. If you must know – and I'm telling you this in the *strictest* confidence' – he was positively glaring at her now – 'that stuff was leaked to me because of a disagreement. They knew there was a spy ring but they couldn't decide what to do with it. The higher echelons wanted to leave it in place a bit longer, and the people lower down thought too much damage was being done. They *used* me, if you like.'

Loretta listened in silence, surprised by Tracey's frankness. It wasn't like him to play down his role in getting a story, particularly one he regarded as a major scoop.

'So there's nothing you can do,' she said at last.

'Nothing. But let's look on the bright side. What if this guy in the churchyard is telling the truth? What if his men didn't

158

do it? Just because he comes on like the Lone Ranger on a bad day doesn't make him a liar.'

'I sup-pose so,' Loretta said uncertainly. 'If he is telling the truth . . . I wonder if Jeremy's still at the police station.'

'Jeremy? That's Clara's husband?'

'Yes, I forgot to tell you. The police hauled him off for questioning this morning. He wasn't very keen on going. But maybe he's back by now. Did you see any lights in the house while you were waiting for me?'

'Oh no, there was no one in. I knocked.'

'I wonder if he did do it . . . but surely he'd have arranged an alibi?'

'Maybe that's what the police are trying to crack. Listen, Loretta, why don't you come back to London tonight? I'll even drive your car down if you're too tired to do it yourself. Now *there's* an offer for you – it'll mean me getting up at the crack of dawn to come and get mine. I've got to be in the office by eleven tomorrow. How about it?'

Loretta considered. Perhaps Tracey was right, and she should wash her hands of the whole affair? Then she remembered something.

'What about Peggy?'

Tracey sighed. 'Sorry, Loretta, I must have missed this bit. Who's Peggy?'

Loretta explained briefly. With the air of one who was beginning to run out of patience, Tracey reached for his cigarettes again.

'So you haven't any proof that she's actually missing? She might perfectly well have gone off of her own accord before the murder?'

'Yes, but –'

'Wherever she is, I don't see what you achieve by hanging around here.' He glanced at his watch. 'It's after ten already. Why don't you start packing?'

Loretta began to get up. The idea of a restful night in her brass bed in Islington was suddenly very attractive. She was letting the cat slip to the floor when she sat down again.

'I can't leave tonight.'

'Why ever not?'

'Robert.'

'Ah.' Tracey had the grace to lower his gaze.

'I'd like to try and sort things out with him before I go.'

'All right, Loretta, I'm sorry about that. I just didn't take to him – he was too damn *proprietorial* about you, if you must know. I know, it's none of my business who you choose to have affairs with. But honestly, I can't imagine *what* you see in him – that posh bloody voice, for a start! I don't know how you stand it. Not to mention – '

'Leave it alone, *please*, John. I'm too tired to argue. I'm going to stay one more night so I can see him tomorrow – I promise I'll be back in Liverpool Road by tomorrow night.'

'Promise? Cross your heart and hope to die?'

'Yes, all that.'

'OK, I'll be off. Lock the door after me, won't you? And ring when you get back to London. If I don't hear by tomorrow night I'll be back. That's a threat!'

Loretta followed him to the door and planted a kiss on his cheek. 'Thanks for coming.'

Tracey hugged her for a moment, then opened the front door. Loretta wondered whether she should move her car, but decided she was too tired. She watched Tracey reverse out into the road, then closed the gates.

'Bye,' she said under her breath, listening to the sound of his engine die away. For a fleeting moment she longed to be in the passenger seat, speeding back towards the safety of the metropolis.

Loretta was packing upstairs next morning when she heard a knock at the front door. It occurred to her that it might be Robert, regretting his abrupt departure the previous evening, and she rushed to examine herself in the dressing-table mirror. She tidied her hair, wishing she had time to put on some make-up; the dark circles had reappeared around her eyes, and her cheerful pink T-shirt and flowered skirt emphasized how wan she had become. There was another knock, louder this time, and she ran downstairs to answer it. She pulled open the front door, smiling in anticipation, then stared at her visitor in disappointment.

'Oh. Hello.'

'Hi.' Jeremy's greeting sounded forced; he was unshaven

and his clothes were crumpled as though he'd slept in them.

'You're back then.' As soon as she'd said it Loretta realized it wasn't a very tactful way to address a man last seen marching off in the company of two burly policemen.

'Yes, I, er . . . got back late last night. They tried the old rubber hosepipe, and let me go when they could see it wasn't going to work.'

'What?' She stared at him in astonishment until the ghastly smile on his face told her he'd been making a joke. She smiled back uncertainly. 'Oh, I see.'

'This came for you,' Jeremy said suddenly, reaching into his jacket pocket. He held out an envelope.

'Thanks,' Loretta said, surprised. She examined the letter briefly, not recognizing the handwriting. The sender didn't seem to know her very well; it was addressed to 'Loretta', no surname, 'c/o Mrs Wolstonecroft's house, near Fitwell, Oxon.' It bore an Oxford postmark. Mystified, Loretta started to open it, then realized Jeremy was still standing in front of her.

'By the way, I'm probably going back to London today. My tenants managed to, er, make other arrangements.' She looked down, embarrassed. 'Will you remember to feed the cat? I've been doing it since . . . um . . . '

'The cat?' Jeremy looked blank for a moment. 'Oh God, him! I'd completely forgotten. I – I'll have to take him to the vet, I can't be lumbered with a cat.'

'The vet?'

'They find homes for unwanted animals, don't they? Or do I mean the RSPCA?'

'You mean – you're just going to dump him?' Loretta was aghast.

'Well, I can't keep him. I'm in – I'm far too busy.'

'What about Imo? Won't she want him?'

'Imo?' For a second Loretta thought Jeremy didn't know who she was talking about. 'Oh, she won't want him, she can't stand cats. It's about the one thing we've got in common.' He pulled a face.

'In that case, can I have him?' Loretta spoke without giving herself time for second thoughts.

'You? Well, I suppose so . . . ' Jeremy seemed surprised, reluctant even.

'I *like* cats,' Loretta told him firmly. 'Don't you want him to go to a good home?'

Jeremy shrugged. 'OK.'

'That's settled then. Has he got a cat basket?'

'A basket?'

Loretta didn't even bother to conceal her impatience. 'To take him to London in! You don't expect me to drive seventy miles with him perched on my knee?'

'Oh, right. I *think* I've seen one.'

'Let's go and look.' Loretta stepped back into the kitchen, still clutching the letter, and picked her keys off the table. She shut the front door firmly, and ushered Jeremy before her down the path.

A few minutes later she returned to the cottage carrying a wicker basket.

'Poor old Bertie,' she said, putting it down on the kitchen table and bending to stroke the cat's head as he strolled across the floor. She straightened up, drew the letter out of her pocket and opened it. She read:

Dear Sister,

The women's peace camp at USAF Dunstow invites you to an important meeting to discuss plans for a vigil for victims of the American attack on Libya. It is very important that you attend this meeting, at which messages from absent friends will be passed on. Please come to the camp at 11 a.m. on Friday morning. This is very important.

In sisterhood, Elspeth (Scottish)

Puzzled, Loretta read the letter a second time. Two phrases, the one about absent friends and the words 'very important', had been underlined. This was the first she'd heard of any vigil, and the tone was quite at odds with the hostility she'd encountered during her trip to the camp on Wednesday night. And who was Elspeth? Then the word in brackets jogged her memory; presumably the writer was the Edinburgh woman she'd met at the camp when she went there with Clara. And – suddenly her heart began to beat faster. Was the reference to absent friends something to do with Peggy? After all, eleven in the morning was an odd time to hold a meeting, and Elspeth wasn't giving her much notice.

Loretta looked at her watch, and saw she had only a couple of hours before she was due at the camp. Why not go there now? For all she knew, she was working herself up over Peggy's absence for nothing – it would be nice to know whether or not there was anything to worry about. She folded the letter, put it in her bag and looked round for her jacket. She was just putting it on when there was yet another knock at the front door. She jerked it open, and found a familiar figure standing there.

'Good morning, Dr Lawson. Were you – ' Loretta watched his mouth move as an F1-11 swooped low overhead. 'Bloody planes,' said Chief Inspector Bailey as the noise faded. 'The jet engine is the curse of the twentieth century. Were you on your way out? I was hoping you'd be able to help us.'

Loretta hesitated. 'You'd better come in.' She stepped back to allow Bailey into the kitchen.

'My sergeant gave me your message,' he said, pulling out a chair and sitting down.

Loretta thought fast; she'd forgotten her attempt to reach Bailey yesterday, and now the reason for it was no longer valid.

'I – just wondered how the inquiry was going,' she said lamely.

Bailey observed her for a moment. 'Very kind of you to take an interest. We have come up with something, as a matter of fact, that's why I'm here. I'd like you to come down to the station and look at some photographs.'

'Photographs?'

'Yes. See if you can identify a couple of people for us. I'd rather not say any more at present – there are rules about these things, as I'm sure you know.'

'You want me to come now?' Loretta asked, dismayed.

'Unless there's a pressing reason why you can't. These identifications are quite important to us.'

'All right.' Loretta gave in. If she left at once, she might just get to the camp in time for her appointment.

'We can offer you a lift – or would you like to follow in your own car?'

'Thanks, I'll take my own.' She didn't relish the thought of having to make small talk with Bailey all the way to Oxford. He stood up and waited for her to open the front door.

'My car's down the lane in the lay-by. I take it yours is the Panda in the road?'

'Yes.'

'Not a good idea to leave it there, if you don't mind me saying so. I've just got to collect something from the house – I'm afraid I didn't come all this way just for the pleasure of your company – and you can follow me to the station. See you there.' He headed across the garden, leaving Loretta to open the gates to the road.

The police station was a modern block in Headington. Loretta followed Bailey's unmarked police car into the car park and reversed into an area marked 'Visitors'. She accompanied Bailey inside the building to a lift; they got in and rode in silence to the third floor.

'This way.' Bailey turned left and led her down a corridor to an office with his name on the door.

'Sergeant Gorringe, Dr Lawson.' He motioned Loretta to a chair at the side of a desk. 'The sergeant's going to show you some photographs – better get WPC Crossley up here before she starts,' he added.

The sergeant, a red-faced man with long sideburns, picked up a phone and muttered into it. He put it down and the three of them waited in silence until there was a knock on the door. Bailey called 'Come in', and a dark-haired woman in uniform entered.

'This is WPC Crossley,' Bailey explained. 'She's here as a witness that the thing's done properly. OK, show her the pics.'

Gorringe picked up a large brown envelope and began placing photographs on the table in front of Loretta. The women in the pictures stared stonily at the camera, united by their determination to give nothing away. Loretta felt uncomfortable, as if she was prying into private grief. Suddenly she gasped.

'Peggy!' The girl's hair was different, shoulder length and brown, but it was undoubtedly the same person.

'Could you tell us where you've seen this person before?' Gorringe asked formally.

Loretta gave Bailey an anxious look, wondering what all this was about. Had they found Peggy, was she all right? What should she say?

'This is Peggy,' she said slowly, 'the woman from the peace camp I told you about. The girl who was staying with Clara.'

'Now you're quite sure about that – no doubts at all?' asked Gorringe.

'Quite sure – her hair's longer here, and a different colour, but yes – that's her. Where did you get this picture? Is she all right?'

'From our colleagues in the Met,' Bailey said, making a sign to Gorringe. The sergeant removed the picture and put it on another desk, collecting together the remaining photographs and returning them to the envelope.

'Now – same thing again,' Bailey said, handing a second envelope to Gorringe.

This time the pictures were of men, and Loretta guessed what was coming.

'Stop,' she said unhappily as they reached the fifth photograph. 'This is Mick – Peggy's husband.'

'Thanks, Dr Lawson, you've been most helpful. Now, if you'll just sign here to confirm your identification of the suspects –'

'*Suspects?*'

'Oh yes. The gentleman you've just picked out is a professional housebreaker, name of Michael James Cummins. Does that answer your question?'

'But Peggy – Peggy hasn't done anything . . . ' Loretta's voice faltered.

'This young lady' – Bailey lifted the first photograph from the desk – 'is Mrs Margaret Cummins. Three convictions for shoplifting, currently serving a suspended sentence. That's why we've got these pics – the Yard routinely keeps photos of convicted felons.'

'Why did you bring me here if you knew who they were already?' Loretta asked bitterly, examining the form that Gorringe had put in front of her before signing her name twice.

'We have to be sure, Dr Lawson,' Bailey said in a pained

voice. 'Bright young PC in Whitechapel recognized your very good description of chummy there, remembered him and his missus. But we have to check these things. We don't want to go asking the public to look out for the wrong people.'

'You mean you're going to give out their names?' Loretta was horrified.

'I'm holding a press conference in half an hour,' Bailey told her.

'But you've got it all wrong. You haven't got any evidence –'

'What would you say if I told you Mr Cummins's fingerprints were in the dead – in Mrs Wolstonecroft's house?'

'I – there must be a mistake.'

'I don't think so. Fingerprinting is a very exact science these days. Shall I see you out?'

'It's all right, I know the way.'

'As you wish. Good morning, Dr Lawson.

'Good morning.'

She walked blindly down the corridor and stopped outside the lift, unable to believe what she'd just been told. Mick's fingerprints in the house! All right, perhaps Peggy's husband was the murderer – but Peggy *couldn't* be involved! The lift doors opened and she moved forward, colliding with someone who was getting out.

'Jeremy!'

'We must stop meeting like this!' Jeremy, still unshaven and now even more haggard than he'd appeared earlier that morning, forced a smile.

Loretta hadn't decided how to respond to this ghastly sally when the man accompanying Jeremy touched his arm and pointed in the direction of Bailey's office. The two men set off, leaving Loretta staring after them.

'Going down?' A man in civilian clothes had got into the lift and was holding the door open.

'Oh – yes. Thank you.' Loretta stepped inside, resisting the temptation to run back and listen at Bailey's door. If the detective was convinced of Mick's guilt – and she had to admit that the revelation about his fingerprints had thrown new light on the case – then why had Jeremy Frere been brought in again? Surely Bailey didn't think all three of them – Jeremy, Mick,

Peggy – were in it together? The lift doors opened and the other passenger stood back to let her out before him. She crossed the foyer, went through the swing doors and down the steps to the car park, trying to construct a theory that would encompass all the disparate pieces of the puzzle. However she looked at it, there was no consistent pattern; it was as though two jigsaws had been jumbled up in the same box. Jeremy's repeated visits to the police station, Peggy's convictions for shoplifting, Mick's presence in Baldwin's, the American plot against Clara – it was like trying to make a landscape with extra pieces thrown in from a jigsaw of a steam train.

She opened the door of her car and climbed in, suddenly overwhelmed by anxiety. If Mick was the killer, what had he done with Peggy? Was she being held somewhere against her will? Had she managed to smuggle out a desperate message to the peace camp? Loretta looked at her watch and started the engine; if she drove quickly, she could be at the camp in half an hour. She waited impatiently behind a police car at the exit while its driver exchanged words with a couple of WPCs, then turned right into the road.

Several unfamiliar cars were parked on the road leading up to the base and, as Loretta approached the clearing, she realized that a meeting was taking place. About a dozen women and a couple of men in clerical clothes were sitting in a haphazard circle round the fire, and Loretta was relieved when the Scottish woman she now knew as Elspeth detached herself and came towards her.

'Let's go into the caravan,' she said in a low voice, gesturing towards the trees.

Loretta followed her in silence, observing as she went up the steps that an attempt had been made to wash off some of the smoke damage around the entrance.

'Have a seat.'

Loretta lowered herself on to a seat which folded down from the wall.

'I hope we can trust you.'

Loretta waited, not knowing what to say.

'I'm sorry about the other night. The girls thought you

were something to do with the police. They come in all disguises, these days. Obviously you got my note?'

'Yes. I wasn't sure what it meant.'

'But you came. I couldn't say too much in case the police were opening your mail.'

'Oh, I don't think they'd do that.'

'Don't you?' Elspeth shrugged. 'I didn't know your last name, by the way. Karen said you left a note with Alison, but she lost it.'

'It's Lawson.'

'It doesn't matter. Peggy needs your help.'

Loretta's heart beat faster but she schooled herself to keep calm; Elspeth's face was grave.

'Where is she? What does she want me to do?'

'She's in London, I'll tell you where in a moment. But first, I want to ask you something. What d'you think happened on Tuesday night?'

'I don't know. Clara was murdered, but I don't know who did it, if that's what you mean. I'm sure it wasn't Peggy.'

Elspeth inclined her head. Loretta felt she'd just passed some sort of test.

'She didn't do it. But she was there.' Elspeth paused.

'And?' Loretta was unable to stay silent.

'I don't know, she didn't say.' Elspeth stopped again, felt in her pocket, and drew her hand out empty. 'I keep forgetting, I've given up . . . Loretta, you've got to understand this is very difficult for us – for the peace camp. So many people are against us and a thing like this – a murder, I mean – is just the excuse they need. RALF, you've heard of them, and all the other upright citizens who want to see women silenced. Do you follow me?'

Loretta wasn't sure she did. 'I don't quite –'

'Let me put it like this. Peggy needs help, but it's too dangerous for us, this thing she's involved in. So it's up to you – only you can help her. We have to stay out of it.'

'All right,' Loretta said impatiently, feeling she could do without the lecture. 'What do I have to do? I'm still none the wiser. How did she get in touch with you, for a start? Is she all right?'

'The police came up here on Tuesday night asking if we'd

seen her. We said we hadn't. That was true. She turned up here a while later, quite a long time after they'd been and gone. She was in a state, it was hard to understand what she was saying. She said she'd been at the house when it happened and she was so frightened she ran away. She wouldn't go to the police – yes, I did suggest it, they have their uses – and she wouldn't say why. She just said she couldn't and she cried a lot.'

'Did she mention Mick? Her husband?'

'She didn't mention any names. She stayed the night here, in the caravan. Karen drove her down to the A40 on Wednesday morning, first thing. She said she was going to hitch to London.'

'And you let her go?' Loretta was incredulous.

'Are you saying we should have kept her here? With the police after her?'

'But – the poor kid! She'd just witnessed a murder!'

'That's her business. This camp, what we're struggling for, is more important than individuals. You've got to understand that. We're here for a purpose, to save the human race. We can't jeopardize the future of the camp for one person.'

Loretta bit her lip, wanting to argue but afraid of further antagonizing Elspeth before she'd found out where Peggy was.

'Did she actually *see* the murder? Do you know that?'

'I don't *know*. Look, d'you want to help or not?'

'Of course I do! Just tell me – what am I supposed to do?' Loretta thought she'd be here all day at this rate.

Elspeth got up and went to the small built-in table at the far end of the caravan. Several empty mugs and a Japanese tea-caddy were standing on it. Elspeth took the lid off the caddy and felt inside.

'Here y'are,' she said, holding out a crumpled piece of paper with tea-leaves sticking to it. 'That's where she's staying. She wants you to go there as quick as you can. Today if you can manage it. And to make sure you're not followed.'

Loretta took the piece of paper, wondering who might go to the trouble of following her and, if she happened to notice, how she'd shake them off.

'How did you get this?'

169

Elspeth sighed. 'There's a woman who takes messages for us in emergencies, we give her number to everyone who stays at the camp. Someone rang her. OK?'

'Not Peggy herself?'

'A friend of hers. Listen, I must get back to the meeting. I've done what I can. I don't want the peace camp –'

' – jeopardized. I've got the picture.'

Loretta folded up the paper, put it in her skirt pocket, and went to the head of the steps.

'I'm sorry about your friend, Clara. She was a good woman.'

Loretta turned and smiled awkwardly. 'Well – thanks for the address.' She went down the steps, skirted the group round the fire, and returned to her car. Once she was inside she unfolded the piece of paper and looked at the address for the first time: 11, Ernie Bevin House, Forman Park Estate, London E9. A council block, Loretta thought, probably one of those crumbling tower blocks built by Labour local authorities in the sixties and named after their political heroes. She had no idea where the estate was, apart from the fact that the postcode suggested Clapton or Hackney. Feeling on the parcel shelf for her *A–Z*, she discovered it under a library book she'd forgotten to return before leaving London. She looked up the name of the estate in the index, discovered it was situated off Well Street in Hackney. She glanced at her watch: eleven twenty-five. With a bit of luck she'd be there in a couple of hours. She looked at the piece of paper again, checking there wasn't a phone number, then fastened her seat-belt and got ready for the drive to London.

8

As the car passed Keeper's Cottage Loretta slowed, wondering whether she should stop and pick up her things. Then she remembered the cat; he had sauntered off across the lawn as she left for the police station and she didn't want to waste time luring him into his basket. In any case, she'd have to come back – she had a half-formed plan of persuading Peggy to talk to John Tracey, after which all three of them would drive to Oxford to confront Chief Inspector Bailey. Peggy must be made to see that, even though Mick was her husband and the father of her child, she was putting her own future at risk by protecting him. A perverted sense of duty, that was the only way Loretta could account for Peggy's behaviour. Or had she quit the scene in a blind panic, stunned by the horror of seeing her new friend shot down by Mick in cold blood? But if that were the case, why on earth hadn't she come to the cottage, where she'd have got a damn sight more help than she was offered by those women from the peace camp?

Loretta had reached the junction with the A40 and flicked on her left indicator. Perhaps she was being unfair; the peace women had given Peggy shelter for the night and a lift to the London road. She pulled out into a small gap in the traffic, picking up speed as a large dark car roared up behind her and flashed its lights. How had Peggy got away from Mick? Maybe he, too, had been horrified by what he'd done. Presumably there'd been a struggle – Loretta remembered the overturned chair in the drawing room which had alerted her to the fact that something was wrong. The scene was beginning to form in her mind: Mick struggling to wrest the gun from Clara, succeeding, then rapidly firing two shots . . . a cry from Clara, maybe one from Peggy, then the blonde girl running full tilt from the room, across the hall and into the garden . . .

A fierce hooting from behind brought Loretta out of this day-dream; she realized her speed had fallen to just over thirty. She pressed down the accelerator, telling herself it wasn't safe to indulge in such speculation as she approached the motorway section of the road. She put out a hand and turned on the radio, hoping Radio Four would provide something to distract her. She was just in time for the midday news, which led on the death in a car crash early that morning of a junior minister at the Department of Trade. Loretta pulled a face as she listened to a brief interview with Mrs Thatcher, in which the prime minister expressed her deep regret at the untimely loss of so *promising* a member of the government; it was followed by another with the Secretary of State, Paul Channon.

The next item caught her by surprise – she hadn't expected Bailey's news conference to be reported so promptly. It was a carefully worded account of what the police had said, including a recording of Bailey reading out full descriptions of Mick and Peggy. Their names were given, as well as the name of the road they'd lived in in Whitechapel. The report also revealed that a man resembling Mick had stopped a passer-by in Flitwell on the day of the murder and asked for directions to Clara's house.

The newsreader moved on to a non-fatal shooting in Belfast and Loretta realized she was clenching her teeth. She took a deep breath, cursing Bailey for making her task even more difficult. How was she to coax Peggy into going to the police when they had all but pronounced her guilty to the media? She started pulling out to overtake a slow lorry when the sound of Jeremy Frere's name riveted her attention back to the radio.

'. . . wife was murdered at their Oxfordshire home on Tuesday evening, is to face several charges in connection with a multi-million-pound art fraud,' the newsreader said. 'Mr Frere is expected to be charged in Oxford some time this afternoon. Police are not revealing details at this stage, but a

Thames Valley spokesman said their inquiries are expected to continue for some weeks. Detectives from Oxford are thought to be working closely with police in London, where Mr Frere owns a gallery, and New York.'

Loretta fell back into the slow lane, taking in this new development. So Jeremy's gallery *was* in trouble, she thought – no wonder he had looked so haggard at the police station that morning. But how had the police got on to him? She remembered the pictures he'd brought to Baldwin's on the morning after her own arrival in Flitwell – the paintings he said he'd assembled for a posthumous show by an American artist she'd never heard of. Did this news mean he'd acquired them illegally? Or perhaps they were forgeries? But wouldn't Clara have known that? Loretta recalled the scene in the kitchen when Jeremy had displayed one of the pictures. Imo had suggested it looked like a Hopper, a comment which had provoked a vehement rebuttal from Jeremy. Loretta couldn't remember Clara expressing any reservations at the time. But then, the man was supposed to be a hitherto unknown painter. But had Clara stumbled on something later, evidence that the pictures were fakes? And had Jeremy – no, there'd been no hint in the radio report that the police were interested in Jeremy Frere for any reason other than the alleged art fraud. And, if Peggy had seen Jeremy murder his wife, why had she stayed silent? She had no reason to protect Jeremy. It was rather bad luck on him, Loretta thought, that the police had stumbled on whatever he was up to in the course of investigating his wife's killing. For a second, she felt a twinge of pity. Then, recalling his callous remarks about dumping Clara's cat on the RSPCA, she allowed it to evaporate. Deciding that she'd never get to Hackney if she carried on at this rate, she turned off the radio, pushed in a Grace Jones tape, and forced herself to concentrate on her driving.

She knew the route as far as St Paul's Road in Islington, and she'd tried to memorize the rest of it from the *A–Z* which lay open on the passenger seat beside her. In spite of its proximity to the part of London in which she lived, Hackney was unknown territory to her and she wasn't sure she could get to

Well Street without getting lost. In the event it was easier than she'd anticipated; instead of the No-Right-Turn sign she'd feared, she was able to turn south into Mare Street when she got to the end of Graham Road. She drove past shops; a magnificent white town hall with a banner across its entrance proclaiming the borough's unemployment figures; terraces of decaying town houses, interspersed with ugly modern buildings, which hinted at the area's more prosperous past. The place was grubbier and more down at heel than Islington, a fact that seemed to be reflected in the faces of the people in the streets. Here and there the anarchist symbol, a letter A in a circle, had been spray-painted on walls, sometimes accompanied by the name of an anarchist group, Class War. At bus stops, men and women leaned resignedly against walls and railings as though they'd long ago given up hope of achieving even a temporary escape from the shabby streets.

Loretta slowed for a set of traffic lights, noticing a cinema that had been converted into a billiard hall just beyond the junction. The lights changed and she was about to carry straight on when she spotted a sign to the left saying Well Street. She moved abruptly into the left-turn lane, provoking a passenger in the car behind to lean through an open window and shout something unintelligible at her. Well Street was narrow at first, flanked by small shops, and the smell of cooking fat floated into the car from the Greasy Spoons to right and left. Then it opened out into a broad road which, to judge by the few remaining houses, had once been flanked by tall, attractive terraces. She came to what looked like a churchyard on her left, although there was no sign of a church, and saw, on the opposite side of the road, a small group of Asian women in saris going into a dingy modern factory with mesh screens over its windows. Then she caught her first glimpse of the Forman Park Estate; it was on the left-hand side of the road and consisted not of the tower blocks she'd expected but thirties mansion blocks.

She turned left into the narrow street that flanked the estate, passing the anonymous sixties pub on the corner. She drove slowly until she came to a wooden board with a map of the estate painted on it; checking there were no yellow lines in the road, she parked and got out of the car. The map was difficult to read: someone had sprayed the letters 'SWP' in red across the middle, and these in turn were partially obscured by the word 'SHIT' in silver metallic paint. Loretta eventually established that Ernie Bevin House was the third block on her right, lying behind others named after Hugh Dalton and Stafford Cripps. When had they been renamed, she wondered, and what had they been called in the thirties?

A narrow path ran along the side of Hugh Dalton House at its far end; she walked along the road, turned into the path, and made her way between the end of the flats and a group of Portakabins to her left. The first of these buildings had a makeshift sign in the window proclaiming it a Neighbour-hood Centre; a poster pasted on to the main door explained the place was closed due to industrial action. The next bore the curious title of South Hackney Unemployment Fightback Centre. It, too, was closed although there was no sign saying why or giving its opening hours. Its dusty air suggested to Loretta that it didn't have any.

Oppressed by the sheer misery of her surroundings – she was beginning to think life in a peace camp wasn't so unbear-able after all – Loretta carried on past Stafford Cripps House and finally arrived at her goal, the block named after Ernie Bevin. She turned right and paused in front of it, observing it to get an idea of the numbering system. It was a deck-access block with a central arch which presumably concealed stair-cases to each floor. The flats on the ground floor to the left of the arch bore odd numbers from one to nine and she carried on, wondering if number eleven was the first flat on the far side of the arch. It wasn't; these were the even numbers. Loretta peered back into the dark archway and hesitated, unwilling to move out of the relative brightness of the over-cast day. As she stood there, irresolute, three boys clattered down the stairs and ran whooping past her, one of them reaching out to punch her in the chest as he went by. Loretta gasped, and turned in time to see them disappear through the rear entrance of Stafford Cripps House. Then she took a deep breath, squared her shoulders, and walked pur-posefully into the shadows of Ernie Bevin House.

There were staircases to right and left, their entrances

liberally surrounded by graffiti. She took the one to her left, climbed the stairs to the first floor, and was relieved to discover that number eleven was the first flat in the row. Some attempt had been made to brighten it up – a plant in a plastic container hung on a wallbracket over the dustbin, and there was a window-box full of red geraniums in front of the kitchen window. Loretta was beginning to feel excited; she rang the bell twice, then stood back and examined the flat next door. The windows were boarded up and planks had been nailed across the front door, presumably to discourage squatters. She thought she saw something moved behind the kitchen window of number eleven, then the front door opened a fraction.

'Loretta?' It was Peggy's voice, but speaking in a whisper.

'Yes, it's me.' She put her face close to the door. It opened just wide enough for her to step inside, while Peggy kept herself concealed behind it.

'You came. You really came.' She sounded as if she could hardly believe it.

Loretta closed the front door and hugged Peggy briefly. To her dismay, the girl promptly burst into tears.

'Come on,' Loretta said, leading her into the small sitting room she could see through an open door. 'Everything's going to be all right.' She pushed Peggy gently on to a threadbare sofa over which someone had thrown a light blue Indian rug. The girl was wearing jeans and her usual pink sweatshirt, Loretta noticed. 'It's all right, everything's going to be all right.' As she repeated the soothing phrase, she hoped sincerely that she was telling the truth. 'Peggy – Peggy, listen to me. I know it's hard, but you've got to stop crying and listen to me. There. Is that better?' She sat holding one of Peggy's hands between her own, and the girl's sobs slowly subsided.

Suddenly Peggy sat up and looked at Loretta fiercely.

'It wasn't me! It wasn't me! They said – on the telly – they said the police are after me and Mick. That's why I ran away, 'cause I knew they'd say I did it. But it wasn't me!'

'Peggy, you've got to tell them the truth, for your own sake. And for your daughter's.' Loretta spoke urgently, her eyes fixed on Peggy's tear-stained face. 'I know he's your husband, but you can't go on protecting him like this – you've got to think of your–'

'What? What're you on about?' The anguish on Peggy's face had been replaced by blank incomprehension.

'About Mick – about him killing Clara.'

'It wasn't *him* that did it.' Peggy's voice was astonished, scornful.

'It wasn't? But his fingerprints were in the house, the police know –'

'Oh yeah, he was *there*. But that was *before*. She saw him off, Clara did, she didn't stand no nonsense from him. Christ, you don't think I'd of protected him?'

'You mean – Mick didn't kill Clara?'

'Course not!' Peggy stared at Loretta as though she'd taken leave of her senses.

'Oh no! I've been such a fool – why did I even *think* he was telling the truth?' Loretta threw her hands up in despair at her own stupidity. 'I'm sorry, Peggy, you're not going to believe this, but I even spoke to an American from the base – he said they hadn't anything to do with killing Clara and I – I fell for it! Listen, this is more complicated than I thought. How many of them were there? Did you see their faces? What actually happened?'

Peggy withdrew her hand from Loretta's and looked at her oddly.

'He isn't American,' she said, 'he couldn't be an MP if he was American, could he? He don't talk like an American, he's all lah-di-dah.'

'You mean – *Colin*? Colin Kendall-Cole?'

'Yeah, that's his name, I couldn't remember it exactly. That's why I run away, see, I knew they wouldn't believe me if I said it was him shot her.'

'But why would Colin . . . ?'

'You don't believe me! You're just like all the rest! I thought you was better, like Clara – well, you can just fuck off out! Go on, out! Leave me alone!' Peggy was on her feet, cheeks flushed, hand pointing to the front door.

Loretta pushed her hair back from her face, swallowed, and held her ground.

'I'm sorry, Peggy, of course I believe you. I thought I'd

worked it all out . . . I'm sorry I misunderstood. I came here because I wanted to help you and I still do – will you let me?'

For a moment it was touch and go, then Peggy sighed and sat down again.

'I – I get upset,' she said. 'I'm sorry. It's 'cause I'm so scared.'

'That's not surprising. Colin – well, it takes a bit of getting used to. D'you feel up to telling me about it?' Anxious as she was to hear Peggy's story, Loretta was determined not to rush her in case she lost her confidence again.

Peggy nodded, then paused. 'I dunno how to start.'

'Why not – why not tell me why Colin shot Clara?' The words seemed fantastic to Loretta; could the girl really be telling the truth?

'It was 'cause of the letter, see.' Peggy was sitting hunched forward, her hands clasped between her knees. 'He was frightened she'd give the letter to a paper, like she said. He told her to give it to him and she wouldn't. I heard him walking round the room, he was going on about his career. Then I heard a noise like he was opening something and he shot her. I couldn't stop him!' she added, giving Loretta an imploring look.

'No, I'm sure you . . . But – didn't he – why didn't he shoot you?'

'He couldn't see me, could he? Not behind the curtain.'

'What curtain – you mean the one in front of the bay?' Loretta was confused. 'Look, let's go back to the beginning. Why was Colin there?'

Peggy waited a moment, getting her thoughts in order.

'You know that bit in the paper? The thing about the women at the peace camp and how they should go back to their husbands?'

Loretta nodded. 'He wrote it, yes.'

'She was so cross about that she rang the paper. Then she rang him. That was in the afternoon, before Mick came. She said she had to see him – maybe she told him about the letter. I don't think so. Anyway, then Mick turned up.' She made a face. 'She let him come in, Mick that is, and she had a chat with him. She said I was staying there for a bit, and how she'd have the police on to him double-quick if he kept hanging around. He shouted a bit, but in the end he took himself off. He knew when he was beat!' She smiled at the memory. 'So then we had something to eat, and we had some wine. Clara said this bloke was coming, and she was going to stop him making a fuss about the camp. She was all sort of . . . *pleased* with herself.

'Then we heard him knock. Quick, says Clara, you go behind the curtains. I'm going to enjoy this, and you will as well. So I sat there like, quiet as a mouse. They both come in, and Clara offers him a drink, but he says no, he can't stay long. They was ever so polite, he says how's your husband and she says how's your wife. So they're sitting there and all of a sudden Clara says, *It's got to stop*, just like that. She really lays into him, says she's had enough of him going on about the peace camp and family life and all that. You're a bloody hypocrite, she says. He says he's got a job to do, and he's not saying the women are wicked, just mis – misguided.'

Peggy stopped for a second.

'And then?' Loretta prompted gently.

'Then she said again, *It's got to stop*.' For the second time, Peggy surprised Loretta by mimicking Clara's voice. 'He just laughed at her, he said things don't happen like that. The peace camp was a nuisance, and he's going to get rid of it. Oh no you're not, Clara said. If you don't stop it, I'm going to the papers with this!' From the way Peggy reported the exchange, Loretta could easily imagine the triumph in Clara's voice.

'This is where the letter comes in, right?'

'Right. He says nothing for a while till he's read it. Then – whoosh! He does his nut. Ranting and raving, swearing and threatening I don't know what. Then he calms down a bit. What's to stop me tearing it up, he says. Don't you think I've got a copy, she says, and anyway, if I go to the papers it won't matter whether I've got the letter. That's just – the icing on the cake. Now, why don't we sit down and talk about this like adults? So they – '

'You mean you don't know what was in the letter?' Loretta could barely conceal her disappointment.

'Oh yeah, I've got it, see? The copy, I mean. It was silly, really, it was only on the mantelpiece, D'you want to see it?'

Peggy started to get up; Loretta put out a hand to restrain her.

'Wait a minute. Just tell me the gist for the time being.'

'Oh, right.' Peggy sat down again. 'Well, it was old, this letter. It was from some girl Clara was at college with, her and this Colin bloke. Somewhere in Oxford, I think it was. It was all about how Colin'd got her into trouble and she was leaving college because he'd paid to have it taken away. Something like that. Christ, he was upset. This could ruin me, he kept saying. You kept quiet all these years – and now you're gonna ruin me. I kept quiet for her, not you, Clara says, and now she's dead. But Connie's a Catholic, he said – that must be his wife?'

'I think so,' Loretta agreed.

'And my career, he said, it'll be the end of it. He kept talking about that bloke who knocked up his secretary, you know the one. The one who had to resign.'

'But why . . . ?' Loretta was doing rapid calculations. She had not been able to see, at first, why this ancient story about an abortion would be so damaging to Colin Kendall-Cole. But Colin and Clara must have been at Oxford a long time before the 1967 Abortion Act. The revelation of his complicity in a backstreet abortion was a scandal that an ambitious politician, particularly one who was playing the family card where the peace women were concerned, would find hard to survive. Not to mention the consequences for his marriage if his wife was, as it appeared, a Roman Catholic.

'And that's when you heard him walking round the room?'

'Yes. I thought he was looking for the letter, I heard him open something. Then he says – sorry, Clara, but I have to do this – and bang. Two bangs. I didn't know it was a gun at first. I heard her sort of sigh, and a noise like she fell. I was so scared then, I couldn't move.'

Loretta leaned forward and put her hand on Peggy's shoulder. The girl sighed heavily.

'Shall I – would you like some tea?' she asked Loretta, clearly needing a break.

'I'll make it,' Loretta said.

She got up, went into the small kitchen, and a few minutes later brought back two cups of tea.

'Is that all right?' she asked, watching as Peggy sipped. 'Or would you like more sugar?'

'No thanks. Shall I tell you the rest?'

'Please.'

'It all happened very fast. After a bit I heard him go out of the room, and his feet going upstairs. I thought, you better get out, girl, get away from here as fast as you can. So I –'

'Just a minute, Peggy. Why didn't you – why didn't you hide till he'd gone and then call the police?'

'What, when he's a bloody MP? And I've got –' She stopped abruptly and Loretta remembered Peggy's criminal record.

'Was it because you . . . you've been in trouble?' she asked hesitantly.

'What d'you mean? Did Clara tell you that?' Peggy was suddenly belligerent. 'She shouldn't have! She promised . . .'

Loretta was about to explain the information had come from Chief Inspector Bailey, then thought better of it.

'Look, Peggy, it doesn't matter, whatever you've done. It's in the past, it's your business. I'm just trying to understand . . . so I can help you.'

'OK, Miss Know-it-all! I'm a shoplifter, right? A thief! The only time the Old Bill's ever been interested in me was when they was arresting me! They didn't care that he'd buggered off and left me with a sick kid and no housekeeping. He used to hit me with his belt till I was black and blue – domestic dispute, they said. So when Clara's lying there dead and the only people in the house's me and a posh bloke like him, who're they gonna believe?' She stared angrily at Loretta.

It was precisely the question that was worrying Loretta. But she decided to put off thinking about it until she'd heard the end of the story.

'I keep telling you, Peggy, I'm on your side – I'll think of something. Just tell me what happened next.'

'OK. Sorry. Sharon left me some Valium but I didn't want to take them.'

'You don't need Valium,' Loretta said firmly. 'Who's Sharon?'

'Me best mate. We was at school together. She works up a shop in Mare Street. She said I could stay here, she's just moved here. It took me a while to find her, I didn't have her new address and I remembered it a bit wrong. Where was I?'

'Behind the curtain.'

'Oh yeah. I could hear him upstairs, I dunno what he was doing but it made a lot of noise. I thought, this is me chance. I dunno how I managed it, I was nearly wetting meself with fright. Soon as I came out, I could see she was dead, I couldn't do nothing for her. I got the letter off the mantelpiece and I went to the door, on tiptoe, like. I ran across the hall into that bathroom, I didn't wanna go in the garden in case he looked out and seen me. Then I heard him come downstairs and I was hoping he'd go out the front door but he didn't. I was so scared, not knowing what he was up to, I dashed into that store place that's off the bathroom. It's got all the garden stuff in it – deckchairs and spades and things. I never went in there before, but it's got a door into the garden. Funny sort of house, it is. I got it open ever so quiet, and then I hid in the trees at the side of the garden. I got down near the gate and I saw a car, a posh one like you see on telly. I listened for a bit, but I couldn't hear nothing from the house. So I dashed up the lane to the road, and I didn't know where to go. Then I remembered the peace camp. I knew they'd help me. I got down on me hands and knees and went past the kitchen window, then I started running. I hid behind hedges and trees when I got tired. One time I heard a police car go by. Then it came back again and I guessed they'd been at the camp, looking for me. So I knew it was safe to go there then. I had to do something, all me stuff was back at the house. I had the clothes I stood up in and twenty-seven pence in me jeans pocket.'

'And you got a lift to the motorway next morning. They told me.'

'D'you wanna see the letter? The copy? I suppose he took the real one with him. It's in me bag in the bedroom. Me new bag, Sharon give it me.'

'In a minute,' Loretta said. 'We must do something. I'm just trying to think . . . ' She got up and looked out of the window, hardly taking in the row of lock-up garages and the small yard behind the flats. 'Peggy, you're not going to like this but it's the only thing we can do. You can't hide for ever, really you can't. The police know how to find people, they'll talk to your mother, your friends, everyone who knows you. And you want to be with your daughter, don't you?'

'Yeah, but – ' Peggy seemed about to argue but changed her mind. She looked warily at Loretta.

'I'm not suggesting we go to the police, not yet. My husband, my ex-husband, he works on a newspaper. If I get him to come here now' – she looked at her watch and saw it was just after three – 'we can tell him your story and he'll help us. You can trust him.' She hoped that Tracey would have more ideas than she did about how to get Peggy out of her predicament: accusing an MP of murder, when the only witness possessed a criminal record and had been on the run, seemed to Loretta a gargantuan undertaking. 'Maybe he could put a story in the paper on Sunday, I don't know. But the more people who know what really happened, the safer you are.'

'What if they arrest me?' Peggy asked flatly.

'We'll get you a lawyer, a good one. Peggy, at least you've got the letter – that's *evidence*. We can prove Colin had a motive. Let me ring John. Please.'

Peggy sighed. 'I got no choice, have I? If I stay here, they'll get me – and I got nowhere else to go.'

Loretta hid her relief. The sooner she had Tracey in on this the better.

'Is there a phone here?'

'No, Sharon hasn't got one yet.'

'D'you know where there is one? What about next door – oh, it's boarded up. What about the other neighbours?'

'Dunno. Sharon keeps herself to herself.'

'OK, we'll have to go and find one.'

'No! I'm not leaving here.' Peggy turned out to be stubbornly resistant to all Loretta's arguments; the flat had come to seem her refuge, and she didn't intend to set a foot outside it.

'Oh, all right,' Loretta said; it had occurred to her that Peggy's picture might be splashed all over the *Standard* by now. 'I'll be as quick as I can. I don't suppose you've got any change? Oh, well . . . See you soon, And try not to worry.' She hugged Peggy briefly and went to the door, leaving her sitting on the rug-covered sofa. 'Bye.' She pulled the front door shut behind her.

Outside the block of flats Loretta stopped and looked around. There wasn't a phone in sight – why, she thought, hadn't it occurred to anyone that the residents of Ernie Bevin House might want to use a phone? – and she decided the best thing to do was retrace her steps to where she'd parked the car. She went back along the path past the South Hackney Unemployment Fightback Centre, came out next to the road and saw a red telephone kiosk to her left at the junction with Well Street, next door to the pub she noticed earlier. Inwardly cheering, she hurried to it, pulled open the door and stepped inside. She ignored the peculiar smell, which was more like vomit than urine, and picked up the receiver. As she was feeling in her bag for her purse, the message '999 calls only' flashed up at her. With a sigh of impatience she punched in 100 for the operator, but the dialling tone continued uninterrupted. Slamming the phone down, Loretta shouldered her way out of the telephone box and looked up and down Well Street. Had she passed a kiosk on her way here? She didn't *think* so. Coming to a quick decision she turned left, going in the opposite direction from Mare Street, and followed the road round to the left. She soon came to a dentist's surgery and some small shops on the left-hand side of the street; on the other was a hall of residence with a couple of battered cars parked outside. Students, here? she was thinking, when she realized she had come to a large, modern branch of Tesco's. Beyond it Well Street became much narrower, and the road itself was closed to traffic because of a bustling street market. There *must* be a telephone box here, Loretta thought, plunging down the street. Her progress was slow, as she had to circumnavigate queues for vegetables, underwear, and one at a stall that sold only damaged tins, but she eventually reached the end of the street. There was a kiosk, sure enough, but there were three people waiting outside it as well as the man who appeared to be having an angry conversation inside. As she stopped to join the queue, a woman with two heavy bags of shopping at her feet turned and spoke to her.

'Fifteen minutes, he's been in there, it ain't fair, is it?'

Loretta's heart sank; she wondered whether she should open the door and plead with the man on the phone, but realized she would have to start explaining her urgency to the people in the queue as well.

'Have you tried Tesco's?' the woman said, seeing the frustration on her face. 'They got one inside. I'd go up there meself 'cept I got these bags to think about.'

'Thanks,' Loretta said fervently, wanting to kiss the woman. 'Thanks.'

She turned and went back up Well Street as fast as she could, jumping over bags and an orange-crate in her hurry to reach the shop. The automatic doors opened as she approached and she rushed inside, peering round towards the check-outs for the phone. She spotted it, then realized the shop was arranged in such a way that she'd have to go to the far end and back up the next aisle to get to it. Muttering apologies right and left, she thrust her way through a dense mass of people doing their weekend shopping and turned back on herself when she reached the bakery counter at the bottom. She headed up the aisle to the nearest till, squeezing past a large woman with a half-full trolley, and flung herself at the phone. The receiver was in her hand before she saw the small notice on the wall announcing it was out of order. Close to tears, she hurried outside the shop wondering whether she shouldn't force Peggy into her car and take her to her flat in Islington. Reluctant to waste more time, she decided to have one more try. She went along Well Street the way she'd originally come, stopping when she came to the Indian grocer's she'd noticed earlier. She went inside, marched straight up to the till and asked the young Asian woman behind it if she could use her phone. The woman looked at her uncertainly.

'Please,' said Loretta, 'it's an *emergency*. I'll pay!' She produced her purse and started pulling out a five-pound note. The woman waved it away.

'OK,' she said with a strong East London accent. 'It's out the back.'

She led the way to a small room at the rear of the shop, and left Loretta to it. Within half a minute she was through to Tracey's desk. A female voice answered and said he was out of the office for the moment.

'Are you expecting him back?'

The woman said she was.

'Tell him his wife rang, and it's urgent. I have to see him. No, I can't leave a number. Tell him I'm in London, and I'll ring again in half an hour.' By then she'd have Peggy safely at her flat. 'Tell him it's very, very urgent, a matter of life and death.' The woman probably thought she was mad, but what did that matter as long as Tracey got the message?

She put the phone down, thanked the shopkeeper on her way out, and set off in the direction of the Forman Park Estate. As she walked, she glanced at her watch and saw that her fruitless trip had taken three-quarters of an hour. What a waste of time, with every police force in the country looking for Peggy! Ernie Bevin House came into sight and she started to run, slowing after a few yards when she got a stitch in her side. She had arrived at the row of lock-up garages behind Peggy's flat, and she realized that if she could scale a wooden fence she could take a short-cut. It was a pity she'd worn a skirt; she felt something rip as she hoisted herself over the palings. Thoroughly out of breath, she hurried across the pitted yard, making her way between an old BMW and a Cortina without wheels propped up on bricks.

Now she was at the rear of the central archway of Ernie Bevin House; she paused to catch her breath and was about to turn right up the stairs when she heard a scream from the first floor. It was repeated, louder this time, and Loretta broke from the trance caused by the first cry, forcing herself up the stairs until she collided with a woman at the top. Loretta struggled to hold the woman, demanding to know what had happened, but the girl went on screaming and fought her off. She turned to look at Loretta from half-way down the stairs, mouthing the word 'ambulance' before disappearing through the doorway at the bottom.

Loretta put her hands to her face, a chill stealing through her bones. Turning slowly, she made herself take the two steps that would bring her to the open front door of number eleven. She paused on the threshold, stifled a gasp, and walked mechanically forward to the door of the living room. There she stopped, unable to believe what was in front of her: Peggy lying on her left side, her head towards the door and her knees drawn up as if she'd fallen forward from the sofa.

Loretta closed her eyes – she thought she was going to be sick, she thought she was going to faint, she put a hand out to the door-frame to support herself. She opened them: the scene had not gone away. This time there was no mistaking the bullet wound over Peggy's right ear, a star-shaped black hole above which a single fly was already buzzing. Loretta's gaze travelled in a line down Peggy's shoulder and right arm to her outstretched hand. It was then, and only then, that she realized that Peggy's fingers had just released an old-fashioned gun whose lack of adornment suggested it might be army issue. Loretta closed her eyes again and began to scream.

9

'You should eat something, you'll feel terrible tomorrow.'

'I'll feel terrible anyway. I couldn't eat, not a thing. I'd be sick.'

John Tracey shrugged and didn't press the matter. Loretta leaned across to the low table in front of her and picked up the brandy bottle. It clinked against the rim of her glass as she poured herself another generous helping. Aware that Tracey was watching her, she sipped it gently instead of finishing it in two or three gulps as she had the first.

'Thanks for rescuing me,' she said, cradling the tumbler on her knees, which were drawn up under her skirt. 'I thought they were never going to let me go. They were even muttering about charging me with – obstructing the course of justice or something.'

'I know,' Tracey said grimly. 'I nearly hit that bastard Bailey. I was there nearly two hours before he'd even talk to me. It was only when I started shouting about *habeas corpus* and getting the *Herald* lawyer that they began taking notice.'

'He must be good.'

'Who?'

'The *Herald* lawyer. If they were frightened of him.'

'He's the best – where libel's concerned, that is,' Tracey said, permitting himself a slight smile. 'I don't know how he is on getting innocent people out of police custody. I think it was the fear of bad publicity that did it, not me being able to get hold of a barrister at eleven o'clock at night. What time is it now, by the way? I took my watch off upstairs.'

Loretta glanced at her wrist.

'Ten to two. And it's – Saturday morning, right? I've rather lost track. I feel as if I've been at that police station for days.'

'Are you sure you should be drinking that? On an empty stomach?'

'Oh John, don't nag. It's been just . . . I can't tell you how awful everything is. I – I don't know what to do with myself.'

'OK, OK. Listen, why not try and get some sleep? I've put some sheets on the bed in the spare room. You're honoured – they're actually clean.'

Loretta ignored his attempt at a joke.

'I couldn't *sleep*. After all that? I feel as if I'll never sleep again.' She raised the glass to her lips and swallowed quite a lot of brandy.

Tracey pulled a face and moved the bottle out of Loretta's reach.

'Well, in that case, do you want to talk about it? Get it off your chest?'

'Yes. But what about your job? You're working tomorrow – today, aren't you?'

Tracey waved the objection away. 'They'll understand. I rang the news editor at home as soon as I got your call. I said you were in trouble – he's a good guy. The story I'm doing can wait, it's not the end of the world if it doesn't appear this Sunday. So – what happened?'

'Bailey says it was suicide.'

'And you say it wasn't.'

'I *know* it wasn't. I left her there while I went to ring you. She was going to talk to you, tell you the whole thing. She wasn't *suicidal*. There was no *reason* for her to kill herself. I'd promised to help her, said we'd get a lawyer and all that. She had less reason to kill herself yesterday than at any time since Clara was murdered.'

'So why does Bailey think . . . ?'

'Oh, *Bailey*. He says she did it in a fit of remorse and because she knew he was closing in on her. It happened just after he'd given her name and description to the press, you see.'

'Remorse? Remorse for –'

'For killing Clara.'

'Did she kill Clara?'

'Of course she didn't! It was Colin, Colin Kendall-Cole. The

MP. The one who turned up on Clara's doorstep just after I found her body. *Pretended* to turn up, I should say.'

'Hang on a minute, Loretta. You're saying that – you're telling me Clara was murdered by a Tory MP?' Tracey couldn't hide the incredulity in his voice.

Loretta glared at him, then jumped to her feet.

'Here you are!' she cried, grabbing the phone and thrusting it at him. 'Why don't you ring for the men in white coats? That's what Bailey thinks – that I'm some sort of loony. And you do, too, don't you?'

Tracey got up, took the phone from her, and propelled her gently back to the sofa.

'Come on, Loretta, you know I don't think anything of the sort. It was just a bit unexpected, that's all.' He returned to his chair and waited while she composed herself. 'Remember, all I know is that I got a frantic phone call from you saying you were at Clapton nick and they wouldn't let you go. Take it slowly.'

'I'm sorry. It's just – he was so awful, Bailey. And the other one I saw, the one who was in charge till Bailey got there from Oxford. That was about half past eight. I don't know why it took him so long. I went through the whole thing with him, the London one, while we were waiting for Bailey. And he said just what you said.' She put on a sarcastic tone. 'You're telling me, miss, that Mrs Wolstonecroft was shot by a *Member of Parliament*? You should have seen his face when I told him Colin shot Peggy as well!'

Tracey leaned over the side of his chair and picked up the brandy bottle. He saw that Loretta was watching him suspiciously and paused before filling his glass. 'Go on, I'm listening. This is all new to me. When I left you last night – I mean Thursday night – you said you had, er, one or two things to do up there' – Tracey suddenly looked embarrassed – 'before you came back to London. I didn't know anything was wrong until I found a piece of paper on my desk saying my *wife* had called. I mean, I thought something was up then. You never called yourself that even when we were living together. But I had no idea . . . when you rang and said you were at Clapton nick my first thought was that you'd had some sort of car accident. I've got a lot of catching up to do.'

'OK.' Loretta thought for a moment. 'It all started when I got a message from Peggy through the women at the peace camp – just where she was and that she wanted to see me. I came dashing up to London, I thought she was hiding because her husband had killed Clara. But he hadn't. He was at Clara's earlier in the evening, before the murder, but Clara sent him off with a flea in his ear. Then Colin arrived. With me so far?'

'I think so.' Tracey was feeling anxiously in his jacket pocket and withdrew his cigarettes. He kept his eyes averted from her as he lit one, his first since they'd arrived at his house from the police station.

'Clara had asked him to come. She was furious about the way he kept attacking the peace camp. She felt very passionately about it, you know. The attack on Libya, all those people being injured, it really horrified her. I suppose Gilbert was right in a way – he was a friend of hers, you don't need to bother about him. I was just thinking about something he said, that Clara had all the zeal of the convert, and he was right. She'd been going along for years not thinking about why the base was there, and then – wham! It suddenly hit her.

'Anyway – she told Peggy to hide behind the curtains. It sounds like she was looking forward to talking to Colin, she knew she'd got him where she wanted him – I suppose she wanted to show off a bit. She told Colin to leave the camp alone, all this stuff about them being lesbians and deserting their families. And she threatened him.'

'I don't understand this bit. How?'

'Well, Colin turns out to have a murky past. Apparently she produced a letter, one she'd kept for years. It was from a friend of hers, a girl she'd been at Oxford with. She'd written to say she was leaving because Colin had got her pregnant and she was having to have an abortion. An illegal one, of course. You can see how damaging that would be to an up-and-coming Tory MP – Victorian values and all that. Especially as his wife's a Catholic.'

'And he knew about this abortion?'

'That's the point. He *paid* for it.'

'Wow.' Tracey inhaled deeply and blew smoke across the room.

'And now the letter's gone.'

'Gone? What do you mean?'

Loretta's face twisted as though she was in agony.

'Peggy had a copy, she had it at the flat. We were going to show it to you, it was our main piece of evidence! But he must've taken it. That's how I know he killed her. This afternoon, while I was trying to find a phone. That and the gun.' She felt in the pocket of her skirt for a handkerchief and wiped her eyes. 'I'm sorry, I'm not telling this very well. You see, she didn't mention anything about the gun when I talked to her, when she told me what happened on Tueday night. I'm sure she would have mentioned it if she'd picked it up. She told me she had the letter, she said it was in her handbag. But when I got back – and she was there, on the floor' – Loretta stopped and blew her nose – 'when I got back the gun was there, by her hand. And the letter was gone.'

'But surely, Loretta, if you're saying he came to the flat in broad daylight, somebody must have seen him?'

'That's what I thought. I made them knock on all the doors near by, the police I mean. But it was hopeless. D'you know what those estates are like? The flat next door is boarded up, the one after that's got an old woman in it who's afraid to open her own front door . . . There were some lads playing around when I first arrived, about twelve years old, two white and one black, but I don't know where they came from. Anyway, it's not the sort of place where people fall over themselves to help the police. Even though Sharon, she's the woman who found Peggy, even though she was screaming blue murder, no one came out to see what was going on till the ambulance and all the police cars arrived.'

'OK.' Tracey stubbed out his cigarette in the ash-tray on the coffee table. 'You're saying this guy Colin killed Peggy with the gun he used on Clara. How did he know where to find her?'

Loretta nodded. 'I've thought about that. When he threw away Peggy's barrel bag in the garden, after he killed Clara, he must have kept her purse. Or her handbag. He was trying to make it look like a robbery, remember. Sharon's address must have been in it – she'd just moved and Peggy said she had trouble remembering it.'

'And when he got to the flat? How did he get in? I presume the door wasn't forced?'

'No, nothing like that.' Loretta's shoulders suddenly began to heave and she put her handkerchief to her face to wipe away a fresh crop of tears. 'That's what I feel so bad about – I think it's my fault!'

'What is?'

'Him getting into the flat. My car was parked in the road, you see. I think he knew I was there – all he had to do was pretend I'd sent him, that he was a friend of mine!' She blew her nose hard.

'But surely Peggy would have recognized him? Even if he – '

'*No*! That's the *point*! She didn't see him on Tuesday night – she didn't know what he looked like.'

'Hang on a minute. Why should he recognize your car? When did he see it before?'

'It was parked outside the cottage the other morning, when I made him coffee. He must have seen it then.'

'Even so . . . how many white Fiat Pandas are there in the world? It's hardly an unusual make.'

'Perhaps he recognized the number, some people remember things like that. And it's got a CND sticker in the back window.'

'That's probably true of half the cars in Hackney.'

'All right, maybe he saw me leaving the flat, I don't know. I was so desperate to find a phone box I didn't waste time looking round for old acquaintances.'

'So you think he got in and overpowered her . . . I *suppose* it's feasible.'

'And the thing about the gun, and Peggy's purse, the stuff he took from Clara's house – I've thought about that as well. The police searched him and his car on Tuesday night, and they didn't find anything. What I think is, he knew of some hiding-place, an old well or something – he used to play with Clara's brother when he was a boy. And Thursday morning, when he *said* he was looking for Jeremy, he'd come to get it back. He was carrying a briefcase, I didn't think anything of it at the time, but that's what it was for. He came back as soon as the police were out of the way and put it all in his briefcase.'

'You have got it all worked out. You told Bailey all this?'

'Not all of it. He wouldn't listen. And some of it I didn't work out straight away, I was too upset. All Bailey kept going on about was how I knew Peggy was there and why I hadn't told the police. I had to make up a story about an anonymous letter, and then he wanted to know why I hadn't kept it. I really did think he was going to charge me.'

'So – the official version is murder followed by suicide. To be fair to Bailey, it is a lot neater than what you've just told me. The idea that someone got into the flat and – wait a minute. What about the husband? How do you know Peggy was telling the truth? How do you know she wasn't protecting her husband, and *he* got into the flat and killed her? After all, you never saw this famous letter.'

A look of anguish passed across Loretta's face. She held out her hands palm upwards, opening and closing them in an expression of her frustration.

'I *know* she was telling the truth, I just *know* it.'

'No you don't, Loretta, you just want to believe it. She could have made the whole thing up to divert suspicion from herself and – what did you say his name was?'

'Mick. Well, at least you aren't convinced it was suicide either.' She gave him a triumphant look.

'I don't – look, Loretta, all I'm saying is that the case against Colin is no better than the one against this Mick. Or, to put it another way, one's as flimsy as the other.'

'So you're saying Peggy went to all that trouble to get me to Hackney and chose that moment to shoot herself?' Loretta was getting angry again. 'In a fit of remorse which just happened to strike the minute I walked out of the door – three days after the murder?'

'OK, OK. This isn't getting us anywhere . . . Even if you're right, you're never going to prove it, you know.'

Loretta looked at him without speaking. Tracey produced his cigarettes again, shook one out and lit it.

'Another thing. If you are right, where does the Yank fit into all this? The character you met in the churchyard?'

Loretta shifted a little on the sofa. When she spoke, her voice was calmer. 'I think he was telling the truth. His men were trying to frighten Clara, but they didn't have anything to do with the murder. I suppose we ought to be grateful they draw the line *somewhere*.' She raised her glass to her lips and finished her brandy.

'Fingerprints,' Tracey said suddenly. 'Did they find any on the gun, or in the flat? Ones they couldn't identify, I mean? That would support your story.'

Loretta smiled briefly and shook her head. 'He's too clever for *that*. The gun had been wiped, the only prints on it were Peggy's. And they found mine and Sharon's in the flat, on teacups and things, plus about one smudge mark from a pair of gloves. Bailey didn't think much of that. Oh, there's something else I worked out about Tuesday night – why Colin went rushing into the drawing room to look at Clara's body. It was so he could explain any fingerprints he'd left in there. He really is *very* clever.'

'Not just clever, if he managed to think of all that – he'd have to be a genius. Anyway, Loretta, everything you've said could apply just as much to Mick. You've got no proof that Colin killed either of them.'

'I have! Oh, all right, it's not something that would stand up in a court of law. But it's – it's enough for me. I *know* Peggy. I *know* she was telling the truth. I saw her with Mick, you didn't. She'd never have protected him. Colin killed her, and now he's going to get away with it.'

Tracey heard the despair in her voice and leaned across to crush the end of his cigarette in the ash-tray on the table.

'I think you've had enough,' he said, avoiding her gaze. 'Think you could get some sleep now? You weren't well even before all this happened. You're all in.'

'I suppose I am.' She spoke absently, watching him toy with the cigarette end. 'John, won't you believe me? I know I'm right.'

Tracey thought for a moment, his head averted. Then he looked up and finally met her gaze.

'I'm sorry, Loretta,' he said, 'I just don't know what to think. I really don't.'

She was woken by a sound that she couldn't immediately identify; even when she'd worked out it was rain spattering on the window directly above her head, she didn't at once remember that she was sleeping in Tracey's spare bed. She groped on the floor for her watch, picked it up, and was astonished to discover it was five to three; she'd slept for just under twelve hours. She sat up and swung her feet to the floor, experiencing a stabbing pain above her eyes that made her wish she hadn't tried to get out of bed. The brandy, she thought, or just the general aftermath of the previous night. She lay back on the pillows for a while, reluctant to move, but was driven to do so by her need for a glass of water. She got out of bed slowly, feeling sweaty from sleeping in her T-shirt and pants, and pulled her skirt over her head. Clean clothes, she thought, that's what I need, then remembered with dismay that her belongings were still up in Oxfordshire. She went downstairs barefoot and headed for the kitchen at the back of the house.

'John? Are you there?' There was no reply, and it occurred to her that he had probably gone to work. Then she spotted an envelope propped against the butter dish on the kitchen table. She picked it up and found a scribbled message in Tracey's handwriting.

'Dear Loretta,' she read, 'I thought it was best to let you sleep. Should be back some time this afternoon. Please' – underlined twice – 'don't go wandering off anywhere. Wait here for me and we'll talk about when we can go and collect your car from Oxford – you're in no fit state to drive. Try and have something to eat. There isn't much food in the house, so I'm leaving some money in case you haven't got any. Love, John. PS I am very worried about you.'

She smiled sadly, grateful for his concern. Putting the envelope down, she saw he'd left two ten pound notes and a spare key on the table. She still didn't feel like eating, but wandered over to the sink and filled the kettle. After a cup of tea, two glasses of water and two paracetamol, she started to feel very slightly better. But as soon as her headache receded, she was flooded with an overwhelming sense of guilt: she was sure that in some way, she wasn't quite sure how, she should have been able to save Peggy.

After half an hour in which she had a bath and dressed, she was able to bear her own company not a moment longer. She decided to take Tracey's advice and go out to buy food; he might well be hungry when he returned from the *Herald* office, and maybe her own appetite would have revived by then. She borrowed his trench-coat from a peg in the hall, and went outside. Tracey's house, which he had bought after the break-up of their marriage, was in a deceptively quiet square close to the heart of Brixton. Feeling like a sleep-walker, or a visitor from another planet, Loretta took the short cut to Brixton Road and found herself among crowds of Saturday afternoon shoppers. The rain had stopped, and a solitary evangelist had mounted an orange-box outside Marks & Spencer and was exhorting its customers to repent. Loretta joined the hecklers, giggling adolescents and two women with heavy shopping bags who constituted his audi-ence, and let the tide of words wash over her, grateful just to be with other people. After a while, the audience began to drift away and Loretta got the uncomfortable feeling that the preacher's words were being addressed directly to her. She turned away and went into the shop, heading for the food section and filling her basket with an almost random selection of things she usually liked. There were long queues at all the check-outs; eventually she paid and, with her purchases in two plastic carrier bags, set off for Tracey's house.

She made herself a couple of slices of toast, hoping they'd prepare her stomach for a more substantial meal on Tracey's return. She wandered listlessly into his drawing room, suddenly realized she was rather cold, and decided to light a fire. She had just got it going and was sitting back on her heels when she heard his key in the front door.

'Loretta! You there?' His voice was anxious.

'In here,' she called, getting to her feet.

Tracey appeared in the doorway, a bag of shopping in one hand and, to her astonishment, a cat basket in the other. Bertie looked up, caught sight of her, and purred loudly.

'How on earth –'

Tracey put down the basket and Loretta knelt to let the cat out.

'I woke up this morning and thought I'd go and get your car,' Tracey said sheepishly. 'I thought it would upset you, going over to Hackney again. You were fast asleep, so I took your car keys out of your bag and got a taxi over there. I was going to come straight back, and then I thought – why don't I nip up to Oxford and pick up her things? This little chap was sitting on the doorstep when I got there. He looked so bedraggled, I couldn't really leave him . . . did I do the right thing?'

'Oh *yes*.' Loretta was still on her knees, stroking the cat as he leaned against her.

'I'll just put this stuff in the fridge,' Tracey said abruptly. 'I got some food in case you hadn't been out.'

'Oh, so did I. Never mind, I'm beginning to feel quite hungry. I haven't eaten properly for days.'

Tracey turned to leave the room, hesitated in the doorway and produced something from a pocket.

'Um . . . this had been pushed under the door,' he said, holding out an envelope.

Loretta got to her feet, took it, and sat down on the edge of an armchair. At her feet, the grey cat was sniffing the carpet, starting to explore. Loretta tore open the envelope and read the single sheet of paper inside it.

'Dear L,' it began, 'I think we both made a mistake – best call it a day. No hard feelings? Yours, Robert.'

'Well . . . ' she began, more to herself than Tracey, who was hovering in the doorway. Why hadn't Robert gone the whole hog and put 'yours sincerely'? she wondered.

'Bad news?'

'Not in the scale of things,' Loretta said, crumpling the paper into a ball and tossing it into the fire. Flames licked round it; it hung in the air for a few seconds, a blackened oblong, then collapsed into fine ash.

'Here, Bertie,' Loretta called, holding out her hand. The cat came to her, jumping into her lap, and Tracey left the room.

A few minutes later he returned, dropping her car keys on the coffee table. 'I put the keys to the cottage in an envelope and stuck it through the door of Clara's house,' he said, taking a seat on the sofa.

'You haven't been to the *Herald*?' Loretta asked, stroking the cat.

'No, I rang in before I left. Watson told me to take the day off, he's a good bloke. Just as well, the time it's taken me. I thought I'd be back long before now. It's not exactly built for speed, your car.'

'Have you – have you seen any papers?' Loretta was

reluctant to bring up the subject of the murders, but it was hanging in the air between them. Anyway, she couldn't avoid it for ever. Tracey had taken that day's papers with him, and she hadn't been able to bring herself to buy any; she had a curious dread of knowing what was in them.

'Nothing about Peggy, if that's what you mean. Apart from the press conference yesterday morning, that is. Police are probably sitting on it till they've tied up all the loose ends. The BBC news is on in a minute. Want to watch it?'

'All right.'

Tracey got up and switched on his small colour television. They watched the end of a programme Loretta didn't recognize, then she heard the familiar signature tune.

'It's just been announced that police have scaled down the inquiry into the murder of Mrs Clara Wolstonecroft, the well-known author of children's books, following the discovery of a woman's body in a flat in east London,' the woman newsreader began in a solemn voice.

'The dead woman, who is believed to have a head wound, had been staying in Mrs Wolstonecroft's house near Oxford prior to the murder on Tuesday night. Police say they aren't looking for anyone else in connection with either death. This report is from the scene where the second body was discovered . . .'

Loretta and Tracey watched as a young female reporter with blonde hair spoke direct to camera from the car park behind Ernie Bevin House. The camera travelled up to the window of Sharon's flat as the reporter gave brief details of when the body had been found. It was clear that the police weren't releasing much information at this stage.

'So that's that,' Loretta exclaimed angrily as the reporter signed off and the newsreader reappeared with a story about a motorway pile-up. 'Clara and Peggy are dead and the whole thing's sorted out without the police having to ask awkward questions. What sort of world are we *living* in?'

The cat wriggled and jumped down from her knee. Tracey said nothing, and she turned back from him to the television. Suddenly a smiling picture of Colin Kendall-Cole filled the screen.

'The Conservative MP for Oxfordshire South-East, Mr

Colin Kendall-Cole, has been appointed junior minister at the Ministry of Defence,' the newsreader continued smoothly. 'Mr Kendall-Cole, who entered the House of Commons in 1979, becomes a minister in the minor re-shuffle caused by the death in a car accident yesterday of a junior Trade minister. He is fifty-two, and married.' Colin's picture disappeared.

'No! They can't! They just can't!' Loretta stared at the screen in anguish. The cat padded back across the carpet towards her and jumped lightly on to her knee. Hardly aware of what she was doing, she put her arms around him and hugged him close. 'They just can't,' she repeated, quietly and without conviction.

Without speaking, Tracey got up and turned off the television.